**"Ms. Duquesne," said Horatio.
"Glad you could join us."**

"You know how badly this has traffic backed up?" she said as she strolled up with a smile on her face. "Even with the flashers on, it took forever. Like playing hopscotch for fifteen miles using one leg."

"I know," said Alexx. "And all the looky-loos slowing down to stare doesn't help." She glared at a Jeep full of college-age kids crawling past, all of them straining for a glimpse of possible carnage.

"Death is the great mystery, Alexx," said Horatio. "You can't really blame people for their curiosity."

"No," said Calleigh, "but we *can* charge admission."

Horatio dipped his head and peered at her over the rims of his sunglasses.

"Taxes," said Calleigh. "The public pays them, we collect our salaries, do our job, and come up with answers. The public may be clueless . . . but *we* aren't."

"No, we're not," Horatio agreed. "As a matter of fact, I have a whole basket full of them, just for you."

Other **CSI: Miami** books

Cult Following
Riptide
Harm for the Holidays—Misgivings
Harm for the Holidays—Heart Attack

Also available from Pocket Books

CSI: Crime Scene Investigation
Double Dealer
Sin City
Cold Burn
Body of Evidence
Grave Matters
Binding Ties
Killing Game
Snake Eyes
In Extremis

and

CSI: NY
Dead of Winter
Blood on the Sun
Deluge

CSI: MIAMI™

CUT & RUN

DONN CORTEZ

CSI: MIAMI produced by CBS Productions, a business unit of CBS Broadcasting Inc.
and Alliance Atlantis Productions Inc.
Executive Producers: Jerry Bruckheimer, Ann Donahue, Carol Mendelsohn, Anthony E. Zuiker, Jonathan Littman
Series created by Anthony E. Zuiker, Ann Donahue, and Carol Mendelsohn

POCKET **STAR** BOOKS
New York   London   Toronto   Sydney

Pocket Star Books
A Division of Simon & Schuster, Inc.
1230 Avenue of the Americas
New York, NY 10020

This book is a work of fiction. Names, characters, places, and incidents either are products of the author's imagination or are used fictitiously. Any resemblance to actual events or locales or persons, living or dead, is entirely coincidental.

CSI: Miami and related marks are trademarks of CBS Worldwide Inc.

First Pocket Star Books paperback edition March 2008

POCKET STAR BOOKS and colophon are registered trademarks of Simon & Schuster, Inc.

For information about special discounts for bulk purchases, please contact Simon & Schuster Special Sales at 1-800-456-6798 or business@simonandschuster.com.

Cover design by Richard Yoo; photo of car by Jim Reed

Manufactured in the United States of America

10 9 8 7 6 5 4 3 2 1

ISBN-13: 978-0-7434-9953-8
ISBN-10:   0-7434-9953-0

This book is dedicated to my colleague, Don DeBrandt. While Rembrandt is something of a maniac, he does have his talents; Coffin Juice, Red Dawns, the Skullbuster, the Church of the Laughing Cow, and the Black Rock City riding crop are a few of his creations.

Oh, and he's not bad as a writer, either.

1

THE WHITE VAN blew past the gray Lexus at nearly ninety miles an hour, dodging crazily from one lane to another. The driver of the Lexus, Stephano Kliomedes, swore and hit the brakes as the vehicle cut in front of him, but the van never even slowed down; it crossed another lane and then swerved back the other way, darting through gaps in the traffic like a running back with five hundred pounds of defensive linemen breathing down his neck.

"That's it! That's *it*!" Stephano roared.

His wife, Grace, sighed in the way that only a twenty-year marriage can produce. "Stephie, calm down," she said. "You don't—"

"I don't? *I* don't? What about him? *He* don't, that's what I say! Not this time!" He stomped on the accelerator and took off after the van, muttering curses in Greek under his breath.

"Leaping, always leaping," Grace said. "Leaping before looking, that's you. What if this maniac is on drugs? What if he has a gun? Or a pregnant wife in the back, going into labor?"

"Then the child will grow up an orphan! *I* have a gun, too!"

"What a *terrible* thing to say. Now you'll go to prison for murder? And what am I supposed to do—grow old without you? Or do we both die in a hail of gunfire?"

"You're *already* old. We're *both* old. And we deserve more respect than this!"

"You want respect, you should have become a fireman. You're a shoe salesman."

"A shoe salesman with a gun!"

Grace's reply died on her lips. There was something in the sky ahead of them—something *large*. "Stephano," she gasped. "You think maybe *that* has something to do with Mr. I'm-in-a-Hurry?"

Directly ahead of them, a hot-air balloon dropped toward the highway. It wasn't exactly *plummeting*, Grace would tell the police later; no, it was more like *sinking*. Sinking in a *Titanic* sort of way, she said, except without the iceberg. Slow and heavy and kind of inevitable.

The basket touched down with hardly a sound, and the balloon proceeded to collapse like a gigantic airborne thespian giving her last and greatest performance. The airbag kept moving as it settled, dragging the basket along the highway at an angle until it wedged between an SUV and a convertible that had stopped to gawk.

The white van slammed to a halt a few feet away. A young man with an unruly thatch of hair and a three-day growth of beard jumped out of the driver's side and sprinted over to the basket, leaving his door hanging open. By the time he got there, the driver of the convertible and the SUV were already out of their vehicles and staring into the basket. Its sole occupant stared back sightlessly with his one remaining eye.

Lieutenant Horatio Caine surveyed the scene, hands on hips. The balloon had been dragged off to one side of the highway, but the basket hadn't been disturbed. Police barriers had been set up to isolate the scene, with a single narrow lane down one side to let traffic by. A steady stream of slow-driving rubberneckers crept past, sometimes snapping pictures with cell phone cameras.

"Alexx, what can you tell me?" asked Horatio. The ME was inside the basket itself, examining the body.

"Looks like a single GSW," Doctor Alexx Woods said, straightening up. "Entry point is the right eye. No exit wound—bullet's still inside." She shook her head. "Nobody shoots themselves in the eye, Horatio. Suicides put the barrel in their mouth, under their chin, sometimes to the temple—almost never to the eye."

"Just because they want to die, Alexx," said Horatio, "doesn't mean they want to see it coming. Time of death?"

"No more than an hour or two. Body temperature hasn't dropped at all, and there's no rigor—not even in his eyelids. Well, eyelid. And there's stippling around the entry wound, indicating he was shot at close range."

"I don't suppose you noticed a gun while you were down there?"

"No. But if he shot himself in midair, it probably went over the edge. Give me a hand, will you, Horatio?"

Horatio helped her climb out of the basket. "I retrieved his wallet while I was in there," said Alexx. She handed it to Horatio and he flipped it open.

"Timothy Breakwash," said Horatio. "Fifty-one, resident of Florida City. Has his pilot's license, which means he can fly passengers as well as solo."

"Well, if he had anyone else with him," said Alexx, "they got out before he did."

Horatio glanced up as a silver Humvee parked at the edge of the barricade. Calleigh Duquesne, dressed in black slacks and a white silk blouse, got out of the driver's seat. She gave them a cheerful wave as she grabbed her CSI kit from the back.

"Ms. Duquesne," said Horatio. "Glad you could join us."

"You know how badly this has traffic backed up?" Calleigh said as she strolled up with a smile on her face. "Even with the flashers on, it took forever. Like playing hopscotch for fifteen miles using one leg."

"I know," said Alexx. "And all the looky-loos slowing down to stare doesn't help." She glared at a Jeep full of college-age kids crawling past, all of them straining for a glimpse of possible carnage.

"Death is the great mystery, Alexx," said Horatio. "You can't really blame people for their curiosity."

"No," said Calleigh, "but we *can* charge admission."

Horatio dipped his head and peered at her over the rims of his sunglasses.

"Taxes," said Calleigh. "The public pays them, we collect our salaries, do our job, and come up with answers. The public may be clueless . . . but *we* aren't."

"No, we're not," Horatio agreed. "As a matter of fact, I have a whole basket full of them, just for you."

"Why, *thank* you, Horatio. You're so thoughtful . . ."

Natalia Boa Vista ducked under the yellow crime scene tape and flashed her ID to the uniformed officer guarding the front door of the house. He nodded and waved her inside.

Natalia hadn't been a CSI for long, but her training kicked in the second she stepped over the threshold. She looked around, not just to the left and right but down to the floor and up to the ceiling. The bungalow was nothing special, just a single-level building in a middle-class Miami neighborhood, but she could already tell that it was occupied by a single male, probably in his forties, no wife or kids; she saw a single pair of sneakers and a light jacket on a hook, but no women's or kids' shoes. *If the eyes are the windows of the soul,* Horatio had told her, *the foyer of a house is the inside cover of a book. Take the time to read it and it'll prepare you for what's inside.*

It didn't prepare her for the blood, though.

The vic was sprawled in the middle of his living room, face-up. Blood soaked his torso and was pooled under the body. Spatter from castoff had decorated one wall and a lampshade with an abstract spiderweb of crimson.

Frank Tripp stood beside the body, jotting down details in a small notebook. He glanced up as she walked in and said, "Oh, hey, Natalia. Got a messy one for you."

"So I see." She realized she hadn't put on a pair of gloves yet, and looked around for a place to set her kit down. *Rookie mistake,* she thought.

If Tripp noticed, he didn't show it. "Vic's name is Hiram Davey. Multiple stab wounds, looks like."

"He looks familiar." She pulled on the gloves, then knelt by the body. The DB didn't have the face of a movie star or the build of an athlete, but she was sure she recognized him just the same.

"If you read the *Tribune*, you'd know him. He writes a weekly column—*Hi Davey*. Humorous local stuff—I was a fan, actually. He made me bust my gut on more than one Sunday morning."

"Well, it looks like somebody busted his," said Natalia. "Medical examiner been here, yet?"

"Been and gone. Had to attend a balloon crash, of all things."

"Yeah, I heard about that." Natalia pulled her camera out of her kit and began taking pictures.

"Kinda thing Davey would have loved. You ever read that column he did on the exploding manatee?"

"Uh—no, I think I missed that one." Natalia surveyed the room. A chair was kicked over and the coffee table upended—Davey had put up a fight.

"It's a classic. Still got it taped to my fridge."

"Any sign of forced entry?"

"No, door was unlocked. His editor was the one that walked in and found the body. Says he was here to give Davey hell for missing his deadline—so to speak."

She glanced around. "Where is he?"

"Took off before we got here, called it in from his cell. Seems he was in a hurry to write it up and get it in the paper."

"Doesn't he know it's illegal to leave a crime scene like that?"

Tripp grunted. "Some journalists seem to think the law doesn't apply to them. I'm gonna swing by his office and re-educate the man."

Natalia grinned. "Wouldn't want to be in his shoes, then."

She knelt and checked the contents of the body's pockets. "Might be a robbery—his wallet's gone." She pointed to a pale band around the DB's wrist. "And so's his watch. Could be they're both somewhere in the house, though; if he works at home he wouldn't necessarily have them on his person."

Tripp shook his bullet-shaped head. "Nah. Davey did all his writing on a laptop in coffee shops and bars—it was a running joke in the column. Claimed he got cabin fever sitting at home."

"Well, if he worked on a laptop it should be here, right?" She looked around. "Did he have a study?"

"Yeah—converted sunroom in the back." Tripp jerked a thumb over his shoulder.

Natalia left the living room and went down a short hall. Several framed writing awards hung along its length, and a tattered brown runner covered the floor. The air had that smell that Natalia always associated with bachelor apartments: a mixture of old pizza boxes, unreturned beer bottles, and dust.

The study was about as messy as she'd expected, crammed floor to ceiling with bookcases, stacked with cardboard boxes overflowing with papers, and festooned with the relics of a misspent youth: a neon beer sign over the door, a poster of the Miami Dolphins cheerleading squad scrawled full of signatures on one wall. There was a desk covered in magazines, books, and bric-a-brac, but no computer.

She returned to the living room. "No luck. Either it was stolen, or he left it somewhere else."

"Anything else missing?"

"Hard to tell for sure. Nothing obvious."

"I'll take a closer look." He hesitated, then said, "Sorry, I didn't mean that the way it sounded. I just meant—"

"It's okay, Frank. New kid on the block, I know. I'll process in here while you look around." She gave him a smile; he nodded and left the room.

She studied the scene carefully, trying to piece together the sequence of events. *The killer didn't break in. So unless the door was already open . . .* She retraced her steps and examined the front door. Heavy-duty lock, plus another lock built into the doorknob and a sturdy slide-action bolt.

Unlikely he would have this kind of security and not use any of it—he must have let the killer in. Someone he knew? Or just someone he thought was harmless?

She went back to the living room and took a closer look at the body's hands and arms. *Defensive wounds. If he fought back hard enough, there's a good chance some of the killer's blood is here, too.*

She was collecting samples from near the wreckage of the coffee table when she noticed something strange about the spatter pattern on the couch. There was a blank rectangular space on one of the cushions, a void outlined in drops of red.

Just about the size of a laptop, too . . .

Natalia went over to take a closer look, then checked beneath the couch.

No laptop—but she did find something else.

"Find anything interesting?" Horatio asked.

"I have," said Calleigh. She handed Horatio a single sheet of paper in a clear evidence baggie. "This was tucked inside an interior compartment."

Horatio read it aloud. "'I have seen enough.' Machine-printed, no signature."

"Well, it's not like we're going to confuse it with anybody *else's* suicide note."

"True—but it's awfully clinical, isn't it? It wasn't even on his person. And the 'seen' part is clearly referencing his being shot in the eye—almost as if trying to explain it."

"I know," said Calleigh. "If he hadn't been shot at close range, I'd say this scene was staged. But how do you fake a crime scene a thousand feet in the air in broad daylight?"

"I don't know," said Horatio. "But while Timothy Breakwash may have seen enough, we're just getting started . . ."

Calleigh finished processing the basket and sent everything she had collected to the lab. What she *didn't* find was a gun; from the look of the gunshot wound she'd guess it would prove to be something small, a .38 or maybe a .22. And, more than likely, it had tumbled to the ground an instant after Breakwash had pulled the trigger.

If he pulled the trigger.

Which meant it was most likely somewhere in the Everglades—anywhere from the top of a mangrove tree to the bottom of a pool of quicksand. It could even be in the belly of an alligator by now— they'd been known to eat all sorts of strange things.

Unless this is a murder, she thought, *and not a suicide.*

It wasn't as impossible as it seemed. Breakwash could have been shot while still on the ground. He *had* been shot in the basket, that much she was sure of; there were no indications of the body's having been moved after being shot—well, other than drifting a few miles though the air—and the pattern of bloodstains seemed to confirm it. So unless he'd been attacked in midair by sky pirates . . . she shook her head and grinned.

"Something funny?" Horatio asked.

"Just the image of sword-wielding brigands bearing down on the balloon in a zeppelin flying the Jolly Roger."

Horatio grinned back. "That seems . . . unlikely."

"Hey, you asked. Anyway, turns out the balloon was only flying a few hundred feet up on a clear day—somebody could have seen something through binoculars or a telescope. What do you think?"

"I'm thinking," said Horatio, looking at the line

of cars still inching past the crime scene, "that sometimes rubberneckers can prove useful."

"Well, they're already lined up. Might as well ask them a few questions as they go through."

"I already have a uniformed officer doing exactly that. If anyone on the road saw something, she'll let us know—in the meantime, I think I'll start with the first person on the scene."

Natalia finished bagging the blood swabs from the living room and joined Frank in the study, where he was searching through each and every book.

"You done?" he asked.

"Yes, I think so. I'm pretty sure the laptop was on the couch when the murder happened—there's ghosting of just the right size. That's not all, though—I found this under the couch." She held up a small digital recorder.

"You think our murder was recorded?"

"Don't know—battery's dead. Could be because it was running for the last few hours—I'll have Cooper take a look at it and see what he thinks. How about you—find anything odd?"

"Thought I'd check for backup files. So far, no luck."

"Used to be a computer disk was fairly easy to spot. These days, though . . ." A sudden thought struck her. She glanced around the room but didn't see what she was looking for. "Just a second, Frank."

Natalia returned to the living room and walked

over to the stereo. An upright CD rack made of wire stood beside it; she ran her finger down the titles until she came to one that looked handwritten. "Ima Novella—Greatest Hits," she said aloud. She pulled it out, revealing a gold CD in a clear plastic case. Scrawled across the front in Magic Marker were the words, DEATHLESS PROSE.

"Funny," she murmured. "But not exactly accurate . . ."

Frank walked up behind her. "CD-ROM?"

"Yeah. I'm guessing this is a backup copy that he hid in plain sight. Sort of."

"Ima Novella. Yeah, that sounds like Davey."

"I'll take it back to the lab. I hope it isn't encrypted."

Frank shook his head. "Knowing Davey, it might just be a collection of traveling salesmen jokes."

"Guess we'll know soon enough." Natalia slipped the CD into an evidence folder. "And if this doesn't give us anything relevant, I guess the joke's on *him*."

"My name's Joel Greer," the driver of the white van told Horatio. "I crew for Mister Breakwash."

Horatio studied the young man with the unkempt hair who wouldn't meet his eyes. The death of his boss had definitely upset Joel, but Horatio could tell there was more to it than that. "I see," he said. "And what, exactly, does crewing a hot-air balloon entail?"

"I don't fly with him," said Joel. He crossed his arms. "I just help get the balloon inflated and then pack it up again at the other end. And I drive the support vehicle."

"So you were present when Mister Breakwash launched?"

"Yeah, of course. And when he . . ." Joel swallowed. "Came down again."

"Was there anyone else there?"

"No, it was just us."

"What about during the flight?"

"I followed him at a distance in the van. He was over the 'Glades, so I couldn't exactly pace him, but he was in sight the whole time. I followed the highway until—well, he was supposed to meet me over here." Joel pulled a battered map out of his back pocket and unfolded it. "Right here in this field. We've done it lots of times. But this time—this time he just kept going."

"Did you try to contact him?"

"Yeah, we have a set of walkie-talkies for that. He didn't answer. I just followed him the best I could after that, until he finally—" Joel broke off and looked away.

"Did you see anything unusual during the flight? Did anything approach the balloon or leave it?"

"I didn't notice anything—but it was pretty far away, and I had to keep my eyes on the road. I called the FAA as soon as I knew something was wrong."

"Yes, I imagine their investigator will want to talk to you, too."

"I didn't do anything wrong, did I? I mean, this isn't my fault, right?"

Horatio eyed Joel calmly for a second. "I don't think so, no," he said. "But we've just started our investigation. Would you mind holding out your hands? There's a test I need to perform."

Natalia took the CD-ROM back to the lab, where she popped it into her computer and discovered it wasn't encrypted—nor was it full of traveling salesman jokes. What it did contain was the outline of a novel, along with a large file labeled NOTES and another called INTERVIEWS. She was halfway through them when Cooper stuck his head in the door. He wore a lab coat over a bright orange T-shirt with the word *POW!* on the chest.

"Hey," he said. "I've been looking at that digital recorder you gave me."

"And?"

"Step into my parlor and listen for yourself."

She followed him back to the AV lab. "Okay," he said. "Here's what was on it." He hit a key and a voice she assumed was Hiram Davey's said, "Maybe move the bit with the flamingo until the end of the chapter? I dunno . . ."

A knock sounded in the background. "Dammit—just a sec—" There was a crashing noise—then nothing.

"Sounds like he was making notes for a book," said Cooper. "And got attacked halfway through."

"That doesn't quite line up," said Natalia. "The killer didn't force his way in, so that crash had to have been part of the struggle. There were no voices, either. It's like part of the tape was edited out—but why bother? Easier for the killer to erase the whole thing or just take it with him."

"I think I can explain the sequence of sounds. He was dictating notes, then hit pause when he heard the knock on the door. If he'd been using an analog recorder, there would've been a noticeable click. I had to analyze the signal digitally, but I found an interrupt signature."

"And the crash?"

"Something or somebody hit the pause button again. Probably happened by accident—maybe the vic dropped it when he was attacked."

She nodded. "I found it under the couch—it might have been dropped then kicked there during the struggle. Did you pull anything interesting from the recording?"

Cooper shook his head. "Sorry. It must have been activated after the vic was already dead—there's no sound of a struggle or any voices. You can hear some very faint breathing after the pause—the killer must have gotten closer to the recorder for a few seconds."

"Probably when he bent down to grab the laptop. Nothing else?"

"Sound of the door closing a minute later. The

person who discovered the body must have shown up after the battery had run down—there wasn't anything else on it."

"Thanks, Cooper."

Frank Tripp glared at the man on the other side of the desk. The man—editor Jeremiah Burkitt—glared back. Burkitt was short and paunchy, with a graying beard and jet-black hair that looked as if it had been polished with shoeshine.

"I did what I had to," growled Burkitt.

"You left the scene of a murder," Tripp growled back. "You know what that looks like?"

"You're the cop. You tell me."

Tripp leaned forward in his chair. "You are getting on my last nerve, Mister Burkitt. I have some questions, and you're going to answer them. Or I will haul you down to the station in handcuffs and stick you in a room with no air-conditioning while I take my own sweet time deciding just what I'm going to charge you with."

"Ask away."

"Why were you at Hiram Davey's home at six in the morning?"

"I told you. He owed me a column and I was there to collect. He wasn't answering his phone, so I went to see him in person."

"And when there was no answer you just walked in?"

Burkitt snorted. "When one of my writers misses

a deadline, they know there's no place to hide. If the door had been locked I would've broken it down."

"Tell me exactly what you saw when you entered the house."

"I saw Davey's body, lying in a pool of blood in the living room. It looked like there had been a fight. I didn't touch a damn thing."

"You didn't check him for a pulse, see if he was still breathing?"

Burkitt's eyes narrowed. "I've seen my share of corpses, Detective. I knew Davey was dead the second I laid eyes on him, and I know enough to not disturb a crime scene."

"Right. Are we gonna find your prints on anything in that house other than the doorknob?"

"Sure. I've been there before. Check the whisky glasses in the rolltop desk he used as a bar—I doubt he ever washed them."

"Any idea who would want Davey dead?"

Burkitt grimaced. "Six months ago I would have sworn the man didn't have an enemy in the world—and that's a rare thing to say about a journalist. Hi was good at making people laugh, and people loved him for it. He got more mail than anyone else at the paper, and it was all positive."

"So what happened six months ago?"

"He signed a book deal. Some kind of crime novel, with a really loopy cast of characters. I thought it was going to be typical Davey stuff, but then I found out he was doing a ton of research and interviews. He wanted people to take his writing more seriously, so he thought he'd ground the book in reality, base it on actual people and events."

"You think some of the people he was planning on using in the book weren't too happy with him?"

"That's what Davey said. He claimed his life had been threatened more than once."

"By who?"

Burkitt shrugged. "No idea. He was being real secretive about the book, wouldn't give me any details. You want to know who was in it, you'll have to read it for yourself."

"I'll do that," said Tripp.

Many drivers reported seeing the balloon drifting over the highway, but none of them had noticed anything fall out of the basket. A few people had spotted the craft earlier over the Everglades, but nobody saw anyone leave it either.

Calleigh talked briefly to the FAA investigator, a thin, harried looking man named Pinlon who'd driven up along the shoulder, bypassing the crawling line and getting more than a few angry honks in response.

"Gunshot?" Pinlon said, shaking his head and entering data in a PDA. "That's a new one. Better than what I usually get, though. Most balloon fatalities happen when they hit power lines. Pow, zap, game over."

"This was more of a blam, crash, traffic jam," said Calleigh. "Fewer fireworks, but more angry commuters."

"They'd be a lot angrier if they got home and their power was out." Pinlon sighed and ran a hand through his thinning hair. "Anyway, seems pretty open and shut to me."

"Looks like it, I know. But we're not so sure . . ."

Pinlon talked to a few more people and then supervised the loading of the balloon itself onto a truck. "We'll have to go over the whole thing inch by inch," he told Horatio. "They may be big and slow, but they're still aircraft. The FAA won't sign off on this until I hand in a full report."

"Let us know if you find anything unusual," said Horatio. "We'll do the same on our end."

"What's next?" Calleigh asked after Pinlon had left.

"We visit the launch site," said Horatio. "Mister Greer tested negative for GSR—let's see if the rest of his story checks out."

Frank Tripp knocked on Natalia's door around two. "Got a minute?"

She looked up from her monitor and giggled.

Frank looked nonplussed. "'Scuse me?"

"Sorry, Frank. But you were right—this guy's *funny.*"

"So that's what you found on the disk? More columns?"

"No, it looks like Mister Davey had higher ambitions. He was working on—"

"A book, I know. I just got back from talking to his editor at the newspaper. Apparently he just signed a pretty sweet deal for a crime novel."

"It's called *Floridosity*," Natalia said. "But referring to it as a work of fiction isn't exactly accurate."

"Yeah, apparently he was basing all the characters on real people—Miami residents he'd interviewed or researched."

"Not only that, he made extensive notes detailing his plans for each character."

"From what his editor said, his portrayals weren't all that flattering."

"Actually, they're *hilarious*." She grinned and shook her head. "But yeah, he doesn't exactly show these people at their best. If he wasn't careful, he could have had a libel suit on his hands."

"I'd say he definitely wasn't careful enough."

"Well, he did manage to leave the disk where his attacker didn't find it—which gives us a shopping list of suspects."

Frank nodded. "How long of a list we talking?"

"There are five main characters in the book. Any one of them could be our killer."

"And we've got the real ID of each of 'em?"

"Right here on disk."

"Then what are we waiting for? Let's go get 'em."

"But—don't you want to read the files, first?"

"Nah. I'm a quick study—you can fill me in as we drive. Besides, *how* bad Davey made our suspects look isn't the important part. It's what they did as a result—and who they did it to."

Natalia took off her lab coat and hung it up. "The facts, not the fiction?"

Tripp grinned. "Couldn't have put it better myself."

2

COLBY DIDN'T NOTICE the yacht at first. He was using a hose to wash down the marina's ramp, where the remains of somebody's half-digested dinner was now forming a scaly puddle. "Geez," Colby muttered to himself. "You couldn't make it six inches farther and hit the water? Maybe the seagulls appreciate it, but I sure don't."

Then he glanced up and saw the boat heading toward one of the marina's slips. Colby wasn't exactly a seasoned mariner—he was working part time at the marina because it paid more than a fast-food restaurant and he was saving up for his first car—but even to his inexperienced eyes there were two immediate problems that leaped out.

First, the boat was going way too fast. Second, the slip it was heading for was already occupied.

"Hey!" Colby said. He looked around wildly, but his boss was nowhere in sight. *"Hey!"* he said again, louder this time. The boat—at least a sixty-footer—continued its steady, resolute charge forward. The bow of the ship proclaimed its name as *Svetlana 2*.

The boat it was heading toward was a small sailboat called the *Feverfew*. Colby had always thought it was a dumb name, but the couple that owned it were nice enough. They weren't aboard now, which was good. Colby hoped they kept up their insurance payments.

"HEY!" Colby hollered. He was yelling at whoever was piloting the yacht now; the boat was close enough that Colby could see the figure up in the wheelhouse, behind the glass. He seemed awfully short—

Colby realized the figure was slumped forward, on top of the wheel itself. And the only glass in the window of the wheelhouse were jagged shards jutting from the edges of the frame.

The yacht slammed into the smaller ship with a sound like a dinosaur stepping on one of its own eggs. It crushed the sailboat between its own mass and the dock, wooden planks splintering and snapping. The pilings held firm, but the sailboat was scrap; it sank in less than a minute.

Colby stared at the wreckage for a full ten seconds, then pulled out his cell phone.

He made sure he took at least a dozen good photos before he called nine-one-one.

*   *   *

"This is obviously not a good day to travel," Alexx said, looking at the wreckage of the yacht from the top of the ramp. She crossed her arms and glanced at Delko and Wolfe, who had just arrived. "First a balloon, then a boat. What's next, a train wreck?"

Delko grinned. "I'm just glad it made it to shore. Means I don't have to suit up and spend the day pulling bodies out of the water."

"I don't know—nice day for a swim," said Wolfe. "Pretty damn hot, actually."

"Then let's get to work," Alexx said. "From what I understand, there's plenty of it."

They made their way down the ramp and toward the makeshift gangplank that had been set up, a long board that stretched from the damaged dock to the yacht itself. A uniformed officer helped them aboard. "It's pretty ugly," the officer, a tall woman with a blond crewcut, said. "Only one survivor, the guy that got the ship back to shore. They took him to Dade General with multiple gunshot wounds, but the EMT's said he'd probably make it."

Alexx sighed. "Well, we're here for all the ones that didn't."

There was no shortage of victims. Bodies were sprawled on the upper deck, on the lower deck, and in the cabin area below. Bullet holes scarred bulkheads like the tracks in a junkie's arm, and blood was everywhere.

Alexx moved quickly and professionally from body to body, confirming death by GSW over and over again. Delko took pictures, while Wolfe collected and documented bullet casings.

"I think," said Delko, "I'm getting a pretty good idea of what went on here."

"Running gun battle," said Wolfe. "Two sides, both of them heavily armed. I'd say it started on the top deck and moved indoors."

"Yeah. Question is, why were they shooting at each other?"

"Well, let's break down the two groups. On one side we have a bunch of young guys with tattoos dressed in Modern Urban Thug; on the other, we see a lot more khaki, at least two suit-and-ties, and actual leather shoulder holsters."

Delko nodded. "Street crew and professional security team?"

"Right. So why were they on the same boat together?"

"Maybe one of them crashed the party."

"A hijacking?" Wolfe considered it. "Could be. Which means there was another boat involved—"

"Guys?" Alexx called out. "Come down here and take a look at this."

They followed her voice belowdecks, through a dining room with a massive, bullet-riddled buffet laid out, and down a hall lined with cabins. She was in the first one on the right, crouched beside a bed with a male DB sprawled on it.

"This makes the fifteenth victim," said Alexx. "But this one wasn't shot."

"COD?" asked Wolfe.

"Skin is pallid, lips cyanotic." She opened his mouth carefully. "Got a lot of liquid in his mouth—might be saliva. No petechia in the eyes, no bruising on the neck or any other obvious wounds. I'll have to get him on my table before I can say."

"Did you hear that?" asked Delko. He looked around.

"Hear what?" asked Wolfe.

"A thumping noise."

"I don't—wait. Yeah, I heard that, too."

Delko and Wolfe drew their guns at the same moment. "Stay here," Delko told Alexx in a low voice.

"They told me the boat had been cleared—" Alexx whispered.

"We'll check it out," said Wolfe.

The two CSIs moved out of the cabin and back toward the dining room. The thumping grew louder.

"Miami-Dade PD!" Delko called out. "Show yourself!"

The thumping grew louder, and now muffled voices could be heard as well—it sounded like they were saying, "Let us out of here!"

"It's coming from the galley," said Wolfe.

The galley was outfitted like an upscale restaurant, with gleaming stainless-steel appliances and marble countertops. The sound was coming from behind a wine rack against one wall.

Delko holstered his gun. "Cover me," he said. "I'm going to try to move this thing out of the way . . . ah. It's on hinges." He swung the wine rack to one side, revealing a metal door with a recessed latch. He pulled it open.

A frosty mist billowed out, obscuring their vision. As it cleared, Delko and Wolfe could see a group of people huddled together in the center of what looked like a large meat freezer. A man stood apart from them, closer to the door. He was dressed in a lightweight linen suit of pale gray, with a black silk shirt underneath. His nose was sharp, the high widow's peak of his hair black shot with silver. He was the only one who didn't look terrified or half frozen.

"At last," he said. "I thought you'd never hear us."

"And you are?" said Delko.

The man smiled and stepped past Delko, into the galley. He ignored Wolfe's gun. "Jovan Dragoslav. I am the owner of this craft."

"You can come out," Wolfe called to the others. There were six of them: four were young, beautiful women, one was a Japanese man dressed in cook's whites, and one was a woman in her fifties in a business suit.

Wolfe holstered his gun. "Why didn't you say something before this?"

Dragoslav turned his palms up in a gesture of apology. "We thought it might be a trick. The pirates, trying to get us to reveal ourselves."

"Pirates, huh?" said Delko, giving Wolfe a look.

The women and the cook filed out, hugging themselves and looking as if they wanted nothing more than to get out into the Miami sun. "I'll take you up and out," said Wolfe. "Follow me closely and don't touch anything." The women nodded, but the cook looked anxious. "I don't think he speaks English," the fiftyish woman said.

"Police," said Wolfe, holding up his badge and letting the cook see it. It didn't seem to make him any happier. "I think he gets it," he said, and motioned for the group to follow him. Delko brought up the rear.

"Oh my God," one of the women gasped when they saw the bodies. Dragoslav's face was impassive.

"All clear, Alexx," Wolfe called out.

She stepped out of the cabin with a concerned look on her face. "Anyone hurt?"

"Maybe some hypothermia. I'll let you look them over up top."

Once Alexx and the passengers were off the ship, Delko took Dragoslav aside. "You want to tell me what happened?"

"Certainly. I and my guests were enjoying a cruise, when our ship was approached by another vessel, a speedboat. They wanted our help, but when we let them aboard, they pulled out guns and began shooting."

"And your men shot back?"

"We defended ourselves, yes."

Delko nodded. "Seems like you were packing an

awful lot of firepower for a pleasure cruise. Were you expecting trouble?"

Dragoslav smiled. "I am by nature a cautious man."

"Not cautious enough, though."

"I suppose not."

"What sort of business are you in, Mister Dragoslav?"

Dragoslav shrugged. "I dabble in the import/ export trade. I deal mainly with Eastern Europe."

"I see. Any idea why pirates might want to hijack your yacht?"

Dragoslav looked away from Delko, at the wreck of his ship. His look darkened. "They are pirates. I have—*had*—a yacht. Would you blame a bank for being robbed?"

"No," said Delko. "Of course not. If you'll excuse me, I have to process the crime scene. An officer will take your full statement."

He nodded at Wolfe, who joined him as they returned to the ship.

"The ladies," said Wolfe, "as you might have gathered by the MTCR, are professional escorts. Except the one in the suit—she says her name is Val Faustino, and she's a business associate of Mister Dragoslav."

"MTCR?" asked Delko.

"Makeup to Clothes Ratio: high on the first, low on the second."

"Right. Well, Mister Dragoslav claims they were

out there for nothing more than a cruise, and claims he doesn't know why the hijackers targeted him."

They went belowdecks once more. "Sure," said Wolfe. "He just happened to have a heavily armed security force with him to make sure the *mojitos* were served on time."

"Dragoslav says he's in the import/export business."

"Shorthand for smuggler. Question is, what's he smuggling?"

Delko headed straight for the galley. "Something valuable, no question. Something you might want to hide in a concealed walk-in freezer."

"Suspect number one," said Natalia, "is Marssai Guardon."

"The citrus heiress?" asked Tripp. He put on his seatbelt as Natalia started up the Hummer.

Natalia grinned. "Right. I'm sure that's the first thing that leaped to mind when you heard that name."

Tripp grinned back. "Okay, so like everyone else in the world, I've heard of the video. But I've never seen it."

Marssai Guardon was in line to inherit her family's citrus empire—supposedly worth billions. She was young, rich, and had grown up in Miami, a playground she rapidly became queen of. Her partying was legendary in Miami's social blender of models, rock stars, and actors—but that notoriety went from local to international when an X-rated video of her having sex in a Miami nightclub got loose on the Internet.

"If that's true, you're probably the last holdout on the planet," said Natalia. She reached down and turned up the Hummer's air-conditioning a notch. "But there's an interesting twist to the story—according to Davey's notes, the video was a fake."

Tripp frowned. "Hold on. If that's true, why would she kill him? Wouldn't she want the truth to come out?"

"That's just it—Davey claims that not only was the video a fake, Marssai was in on it."

"Why?"

"His notes were a little vague on that part. I can tell you why the fictional version of Marssai Guardon participates in the hoax: She wants to embarrass her family because they've reduced her allowance. He writes her character as shallow, stupid, sex-obsessed, and greedy."

"So the book could not only make her look bad, it could get her in hot water with her folks. Think that's enough to trigger a murder?"

"Depends on how accurate it is."

Tripp nodded. "Where we headed?"

"The Glitteratti Hotel. Marssai's publicist says she's staying at a suite there."

"Publicist? What does she need a publicist for? I'd think more publicity is the last thing she'd want."

Natalia shook her head. "People that grow up under a spotlight aren't like everyone else, Frank. It's like they breathe a different kind of air. It's around them all the time, so they take it for granted—until something takes it away. Then they realize how much they need it."

"Sounds like you know a little something about the subject."

"I've—known people like that, yeah."

Frank heard the tone in her voice and didn't pursue it. "So . . . how about the bloodwork?"

"No hits from CODIS—but I don't think she's in the system."

They pulled up in front of the Glitteratti, a brand-new Miami hotel a block away from Ocean Drive. Its green-tinted windows and angled top made it look like a spaceship carved from a single, immense emerald.

The lobby was opulent, with a gold-veined black marble floor and a huge fountain shaped like a globe of the world done in blue glass and illuminated from within. Tripp strode up to the front desk as if he'd just pulled the clerk over for speeding, flashed his badge, and asked for Marssai Guardon's room number. The clerk gave it to him without an argument.

"Think she'll be there?" Natalia asked as they rode up in the elevator.

Frank checked his watch. "It's almost three. Should be out of bed by now."

Natalia couldn't tell if he were joking or not.

Tripp rapped on the door to the suite, noting the two empty room service trays outside the door, each one holding several empty champagne bottles and glasses.

"Looks like Miss Guardon was celebrating last night," said Frank.

The door opened. A young blond woman stood there, dressed in a short pink robe and blinking sleepily. "Yes?"

"Miss Guardon?" said Natalia. "I'm a crime scene investigator with Miami-Dade PD, and this is Detective Frank Tripp. Can we come in and ask you a few questions?"

"Uh—can you give me a minute to put some clothes on?" she asked.

"Go ahead," said Tripp. "We'll wait out here."

She shut the door. Frank glanced over at Natalia. "When I was a beat cop, we called this part the Bathroom Break."

"I don't get it."

"This is when the perp flushes all his drugs down the toilet. If there's already a warrant for his arrest, he tries to climb out the bathroom window."

Natalia frowned: "If you *know* he's going to flush the drugs or run, then why—"

"On a serious bust, we wouldn't give them any warning. But if we're just making inquiries, it does two things: makes them nervous, and gets rid of the drugs. Two birds, no stone."

"So you think she's—tidying up?"

"Could be. Keep your eyes open."

The door opened again. Marssai Guardon had thrown on a tracksuit of dark purple, but was still in her bare feet. She smiled at them and said, "Come on in."

The suite was large and luxurious, with a full bar at one end and a large, sunken hot tub in the center of the room ringed by curving couches. If anything illegal had been going on, there was no trace of it now. Marssai led them to a large, glass-topped table and sat down in one of the chrome-and-leather chairs around it, motioning for them to join her. "What's this all about?" she asked.

"Did you know a man named Hiram Davey?" asked Natalia.

"Hi Davey? Sure. I met him at a party—about six months ago, I think. He's *funny*."

"Not anymore," said Tripp. "He was found dead this morning."

Marssai's large blue eyes got even wider. "Ohmigod. What happened?"

"We're trying to figure that out," said Natalia. "Were you aware that Mister Davey was planning on writing a novel?"

"Well, yeah. He mentioned it at the party. Said he was going to fill it with crazy Miami types—it made him real popular. Everybody wanted to be in it."

"Did you know," asked Natalia, "that *you* were in it?"

"Really? No—no, I didn't know that."

"That's strange," said Natalia. "Because among his files were a number of interviews—including an interview with you."

Marssai sighed. "Do you have any idea how many interviews I do? When I had a part in that gross-out comedy last year, I did, like, a *hundred* of them in one week. They all kind of blur together after a while."

"I didn't know you were an actress," said Natalia.

"Well, it was only a small part—my character drowns in a vat at a vodka distillery. I just did it as a favor to the director."

"So you don't remember doing the interview?" asked Natalia.

"No."

"Where were you between midnight last night and noon today?" asked Tripp.

"I was out clubbing until three—I don't remember all the places I went to, but I could put together a list if I talked to some of my friends. I came back here with some of them, and we were up till about six. Then I crashed."

"Alone?" asked Natalia.

"No," said Marssai. "I was with Rudolpho, a friend of mine. A friend with benefits, you know? He was gone when I woke up—I don't know what time he left."

"Rudolpho and your other . . . *friends* can verify your whereabouts?" asked Natalia.

Marssai shrugged. "Sure. I can get you cell phone numbers if you want to talk to them."

"We'd appreciate that," said Tripp.

"What the *hell*," said Wolfe slowly, "is *that*?"

He and Delko stood in the chilly confines of the concealed freezer. At the very end was a plastic sheet hanging from the ceiling; they had pulled it aside to reveal what hung behind it on a hook.

It stretched from floor to ceiling, looking like a whale that had been run over by a steamroller. One flat, triangular fin was folded across the huge, disk-shaped expanse of flesh, while a single eye stared blankly at them from near the floor. Its skin glistened wetly.

"It's a mola mola," said Delko. "Also known as a sunfish or moonfish. They're native to these waters, but they're not a sport fish."

"Are they edible?" Wolfe asked, eyeing the thing dubiously.

"Not particularly. In fact, I have no idea why someone would go to the trouble of catching one, let alone keeping it."

"Well, it must be here for a reason."

"It's a big specimen," said Delko thoughtfully. "Moonfish can run as large as five thousand pounds—this one looks close to that. Maybe it's here because of its size."

Wolfe nodded. "As a container, you mean? Like drug mules swallowing condoms filled with heroin?"

Delko ran one gloved hand along the fish's right edge. "More like a turkey full of illegal stuffing. It's been cut open—give me a hand, will you?"

They each grabbed an edge of the incision and pulled in opposite directions, opening a gaping hole. Delko shone his flashlight into the wound. "Nothing but entrails. If there was anything in here it's already been removed."

"Or hasn't been placed yet," said Wolfe, releasing his edge. It slapped back into place with a wet smack.

"You notice the temperature in here?" asked Delko.

"Yeah, it's nice and cool. I wish the rest of the crime scene were this comfortable."

"Cool, but not cold. The fish isn't frozen—obviously, they didn't plan on it being here for long. We need to get it back to the lab and take a closer look. If there was contraband in there, it may have left some transfer."

"Great. Think Alexx has a drawer big enough?"

Natalia and Tripp collected the names and numbers of Marssai Guardon's friends, thanked her, and left.

"Think her alibi will pan out?" Tripp asked as they got back in the Hummer.

"Depends on how loyal her pals are. They'll back her up about being out in public—it's what happened afterward I'm not so sure about."

The first name on the list was Rudolpho Senzo, the one who had supposedly spent the night with

Marssai. Rudolpho was a male model who was staying at another expensive hotel, the Shoremont. The lobby of this one was done in classic Art Deco, with lots of fluted silver piping and sweeping marble arches; the front desk looked like a counter from a 1950s diner that served nothing but caviar burgers and champagne milkshakes.

They had some trouble locating Senzo's room at first—he wasn't registered under his own name. The desk clerk, a perky young woman named Alyssa, finally figured out that the room had been charged to his agency, Adonissy, Inc.

A young woman with pink hair answered their knock. She was wearing even less than Marssai had been, just a white T-shirt with a picture of an attractive woman on it. The picture, Natalia realized, matched the face above it.

"Rudolpho? He's, ah, still asleep," the woman said, tugging her T-shirt down. "Can you come back later?"

"Afraid not," said Tripp. "Tell him this is his official wake-up call."

She disappeared into the bedroom, leaving the door open. Natalia glanced at Tripp and shrugged, then walked in.

The suite wasn't quite as upscale as Marssai's, but then, Rudolpho actually worked for a living—*if*, Natalia thought, *you can call being paid thousands of dollars a day to look beautiful work.*

The pink-haired woman came back, wearing a

fuzzy green terry cloth robe. "He says he'll talk to you in there," she said.

"Okay," said Natalia.

Rudolpho Senzo sat upright in bed, knees bent, rumpled bedclothes gathered around his waist. His bare chest and arms were smooth, muscular, and perfectly tanned. His face had the sort of sharp-boned generic beauty that somehow made him seem less than human; it was like looking at a magazine ad that had learned how to talk. Later, Natalia's memory would insist on portraying him in black and white.

"What's this all about?" Rudolpho said. His accent hinted more at New Jersey than Italy.

Tripp and Natalia identified themselves. "We're conducting a criminal investigation," said Natalia. "We were wondering if you could tell us where you were last night, starting around midnight."

Rudolpho scratched his dark, tousled hair. "Let's see . . ." He thought for a moment, then rattled off a list of nightclubs. "We wound up in Marssai's suite around three, I guess."

"Who's we?" asked Tripp.

"Me, Kirsten, Violetta, Chad, and Beemer."

Natalia nodded—that was the same list Marssai had given them. "And you left at what time?"

"Uh—around eight, I guess."

Natalia raised her eyebrows. "Weren't there very long, were you?"

"I had things to do."

Tripp stared at him, arms crossed. "According to

Marssai Guardon, you two hit the sheets at around six. Two hours is a pretty short night."

Rudolpho gave him a dazzling, perfect smile. "Long enough, if you know what I mean."

"So you two have your jollies," said Tripp, "and you take off when you're done."

"Yes and no."

Natalia frowned. "What's that supposed to mean?"

"What it means is, I wasn't exactly done." For the first time, Rudolpho looked uncomfortable. "See, I took these pills. Me and Marssai had a lot of fun, but then she just wanted to go to sleep. I was still . . . you know."

"Primed?" asked Tripp.

"Yeah. So I called Kim—she's a morning person. Thought she might be interested in a little early AM delight."

"Uh-huh," said Tripp. "From the looks of things, she was up for it."

"And I'm guessing," said Natalia, studying the blankets bunched around Rudolpho's waist, "That *you* still are."

Rudolpho blushed. "The stuff takes a long time to wear off, you know?"

"Not this long," said Natalia. "Are you familiar with a condition called priapism?"

"No. Is—is it serious?"

"I think you better see a doctor," said Natalia. "Or you might have worse problems than whether or not you can fit into your pants."

3

THE FIELD where Timothy Breakwash had begun his last flight was just outside Florida City, abutting a large, sprawling ranch-style house. Horatio pulled in and parked the Hummer behind a station wagon that had seen better days. A hand-painted wooden sign at the head of the driveway had proclaimed BREAKWASH BALLOONING, but that was the only indication of the business.

"Not exactly busy," Calleigh said as they got out.

"Joel Greer told me it was more a sideline than Breakwash's primary source of income," said Horatio, taking off his sunglasses and slipping them into his breast pocket. "According to him, Timothy Breakwash was an environmental consultant. He was a little unclear on the details, though."

As they approached the front door, they could hear the barking of a small dog inside. The woman who answered Calleigh's knock was in her early forties, with salt-and-pepper hair in a long braid down her back. She wore a simple blue sundress and sandals, and had a mug of tea in one hand. Her eyes were red.

"Yes?" she said.

"Ma'am," said Horatio. "My name is Lieutenant Horatio Caine, with the Miami-Dade Police Department. I know this is a difficult time for you, but we need to ask you a few questions about your husband."

"Of course," the woman said. Despite the redness of her eyes, she looked quite composed for a brand-new widow—but Horatio knew better than to judge her by a first glance. Grief worked in powerful and unpredictable ways, and it was possible the woman was in shock or even denial.

"I'm Randilyn," the woman said, ushering them into a large living room that held several over-stuffed chairs and two couches. "Watch out for the newspapers on the floor—we're trying to paper-train a puppy."

At that moment the puppy in question came charging into the room, barking excitedly. It was a white bulldog, with a squat body and a jowly face.

Horatio went down on one knee, and the puppy tried to climb onto him, licking his hand and wriggling as much as its short, thick body would allow. "Hey, pal," said Horatio with a smile, scratching behind the dog's ears. "You look like a real people-eater."

"Oh, she's ferocious," said Randilyn. "She may lick you to death. She licks everything—people, furniture, stuffed animals, walls. I caught her licking the TV screen once."

"What's her name?"

"Chiba. She's an Olde English Bulldogge, a breed that was developed in the nineteen-seventies to bring back some of the qualities of the eighteenth-century English bulldog. Oldies are very affectionate, but stubborn." She sighed. "A lot like Tim—I guess that's why he loved the breed so much. He was very protective of Chiba—wouldn't even let her out of the house, you know?" Randilyn sat down, her gaze suddenly distant. She took a long, slow sip of tea from her mug.

Calleigh and Horatio sat on one of the couches, Chiba happily following Horatio and lying down near his feet. "Mrs. Breakwash," said Horatio, "were you present this morning when your husband launched the balloon?"

"No," she said quietly. "Balloon launches are usually very early—around dawn—and I like to sleep late on weekends. He didn't even wake me when he left; the last time I talked to my husband was last night."

"How did he seem?" asked Calleigh.

"He was . . . a little down. Tim always had some scheme going to make us money, but he was more of a dreamer than a businessman. That's why we got Chiba—when Tim heard that Olde English Bulldogge pups could go for as much as three thousand dollars, he decided he wanted to breed them." She shook her head. "He didn't check into why they were so expensive, though. Turns out they suffer from a condition called anasarca. Bulldogs that have it produce fetuses that retain two to three times as much water as they should, meaning the puppies swell up in the womb. It makes delivery extremely difficult and hazardous, so much so that most bulldogs give birth through Caesarian surgery."

"Which isn't cheap," said Calleigh.

"No, and neither is ballooning—at least, not when you don't have any paying customers," said Randilyn. "But Tim loved to fly, especially over the 'Glades. He'd go up even without any other riders to help defray costs."

Horatio nodded. "I understand that Tim also worked in environmental science?"

"Off and on. He'd get hired to take samples from the 'Glades and measure them for pesticide levels, things like that. He had a degree in environmental science, but what he was doing wasn't very sophisticated—any grad student could have done it."

Calleigh leaned forward. "You said he was feeling down?"

Randilyn hesitated. "Yes. He'd been depressed for a while, actually. I think the gap between his dreams and his plans was finally starting to sink in. I tried to talk to him about it, but he insisted he was fine."

"Did his ballooning work have anything to do with the research?" asked Calleigh. "Was he maybe using the balloon to look for something?"

"No. I mean—I don't think so. If he was, he never mentioned it to me." She put a hand to her forehead and winced. "I'm sorry," she said. "I'm not feeling very well. Bit of a headache."

Calleigh glanced at Horatio, and he gave her an almost imperceptible nod. "We understand," said Calleigh. "Before we go, we're going to need access to Tim's printer and computer. Actually, we're going to have to take them with us."

"That's fine," said Randilyn.

Once they were back in the Hummer, the first words out of Calleigh's mouth were, "She's hiding something."

"I'd say so, too. Her denial that the balloon was connected to her husband's research wasn't terribly convincing."

"You think maybe Breakwash was killed because of something he found out?"

"Possibly. Which means that whatever *he* found out, we have to find out as well."

Horatio fell silent as he drove. Calleigh could tell he was thinking, but there was something in the quality of his silence that made her quiet as well.

When Horatio finally spoke, the subject wasn't what Calleigh expected.

"Did you have a dog when you were growing up, Calleigh?"

"No, I was always more of a cat person. But I had an uncle with a pair of prize bloodhounds—they were great dogs. I used to love playing with them when he visited."

"I haven't had a dog since . . . since I was very young." Horatio paused. "I called him Scrappy. Not really sure what breed he was—my mother used to claim he was half Jack Russell and half raccoon."

"Liked a nice garbage-can buffet?"

"You could say that. It was a habit that eventually . . . proved fatal."

"Did he get a chicken bone stuck in his throat or something?"

"No. My father came home from work one day and found that Scrappy had gotten into the trash can in the kitchen, made a real mess." Horatio paused. "My father kicked him to death."

"That's horrible. I'm sorry."

"It was a long time ago. And my father did far worse things . . ."

Horatio didn't say anything else, and Calleigh didn't ask.

"Okay," said Natalia. She and Frank were grabbing a quick bite to eat—after a protracted negotiation that had Tripp holding out for chili dogs and Natalia favoring someplace that didn't use paper napkins, they had settled on Auntie Bellum's, a diner a short distance from the CSI lab. "I think I've found something interesting." She had her laptop set up on the table and was picking at the keyboard and a salad at the same time.

"Something in the novel?" asked Tripp. He added some more Piri sauce to his chili.

"No, online. Seems that Marssai Guardon is about to launch her own website."

"So? Everybody has at least one, these days."

"Not like this. It's a pay site, and the buzz on the message boards is that it's going to be X-rated."

"Porn?" Tripp stirred his chili with a spoon. "Seems kinda low-rent for an heiress."

"Maybe not. With the right promotion and material, it could be worth millions."

"Might be even more valuable as a tool to embarrass her folks."

Natalia jabbed a fork full of salad at the screen. "But then why would she kill Davey? A porn site trumps a trashy novel for shock value."

"Maybe that's it. Spoiled rich girls don't like playing second fiddle."

Natalia frowned. "She didn't come across as spoiled to me, Frank. A little wild, sure. But anybody with the business savvy to launch a project like this isn't going to fly off the handle and kill someone for creating a fictional version of her—not when she's already trying to play up the sleaze angle herself."

"Yeah, it doesn't really add up. Except for one thing."

"What's that?"

Tripp took a big mouthful of chili and swallowed it before answering. "Only one thing beats sex, when it comes to publicity."

Natalia nodded. "Murder."

Eric Delko was no stranger to working marine crime scenes; usually, though, this involved his putting on a wetsuit and scuba gear to recover a body underwater. Working on a yacht—even one that had run aground—was a change of pace.

He stood in the freezer, considering the sunfish. *It must have taken several strong men and some kind of equipment to wrestle it down here,* he thought. He'd encountered live sunfish before while diving; the immense creature looked like something out of a science-fiction movie, with its huge, flattened body.

Something moved on its skin.

Delko leaned in closer. It was a small, crablike creature, hanging on to the gill slit near the eye. It reminded Delko of something, something he'd heard about moonfish but couldn't quite remember.

"Parasites," he said aloud. *Moonfish are extremely susceptible to parasites. That's why they float on the surface on their sides—so seagulls will land on them and pick the parasites off. But there was something else . . .*

It wouldn't quite come to him. He shook his head in frustration. Whatever it was, it just reinforced his impression that the fish was important to the case. He needed to get it off the ship and onto a necropsy table.

"You know," said Wolfe, who had walked up quietly behind him, "if this were a movie, this would be the part where the alien bursts out covered in fish guts."

"This isn't a movie, Wolfe."

"Exactly my point. It's a crime scene—a very large, messy, and also unstable crime scene. We've got more than a dozen bodies to process, what looks like hundreds of rounds to collect and document, and the ship we're on might just sink at any moment. And you're in here, studying a fish."

"The ship isn't going to sink. And this fish is important—I'm not sure why, but it is."

"Aye, aye, Captain Ahab." Wolfe gave him a sarcastic salute. "And they say I'm compulsive . . . look, just give me a hand as soon as you can, all right? There's a lot to do out here, that's all I'm saying."

"Sure." Delko pulled out his cell phone.

"Who are you calling?"

"Miami PD motor pool. We're going to need a refrigerated truck to move this, and I think I saw one in the impound lot the other day."

Wolfe rolled his eyes. "Right. Let me know when you're available for some genuine CSI work, all right?" He turned around and stalked off.

*   *   *

QD stood for Questioned Documents, and it was the department of the crime lab that examined everything from bad checks to falsified contracts. Calleigh headed there to talk to Cynthia Wells, the technician who was examining Timothy Breakwash's suicide note.

"Hey, Cynthia," said Calleigh. "Got anything for me?"

Cynthia, a young, attractive brunette, looked up from the piece of paper she'd been studying. "Well, I can tell you it was printed by the printer you brought me."

"Is that all?"

"I can also tell you that there were no prints on it—not even smudged ones."

"That's odd."

"Not if your vic never touched it. You didn't find it on the body, right?"

Calleigh frowned. "No. It was stuck in a pocket of the balloon's basket."

"Then unless the vic wore gloves to handle his own suicide note, I very much doubt that he actually wrote it."

"But someone with access to the balloon and his printer probably did. Thanks, Cynthia."

"Any time."

"What we have here," Calleigh told Horatio, "is a good old-fashioned locked-room mystery."

They were in the break room, going over the

case. Horatio smiled and took a sip of his coffee. "Right. A man goes up in a balloon, alive and alone. He comes down dead, shot at close range. So what rules out suicide?"

"The note, for one. QD says that though it came from Breakwash's printer, it had no fingerprints on it at all."

"And no signature. Suspicious, but not definitive."

"Joel Greer could have shot him in the basket. Or there could have been two people in the balloon and one jumped out after shooting Breakwash—though I don't know how they would have kept from being seen."

Horatio leaned back and rested an elbow on the top of his chair. "Either way, Joel Greer would have to be lying. And it's likely he had access to the vic's printer, as well. Motive?"

Calleigh shrugged. "An affair with the wife? He's young and cute, she's stuck in a marriage with someone addicted to get-rich-quick schemes. They could have planned it together."

"He tested negative for gunshot residue, but he had enough time to wash his hands . . . what we need is something to tie him to the weapon."

Calleigh sighed. "Which we don't have. Guess I'm pulling on my hip waders."

"Don't book an airboat just yet. Talk to Alexx first and see what the bullet tells you."

Calleigh gave him a bright smile. "I always do . . ."

*   *   *

Doctor Alexx Woods handed Calleigh a small, de-
formed piece of metal with a pair of tweezers.
Calleigh took it carefully with a gloved hand.

"That's what killed him," said Alexx. "Went in
straight along the optic canal and through the chi-
asmatic groove, bounced off the back of the skull,
and lodged in the parietal lobe."

Calleigh examined the bullet closely. "Looks like
a twenty-two. Anything bigger probably would
have punched right through."

"I can't believe anyone would shoot themselves
in the eye while over the Everglades; it's such a
beautiful place." Alexx shook her head. "Maybe
that's why he did it. He wanted the last thing he
saw to be something magnificent."

"Or maybe someone else did," said Calleigh.
"This may not be a suicide."

Alexx frowned. "Well, it looked like one to me,"
she said. "So I followed protocol and swabbed his
hands for GSR. His right was positive."

Calleigh considered it. "Doesn't mean he shot
himself, though—just that he fired a gun."

"I suppose," said Alexx. "But if he was up in a
balloon, what was he shooting *at*?"

"Good question," Calleigh admitted. "Anything
else I should know about?"

"He was in good health for his age, and I didn't
find any other suspicious bruises or marks. Tox
screen isn't back yet."

"Thanks, Alexx. Let me know when it comes in, all right?"

"Sure thing, sweetie."

When Calleigh's cell phone rang, she hoped it was good news; so far, her theory that Timothy Breakwash had been murdered was getting weaker with every fact she uncovered. "CSI Duquesne."

"Uh, hello? I was told you were investigating that balloon that crashed?"

"That's correct."

"I, uh, saw it."

"The crash?"

"No. I was watching the balloon with my telescope while it was over the Everglades. Then it got lower and I couldn't see it anymore."

"Can I get your name, sir?"

"Sure. It's, uh, Sebastian. Sebastian Mundy."

"How long were you watching the balloon for, Mister Mundy?"

"Uh, from about seven A.M. I saw it go up."

Calleigh paused. "Mister Mundy, did you see any movement from the pilot of the balloon during the flight?"

"Well, I couldn't tell what he was doing—he was too far away."

"I understand that. But did you see him *moving*?"

"Sure. He was wearing a dark jacket, so I could see him against the sky when he went from one side of the basket to the other. No details, though."

"Mister Mundy, I'm going to need to get an official statement from you. Can we meet?"

"Uh, sure. I'm at home—can you come here?"

"Just give me the address."

She jotted it down. "Thank you very much, Mister Mundy—this is important information. I'll be there in about half an hour, all right?"

"Yeah, okay."

She disconnected and shook her head. If someone had seen Breakwash alive while the balloon was aloft, that just about put the last nail in the coffin of her murder theory. *Well, there's always the zeppelin pirates,* she thought. *They'd have to be invisible, of course, but hey—I understand the new zeppelin stealth technology is scalable.*

Even the bullet wasn't helping—a phone call to Randilyn Breakwash had confirmed that her husband did own a .22, but she couldn't locate it. If Joel Greer owned the same kind of gun, she couldn't find any record of it.

She sighed. It was beginning to look as if the case, despite its exotic trappings, was no more than that of a disillusioned dreamer who'd decided on an unusual setting to kill himself. Maybe the note was part of that—a last attempt to gain a little notoriety by leaving behind a cryptic, mysterious message.

She stopped in at Horatio's office on her way out. "H? I'm going out to interview a witness." She gave him a quick rundown on what Sebastian Mundy had told her.

"Good," said Horatio. "Give me the details when you get back."

Sebastian Mundy turned out to be a tall, lanky teenager, with short, spiky black hair and rimless glasses. He answered the door dressed in sandals, shorts, and a baggy T-shirt in blue-and-orange Desert Storm camo patterns.

"I'm CSI Calleigh Duquesne," she said, showing her badge.

"Uh, hi," he said. "C'mon in."

He led her into the living room and then stood there, looking awkward and nervous. Calleigh glanced around; middle-class neighborhood, middle-class house, middle-class furniture. "So," she said, "you saw the balloon take off?"

"Not exactly. I saw it sticking up over the trees— I guess it was still on the ground then, but I couldn't really tell. Then it started rising, and I could see the whole thing. I mean, I couldn't see the bottom part before."

"The basket."

"Yeah." He shuffled from foot to foot. "I was kinda bored, so I watched it for a while. Couldn't see much, but I didn't have anything else to do." He glanced at his feet, then up again.

"And you're sure you could see someone in the basket? Someone moving around?"

"Uh, yeah. Like I said."

"Could there have possibly been more than one person aboard?"

"Yeah, uh, no. I mean, unless they were crouched down or something. I didn't see anyone else, I know that."

"How long did you watch for?"

"Ten, fifteen minutes. Then I got bored and went downstairs to watch TV."

"Okay. Can I see where you were watching from?"

"Sure. It's up in my room. Uh, it's a little messy."

Calleigh smiled. "That's all right. I don't arrest people for being messy."

Sebastian's room was at the top of the stairs. Its single window faced west, with a small telescope on a tripod set up beside it. Calleigh went over and checked the sight line, confirming that the flight path of the balloon would have been visible.

She straightened up and asked, "Did you see anything fall out of or approach the basket?"

He looked at her with a confused expression. "You mean like a bird or something?"

"Anything at all."

"No. I didn't see anything like that."

She sighed. "Thank you. Let's go downstairs so I can write up a formal statement and you can sign it, okay?"

"Uh, yeah, sure."

Calleigh glanced out the window. A young

woman was just leaving from the neighboring house, locking the door behind her. "You mind if I ask you one more question?"

"Go ahead."

"It's the middle of summer vacation. Why were you up so early?"

He reddened. "No reason."

"Uh-huh. Some people get up early to work out—you know, go jogging or do yoga?"

His blush deepened toward crimson. "I guess."

"I had a telescope when I was a kid. You know the most important thing I learned from it?"

He shook his head.

"That to do good science, it's important to have good tools—and use them properly. Right?"

He nodded.

"Okay. Let's go fill out that report."

A teenage Peeping Tom, she thought as they headed back downstairs. *Not so much an invisible sky pirate as an unseen privacy invader. Well, it's in the ball-park, anyway . . .*

4

WOLFE SURVEYED THE RUINS of the yacht's buffet and shook his head. "Looks like they were just getting ready to eat when the attack happened. What a mess."

Delko grinned and opened his kit. "What, you're complaining about a little spilled food? You'd prefer decomposing body parts?"

"That comes with the job. This just seems . . . unnecessary."

"I don't think they were too concerned with proper etiquette."

"Quite the spread, though. This is a few steps beyond macaroni salad—lobster, foie gras, enough champagne to drown a sheik."

"And enough bullets to . . . kill a camel."

Wolfe gave Delko a skeptical look. "That would be *one*, wouldn't it?"

Delko shrugged. "Hey, it was the best I could do. A herd of camels? A really, really *tough* camel? All I know is, I see a whole lot of casings and a whole lot of holes."

"What do you want to take, casings or bodies?"

"I'll do the bodies, if that's all right."

"Yeah, sure."

They worked their way through the boat slowly and methodically, putting down numbered markers beside blood pools or bullets and snapping pictures, examining each body and how it was placed, bagging evidence as they went.

"Take a look at this," said Delko, holding up a large handgun. "It's a Russian Makarov—third one I've found, all on the guys in suits."

"Eastern European owner, Russian weapons—you think Dragoslav is Red Mafiya?"

"Could be. The other crew seems Cubano—they could be part of one of the larger gangs but not flying their colors. Seem to favor machine pistols."

"You know what's missing, right?" Wolfe asked.

"Two things."

"Exactly. Two things. Whatever the pirates were after—"

"—and the boat they took it away with."

Wolfe shook his head. "Hang on. What makes you think they found it?"

"Well, neither one's here."

"No, but in a gunfight like this all sorts of things could have happened. The boat could have been sunk, or left adrift. Maybe the pirates didn't have a chance to grab whatever it is they came for."

"Or whoever?" Delko suggested. "The motive might have been kidnapping—or even straight-out assassination."

Wolfe sighed. "Yeah, we really don't know enough yet. And I get the feeling Dragoslav and his locker-room pals aren't going to be too forthcoming."

"Dragoslav, no. Maybe we can lean on one of the working girls, though."

Wolfe snorted. "With what? We can't charge them with anything, and if Dragoslav really is Red Mafiya, they're going to know enough to keep their mouths shut."

"How about the guy that drove the boat into the dock? Last I heard, they said he was going to make it."

"Depends on how loyal he is, I guess."

"Yeah," said Delko. "And to whom."

Horatio Caine had realized long ago that the city of Miami and the Florida Everglades were inextricably linked. Despite the glittering skyscrapers, despite the limousines and SUVs and sports cars, despite all the beautiful people and the opulent places they frequented, at its heart Miami was a swamp. It had a very specific ecology: it had predators and prey, it had diurnal and nocturnal schedules, it had environments that nurtured some creatures and were deadly to others. Sometimes, tracking a killer through Miami's terrain felt more like big-game hunting than detective work.

Some game, Horatio thought to himself, *is bigger than others. And some is much, much smaller.*

"*Pfiesteria piscicida,*" CSI tech Laura Lamas said. She was a dark-haired, exotic-looking woman with African-American, Cherokee, Italian, and Irish blood; Horatio had gone to her for help in analyzing Timothy Breakwash's professional work. "Also known," she said, handing Horatio a photograph, "as the cell from hell."

Horatio studied the picture. It showed an oval spheroid with a curly belt around its middle, reminding him more than anything of a cartoon hamburger with lettuce sticking out between the buns. "This is what Breakwash was researching?"

"According to the files on his computer, yes. When it was originally discovered in 1991, this organism was called an ambush attack dinoflagellate. It's a nasty little critter—*piscicida* means fish-killer." Lamas handed him some more photos. "This is the same organism—and so is this . . . and this . . . and this."

Horatio looked through them quickly. "These all look very different."

Lamas nodded. "*Pfiesteria* has a very complex life cycle—twenty-four different unicellular stages. Not only that, but in some of the stages it appears to be a plant, and in others it's an animal."

"So what makes it so dangerous?"

"Crap."

"Excuse me?"

She smiled. "Sorry. Fish crap, to be exact. When the cell is in the presence of a large amount of fish excrement—a condition usually found in shallow, warm waters like a river estuary—it feeds and reproduces rapidly. This is called a bloom. When a bloom occurs, the cells transform into their animal-like, mobile state, and release a toxin. The toxin causes open, bleeding ulcerations in fish, and the *Pfiesteria* feed on the skin and blood that slough off. Once the fish actually die, the *Pfiesteria* transform again, into a kind of amoeba that feeds on rotting flesh."

"The cell from hell, indeed," Horatio murmured.

"It's also extremely hard to detect—the bloom process, from start to finish, only takes a few hours. And the initial organism bears a strong resemblance to other, more passive organisms—the only way to ID it for sure is to strip the outer coating off and study it under an electron microscope."

"So it's a master of disguise, a ruthless killer, and a consumer of rotting flesh."

"More or less."

Horatio handed the photographs back. "Has this organism shown up in Florida?"

"Not yet. It's been reported in nearby states, though: Virginia, North Carolina, Maryland. It's caused massive die-offs in fish populations and a fair amount of worry about possible effects on humans."

"So news of *Pfiesteria*'s presence in local waters would be big news."

Lamas nodded. "Definitely. If Breakwash found evidence the organism had shown up here, he would have been sitting on a huge story."

"Or," said Horatio, "a ticking bomb."

Once Wolfe and Delko were finished with the inside of the boat, they inspected the outside. "I've got paint transfer right here," said Delko, pointing to a blue slash about two feet above the yacht's waterline.

"Could be from the pirates' boat—or should that be ship? Pirates always have a ship, right?"

"Knock off the skull-and-crossbones stuff, huh?" Delko smiled. "This is serious."

"Okay, okay. Yeah, that looks like it's at the right height."

"So we're looking for a blue boat," said Delko, scraping a sample into a vial, "or a boat with blue trim."

"Which might be on the bottom of the bay."

"Or halfway to the Bahamas by now." Delko shrugged. "We'll see what turns up."

Wolfe studied the ship's chrome railing. "I've got two sets of deep scratches here, about two feet apart. And some kind of tool marks—looks like something might have been clamped on."

"Could have been some kind of grappling device, keep the ships together."

A large white panel pulled into the marina's parking lot. "That'll be my truck," said Delko, waving them over.

"You're really going to move a two-ton fish from a wrecked boat into the back of a truck? This I have to see."

Delko's smile turned into a grin. "Oh, you'll do more than see. You're going to help—this is a four-man job, at least."

Wolfe stared at him incredulously. "But—this is a brand-new jacket."

"Well, after today it'll definitely be broken in. Did I happen to mention that the skin of a sunfish is as rough as a shark's?"

"No. No, you didn't."

"Don't worry about it. They have a thick layer of mucus over their entire body that pretty much protects you from the sandpapery stuff underneath."

"Lovely," Wolfe said under his breath.

Laura Lamas had restricted her analysis to the computer files labeled as work; Horatio himself had gone through the rest, looking at Breakwash's address book, email folders, and personal files. He hadn't found anything terribly incriminating, but it had given him a sense of Timothy Breakwash, of the kind of man he was.

Horatio used to think that searching someone's house from top to bottom was the biggest intrusion of privacy an investigation demanded, but sifting through a few hard drives had changed his opinion. Computers had gone from being a glorified file cabinet to something approaching a second brain, storing ever larger amounts of information. But it wasn't the amount of information that Horatio found intriguing; it was the quality. Once, something had to be truly important to write it down. Now, a few clicks of a mouse button and you had a permanent link to a vast amount of data on virtually any subject, which meant the most trivial of minutiae or the most ephemeral curiosity could be recorded forever; the whim made concrete.

Timothy Breakwash had been a bookmark junkie, recording the URL of almost any site that caught his fancy. Scuba diving, live theater, sock puppets, horticulture, dog breeding, Scottish history; the man's interests seemed as broad-ranging and indefinable as the Everglades themselves. There were sites on ballooning, of course, and environmental science—but these were scattered among web pages concerned with treasure hunting or Miami history or sixteenth-century art.

The private files were even more revealing. Breakwash had written up details for over a dozen money-making schemes, ranging from a plan to sell hermit crabs as pets to a grandiose idea involving generating electricity from tiny water wheels installed in every drainpipe and eavestrough in Miami.

That last idea seemed to typify not just Breakwash's thinking, but the thinking of every get-rich-quick dreamer who found his way to Miami. Seen through the right eyes, it was a place of endless potential; a sunny and fertile ground to plant your magic beans and watch the beanstalk grow. And sometimes, that's exactly what happened—Miami had been built by dreamers like that, had been transformed more than once. It was a city that periodically fell into decay, consumed by its own decadence and popularity, then bloomed again. It was an orchid in a swamp, as dependent on the forces that could destroy it as on the ones that nurtured it; a city of storms and sunlight, of decay and rebirth.

Timothy Breakwash had sought the sun, and found the storm.

And now, Horatio thought, *all that's left of his aspirations are these files. Sketches of a life dreamed but not lived. Hopes and desires, in PDF format.*

It was a profile he'd seen before, a common element in a volatile mix. Con men, thieves, and killers were the other elements, drawn as inevitably toward opportunity as the dreamers. The dreamers thought they could spin straw into gold, and the predators were always there waiting to take it away from them. That's how it looked on the surface—but like any ecosystem, it was far more complex underneath. Predators could become prey. Horatio had seen a picture of a large Burmese python someone had released into the Everglades, where it had become a meal for a medium-size gator. What made the picture memorable was that while the gator was busy eating the snake, the python had managed to swallow half the gator.

Dreams unrealized lead to frustration, desperation, and sometimes violence. The most dangerous man is one with nothing to lose . . . and when a man loses his dreams, nothing is what's usually left.

He wondered about Randilyn Breakwash. It took a special kind of person to stick with a dreamer; most couldn't handle the endless cycle of promise and disappointment, of a life of anticipation that was never rewarded. The couples that made it, Horatio had found, were the ones that had some sort of stability to keep them going—either financial, spiritual, or emotional.

Everybody needs an anchor. What was Randilyn Breakwash's? They didn't seem to have children, she didn't strike me as being especially religious—could it be she simply loved him that much?

He had no ready answer, and her husband's computer files had provided no clue—not to that question, anyway. But they had yielded a potential suspect: Sylvester Perrone. Perrone was the CEO of Sweetbright Aquaculture, a company that marketed seafood, and according to Timothy Breakwash's files he and Perrone had met several times in the last two weeks at one of Sweetbright's fish farms. There were no notations for any of the meetings, beyond the fact that they were business-related.

Horatio was still thinking about the Breakwashes when he pulled his Hummer off the highway just outside Florida City, a small suburb of Miami with a primarily African-American population. Florida City was right on the edge of the 'Glades, and the aqua-culture operation was located at the very border of the city. Horatio drove up to a chain-link gate, got out of his vehicle, and hit the button on the small intercom mounted beneath the security camera. A curt voice asked him who he was, and the gate opened without further comment when he produced his badge and held it up to the camera.

A short drive led to a concrete-block building abutting a large, corrugated-tin warehouse. Horatio parked and headed for the smaller structure.

Inside, a slight, sunburned girl with improbably white hair looked up from her desk beside the front door and asked him who he was here to see. Horatio smiled, told her, then waited patiently while she called her boss, taking in the office space. It was one large room, with the feel of a scrappy start-up rather than a corporate leviathan; the office furniture was mismatched, the carpet new but cheap, the computers on the desks a few years behind current. People behind the desks looked busy; there were about a dozen of them, talking on phones or tapping at keyboards or both.

A door opened to Horatio's right, and a man in a white shirt with the sleeves rolled up stepped out. He was in his forties, handsome, with the broad shoulders and chest of a football player. His skin was deeply tanned, his hair a short, glossy brown that looked too perfect to be real. He strode up to Horatio and put out his hand.

"Sylvester Perrone," he said as they shook. His voice was as deep as an empty barrel, with just a touch of Texas in it.

"Lieutenant Horatio Caine."

"Come on into my office, Lieutenant. We can talk there." He motioned Horatio inside.

Perrone's office was about what Horatio expected; his desk was a little bigger, his computer a little newer, but overall it gave the impression that Perrone worked just as hard as his employees. A gigantic mounted sailfish took up most of one wall, but other than that the only decorations were a clock on the wall and a company calendar.

Perrone sat behind his desk and Horatio took the only other chair. "Now, Lieutenant—"

"Horatio, please."

"Okay, Horatio. How can I help you?"

"It's about someone who was doing some ecological consulting for you—Timothy Breakwash."

Perrone nodded. "I heard about what happened to him. Never thought of ballooning as being that dangerous."

"It's not. Mister Breakwash was shot."

Perrone's eyebrows went up. "You mean someone *shot* him while he was up in the air? That wasn't on the news."

"There are a number of unanswered questions about Mister Breakwash's death, Mister Perrone. I was hoping you could shed some light on the work he was doing for your company."

Perrone settled back in his plush leather chair—the only nod to luxury Horatio could see. "Well, the work he was doing for us was pretty standard—evaluating levels of phosphorous and nitrogen in our runoff, making sure we're up to EPA standards."

"I see. How about finding evidence of *Pfiesteria piscicida*?"

The statement had the desired effect. Perrone's eyes widened ever so slightly, there was a barely discernible pause, and his smile suddenly became even more friendly. Subtle signs, but to Horatio the man might just as well have put up a sign saying, *The next words out of my mouth will be a lie.* "The cell from hell? I've heard of it, sure, everybody in the fish business has, but it's not the kind of thing that we worry about. It's an algal bloom, happens in the wild under very specific conditions; we raise our stock in concrete tanks and control every aspect of their environment. It's like worrying about an outbreak of malaria on the space shuttle."

Horatio smiled. "And you're not the worrying type, Mister Perrone?"

Perrone spread his hands in a universal "who, me?" expression. "Hey, I raise fish for a living. People fish to *forget* their worries, right?"

"Uh-huh. Perhaps you're simply not worrying about the right thing, Mister Perrone. Such as the consequences of lying to a police officer." Horatio met the man's eyes, let him see what was in his own. After a second, Perrone looked away. "I have Timothy Breakwash's files, and I know what he was doing for you. So let's drop the *aw, shucks* act, shall we?"

"All right, all right." Perrone's voice was much more subdued. "Tim was analyzing our runoff to make sure we weren't at risk. You have to understand, this is all about public relations—when a bloom hit Virginia last year, sales of fish from that state dove like a marlin trying to break a line. People hear the words 'red tide' and all of a sudden anything with fins is poison. Even the rumor that our tanks might be contaminated would be enough to cripple business; I was trying to stay under the radar by going to an independent contractor instead of a big commercial lab. Tim told me he could do it himself and keep the results quiet no matter what they were."

"And what were those results?"

Perrone shrugged. "You tell me—you said you have his files. I was waiting to hear from him when I heard about his death."

"When was the last time you spoke to him?"

"Yesterday afternoon. I called him about the tests and he said he was waiting to hear back from his subcontractor."

"Subcontractor?"

"Yeah. Identifying *Pfiesteria* takes an electron microscope, and they're not cheap. Tim said he had a friend with access to one, somebody he trusted."

"Do you have a name?"

"Yeah—Lee Kwok. I think he was an old college buddy or something."

Horatio nodded. "Tell me, Mister Perrone—how much would Timothy Breakwash's silence have been worth to you?"

Perrone sighed. "A lot. But if you're suggesting he would have blackmailed me, you didn't know Tim. He was—well, he wasn't a very practical guy. Head in the clouds, in a very literal sense. He'd devote every second of every day to some crazy idea that was going to make him rich, but stabbing a friend in the back just wasn't in him."

"Maybe not," said Horatio, getting to his feet, "but that doesn't mean it wasn't in someone else."

"What the *hell*," Alexx said, looking down at the huge fish Delko and Wolfe had just wheeled in, "do you expect me to do with *that*?"

"I was going to suggest a nice beer batter, maybe some fries on the side," said Wolfe, "but Eric tells me they're not really good eating."

"Take it easy, Alexx," said Delko. "I've got a guy from Fish and Game coming down to do a necropsy. I just need someplace cool to store it until he gets here."

Alexx raised her eyebrows. "Let me get this straight—you think someone *murdered* this fish?"

Wolfe's grin got even wider. "That's right. We've

got a BOLO out on a guy with a wooden leg. He may be armed with a harpoon."

"Oh, you two are hilarious," said Alexx. "You should take your act on the road, maybe do the cruise ship circuit."

"Don't have the time," said Wolfe. "I have witnesses to interview." He glanced at Delko. "None of which can breathe underwater."

"Go," said Delko. "At least the fish jokes will stop."

"Only until I get back," said Wolfe. "Then it starts aaaall over again . . ."

Wolfe left the autopsy theater and headed for the interview rooms. He'd asked that the survivors of the attack meet with him there individually after giving their initial statements; he wanted to test each of their stories separately, see how consistent they were.

First up was Jillian Kastel, one of the working girls who was trapped in the freezer. She was a tall woman, with sharp Slavic features and dark hair with violet highlights. She had regained some of her poise since the last time Wolfe had seen her, and now regarded him with a mixture of icy politeness and slight amusement, her back straight as a lamppost.

"Ms. Kastel," said Wolfe, sitting down across from her. "I was wondering if I could just ask you a few more questions to clear up some details."

"I'll tell you what I told the other officer," said Kastel. Her voice was deep and rich, with just a hint of Eastern Europe in it. "I didn't see a thing. I was with Mister Dragoslav in his cabin when the shooting started. He told me to follow him and we ran into the galley, then hid in the meat locker. We heard more shooting, then it stopped."

Wolfe glanced down at his notes. "Right. And you were in there for how long?"

"About half an hour. Then there was a big impact and we were all thrown to the floor. I thought we'd been rammed."

"Weren't you worried the boat might sink?"

She gave him a cool, appraising look before answering. "I was, yes. But Mister Dragoslav calmed us down, assured us that if that were the case he would be able to tell."

"You must have a lot of faith in him."

"He is a . . . persuasive man."

"And a generous one?"

Her eyes became noticeably colder. "Very."

"So, after half an hour you're still in the freezer. You're not sinking, so you must know you've run aground. You still don't come out, even after the boat is searched by police officers—why?"

"It was Mister Dragoslav's decision. He said he thought the pirates—"

"—might be trying to trick you, right. That doesn't really hold up. I mean, waiting a half hour, sure, that I could see. But after you've run aground? Dragoslav must have known you were safe at that point."

"I don't know. He wanted to wait. We didn't start calling for help until we tried the door and found out the crash had jammed it."

Wolfe nodded. He thought he understood—Dragoslav's plan had been to slip ashore without alerting the police, if at all possible. "So, I understand how you and Dragoslav wound up in there. How about everyone else?"

"Mrs. Faustino was in the galley with the chef—they followed us in. The other girls were with me and Mister Dragoslav."

Wolfe raised his eyebrows. "All four of you?"

She gave him a tolerant smile. "As I said—he's *very* generous."

"So this isn't the first time you've . . . *entertained* Mister Dragoslav."

"I don't see how that's relevant."

"Just trying to establish the nature of your relationship, Ms. Kastel."

"Is there anything else? I've told you everything I know."

"Oh, I doubt it." Wolfe gave her a smile as cold as her own. "But I'm used to that. And you know what? I wind up finding things out, anyway."

The next woman he talked to was a blonde named Tammy Butcher. She was considerably less composed than Jillian Kastel, and burst into tears at the very start of the interview. *Post-traumatic stress,* Wolfe thought, and told her he'd take her statement later. Tammy thanked him while blowing her nose and trying not to sob.

That left two, Devon Masters and Ivy Shen. Devon was an African-American woman with hair so short it looked painted on, and she was about as much help as Jillian Kastel had been. The last one, Ivy Shen, was a Vietnamese immigrant in the process of becoming a citizen; she acted bored, but Wolfe could see the nervousness she was trying to hide.

"Ms. Shen," said Wolfe. "I'd like to hear your version of the events."

"What's to tell?" she said. Her English was flawless. "I was stuck in a freezer for an hour."

"An hour? Really? One of the other girls said it was only half an hour."

She shrugged. "I wasn't wearing a watch, I don't know. Seemed like an hour."

"Must have been frightening."

"I guess."

"Mister Dragoslav seem scared?"

The question wasn't one she'd been expecting. "What? No, I've never seen him scared."

"So you've known him for a while."

"I—yeah, I've met him before. Never been on the boat before, though."

Wolfe nodded. "He probably brings you around on special occasions, right? When he's celebrating something?"

She smiled, but it was automatic reflex, as devoid of real emotion as an infomercial. "He likes to have a good time. I don't ask why."

"No, but I can see you're intelligent—you must have some idea what he was celebrating."

"It was some sort of business deal, I think. I don't know any details."

"What kind of business is Mister Dragoslav in, exactly?"

And now the smile was practically frozen on her face. "I don't know."

Wolfe shook his head and pushed his chair back from the table. He could see this was going nowhere—at least he'd gotten the detail about the business deal, though it was so vague it wasn't worth much. "All right, Ms. Shen, you can go. If we have any more questions we'll be in touch."

She thanked him in a detached way and left. Wolfe sat at the interview table a while longer, gathering his thoughts.

Dragoslav takes a group of hookers and a business-woman out to party in his yacht. They're attacked at sea and there's a massive shootout, which wipes out both sides except for seven people who hide in a concealed meat cooler. We search the boat and don't find anything obviously illegal. No drugs, no weapons other than the ones used in the battle, no stolen merchandise or counterfeit money or anything else unusual—except one ugly, overgrown tuna.

It didn't add up. Something smelled rotten, and it wasn't the fish . . .

5

"HEY, NATALIA," said Cooper, knocking on the door jamb to the layout room. "Wanna go watch some porn?"

Natalia looked at him and blinked. "Why, Cooper, you smooth talker," she said. "I thought you'd never ask. Are we going back to your place, or are you going to spring for the back row of a sleazy theater?"

Cooper grinned. "I was thinking more along the lines of the AV lab. I like my own equipment, if you know what I mean."

"Not sure I want to," said Natalia. "But lead on."

They talked as they walked. "Okay," said Cooper, "I've been checking out Marssai Guardon's sex video."

"What a surprise."

"Ah, but there *is* a surprise. Guardon's always claimed the video was made without her consent, but she's never denied it was her."

"Are you saying it isn't?"

"Yes . . . and no. You'll see."

They reached the AV lab. Cooper pulled an office chair on wheels up to a large monitor and motioned Natalia to sit down. He stayed standing, but leaned over to tap on the keyboard to one side of the screen.

"Okay. Now, this was apparently shot in a Miami nightclub called Morrocko. They have private VIP booths in the back, sort of semisecluded—private enough that the public can't get at the celebrities to bother them, but exposed enough that people can see that yes, they are actually in the same room as someone rich and famous."

Natalia studied the screen. There was a shot of a booth, with a long table and a curving, black leather bench seat behind it. She recognized Marssai Guardon as the one sitting in the middle, with an attractive woman on one side and a handsome, male-model type on the other. They were drinking something out of oversize martini glasses, laughing and talking about some movie premiere.

"So far," said Cooper, "all nice and innocent. Then Mister Two-Hundred-Dollar Haircut slides under the table . . ."

"Hmmm. Oh, my."

"Yeah." Cooper tapped a key and the image froze. "Now, what's the first and most obvious question about this little scenario?"

Natalia grinned and raised her eyebrows. "You

mean *besides*, 'Where can I get one of those?' Who's filming it, of course."

"Exactly. The picture doesn't jump around the way something handheld would, so the camera was in a fixed position. There are different theories as to where—some think a camera was hidden in a nearby planter, others say a rigged dessert cart was carefully positioned—but I'm going to go out on a limb and say it was a good old-fashioned tripod."

"What, behind a mirror or something?"

Cooper leaned back and crossed his arms. "Nope. Right out in plain sight."

Natalia frowned. "You're saying this was staged. Everybody involved knew exactly what they were doing the whole time."

"I'd bet on it. See, everything *below* the table is X-rated, but everything *above* the table is strictly PG-13. Well, maybe Restricted—Marssai and her girlfriend play a little tonsil hockey at one point."

"So? The other people in the club can't see what's going on beneath the table, right? All they see is Marssai doing her *When Harry Met Sally* Meg Ryan impression."

"And that's the impression they're *trying* to give—that they're doing something naughty right out in public. Did you know they charge five hundred dollars to eat in that booth now?"

"I'll resist the urge to ask what's on the menu."

"In this case," said Cooper, "a great big serving of

body double." He leaned over and tapped the monitor's screen, right at the thin edge of the table. "This isn't a single piece of footage. It's two pieces, carefully edited together. In one, Marssai Guardon and her female friend sit down, have a drink, and make out a little before Marssai fakes an orgasm. In the other, Haircut Guy sits at the same table with someone else. When he goes . . . downtown, it's not Marssai Guardon he's expressing his affection for."

"How can you tell? That it's a fake, I mean?"

"If you're referring to the recording itself, I'd love to be able to dazzle you with a highly technical explanation . . . but I don't have one. No, two things tipped me off, both of them fairly mundane." He tapped at the keyboard, zooming in on one sector of the image. "First, I noticed that Marssai doesn't move her upper body at all during the scene—that's to keep her positioned so the double can match her exactly."

"Yeah, her posture is a little weird—even when she's making out with the other girl she doesn't lean over."

"The second thing was her legs. The double's legs, that is—they're too long. I took measurements and compared them against other photos of Marssai, and if the legs under the table were hers, she'd be six inches taller."

Natalia gave Cooper an appreciative nod. "Nice work. So there's no way this could have been done without Marssai's cooperation, right?"

Cooper hesitated. "Well, I'd say it was highly unlikely—but I can't *prove* she knew what was going on. That's the problem with art, right? It's all subjective."

"I think that refers to whether or not something *is* art. In this case, I just need to know whether the artist is being honest with her public."

"You'll have to ask her. But be careful where you sit when you do."

"Good-bye, Cooper."

Natalia spotted Frank in the CSI break room, hunched over a small and battered laptop. She walked over and sat down.

"Oh, hey, Natalia. Thought I'd hide out in here and catch up on the case. Try to do this at my own desk and people keep wanting my attention."

"Reading the Davey files?"

"Yeah, just about finished. Sounds like it would have been a funny book."

"I thought you said you weren't interested in the fiction?"

He shrugged. "Figured this was my last chance to enjoy his stuff. Besides, you never can tell what might prove useful in an investigation—you guys taught me that."

"Well, the audio on the tape recorder didn't give us anything—but Cooper managed to redeem himself." She told Frank about the faked video.

Frank looked thoughtful. "Hang on. So she

helped make an X-rated video about herself, then denied it in public but didn't mention the fact it wasn't her?"

"So it seems."

Frank shook his head. "That make any sense to you? 'Cause from where I'm sitting, it's about as crazy as a soup sandwich."

"Maybe she's covering up for someone else."

"Someone who uncovered her? Then why make the thing in the first place?"

Natalia frowned. "Maybe somebody got cold feet after the fact. Somebody with more to lose than Marssai Guardon."

"Could be. If so, we don't know who she is."

"No," said Natalia. "But we *do* know someone who does."

The Fish and Game representative was a short, scrawny man named Quinkley, with an egg-shaped balding head and thick, tortoiseshell glasses that looked like they'd been made three decades ago. He walked into the lab wearing an old beige trenchcoat and a shapeless gray fedora, a beat-up black suitcase in one hand. He ignored the receptionist's desk and instead waved down the first person he saw— Calleigh.

"Excuse me, young lady," he said. His voice was a dry rattle. "Could you be so kind as to direct me to the morgue?"

"Certainly," said Calleigh. "But visitors need a badge. You can get one from reception."

"Oh, I have one." He fumbled in a pocket and pulled out an ancient rectangle of yellowed plastic with a pin on the back. He was trying to pin it to his lapel when Calleigh stopped him.

"That one's a little out of date," she said with a smile. "We use lanyards now. Come on, I'll help get you checked in."

"Thank you." He peered at her with eyes that looked like plums through his glasses. "You're very kind.

"I haven't been here since you remodeled," Quinkley said as he filled out the form at the reception desk. "Building looks more like an art gallery than a lab."

"Best antidote for evil is sunshine, my father used to say," said Calleigh.

"Science isn't about evil," said Quinkley, handing back the form. "It's about knowledge. How can you get anything done with all these—these windows? In my day, science was done in a sealed room. If we wanted light, we turned one on."

Calleigh smiled despite herself. "What are you here for, Mister Quinkley?"

"Necropsy on an ocean sunfish. Nobody at F and G knows much about them, so they called me."

"You're a consultant, then?"

He nodded. "I teach at Florida State—marine

biology. I know a little something about the *Molidae* family, so they contacted me."

"I saw them bring it in. It's quite the specimen."

"Largest bony fish in the world. I understand this specimen is around four thousand pounds."

Calleigh whistled. "Well, good luck."

"Luck? Luck has nothing to do with science, either."

Quinkley found the autopsy theater without any trouble. The sunfish was lying flat on two large wheeled tables; Eric Delko was holding its mouth open with two gloved hands and peering inside.

"Watch out for the sea lice," said Quinkley, shrugging out of his trenchcoat.

Delko looked up. "Excuse me?"

Quinkley opened his suitcase and pulled out a white lab coat. He slipped it on and said, "Sea lice. You can find them all over the *mola mola*—even on the tongue."

"You must be Doctor Quinkley."

"I am. Are you in charge?"

"I'm Eric Delko, the CSI conducting the investigation, yes."

Quinkley pulled out his own pair of gloves and pulled them on. "All right, CSI Delko—what can you tell me about this fish?"

Delko filled him in on the relevant aspects of the case. "I think this fish might have been used to smuggle something, but so far I've come up empty. Anything new you can tell me might help."

"*Schwimmender kopf.*"

Delko blinked. "What?"

"It's what the Germans call them. It means *swimming head.*"

Delko grinned. "Okay, I didn't know that."

Quinkley looked around, then picked up his briefcase and put it down on a stainless-steel counter. "*Bezador* in Spain, *Manbo* in Japan, *Putol* in the Philippines. But my favorite is from Taiwan— they call it the toppled-car fish."

"Yeah, it does sorta look like a Volvo fell on it."

Quinkley undid some latches on the side of his suitcase and splayed it wide open, displaying rows of gleaming chrome instruments held in place by strips of black elastic. "I brought my own tools, if that's all right?"

"Fine by me."

Quinkley selected a hacksawlike tool with a wickedly serrated blade. "Then let's begin."

"Delwyn Keith?" Natalia asked, holding up her badge. "I'm Natalia Boa Vista, from the Miami-Dade crime lab. I have a few questions for you."

The tanned young man lying on the sunlounger at poolside studied her through extremely expensive sunglasses. "Crime lab? What is this, a gag? Come on, where's the camera?" He glanced around, a broad smile blooming on his face.

"I could ask you the same thing," said Natalia. Frank Tripp stood behind her, his arms crossed.

"But I already know where the camera was. What I don't know is who was behind it."

A frown wrinkled his forehead. "Huh?"

"The video with Marssai Guardon, the one that gave you your fifteen minutes of fame—I know it was faked. I want to know the names of everyone else involved."

The frown went away, replaced by a blank smile. "Hey, I don't kiss and tell. Marssai's lawyers talk to my lawyers and I pay their lunch bill—that's about all the involvement I have."

"Don't try to con me, Delwyn." Natalia crossed her own arms. "I do research for a living, and I'm pretty hard to fool. Despite all the uproar in the press, Marssai Guardon never filed suit against you. Why do you think that is?"

He shrugged, the smile still in place. "Gratitude? I mean, it's not like I didn't show her a good time—"

"It was all scripted, and her orgasm was as phony as the video itself. You and another woman were edited in after the fact, and Marssai knew it."

"Yeah? If that's the case, why doesn't Marssai say something?"

"Timing," said Tripp, taking a step forward. "See, she wanted to make sure she wouldn't get in trouble for breaking Florida State Ordinance 73-B. It restricts sexual behavior in public places, specifically bars and restaurants. If she was really having sex in that booth, she could be charged; if it wasn't her, she had a legal out. But you, my friend—you have no such protection. And neither does your partner."

Delwyn's perfect smile dimmed a little. "But— but nobody ever told me it was *illegal*. Marssai and Gwen are both over eighteen—"

Natalia cut him off. "Ignorance of the law is no excuse, Delwyn. The only reason you haven't been charged until now is that Marssai has friends in high places—but they've had a sudden change of heart. See, Marssai knows how to cut a deal . . . and you've made it real easy for her to throw you to the wolves."

"But—but—that *bitch*!"

"Maybe so," said Tripp, "but she's a smarter breed than you are."

"Look, I can give you more than she can," said Delwyn. The slightest note of panic had crept into his voice as he saw Tripp pull out his handcuffs. "Oh, God. That's not necessary. Look, all I did was show up and *perform*, okay? The whole thing was Marssai's idea—she hired the cameraman, she got two of her friends to be in it. I didn't *know*, all right?"

"Names," said Natalia.

"The cameraman was this guy named Jeremy Fontwell, some friend of Marssai's. Cherise Dameo doubled for Marssai—part of her, anyway."

Natalia pulled a notebook and a pen out of her bag and handed them to Delwyn. "I need contact numbers and addresses. If what they say corresponds with what you just told me, I might be able to help you."

"Yeah, yeah, okay. I can't go to jail, all right?" He grabbed the pen and started writing. "I get fan mail from way too many convicts already."

Natalia did her best to hide her grin until she and Tripp had left the hotel's pool area. "Nice job," she said. "Florida State Ordinance 73-B?"

"It's my locker number at the gym," said Tripp. "I took one look at our boy and figured he was about as streetwise as a pet hamster. Thought I'd rattle his cage a little."

"Well, it didn't take long for him to give up his friends. What do you say we go have a talk with them, next?"

"Sounds good to me."

"As you can see," said Quinkley, "sunfish are an ecosystem unto themselves."

Delko shook his head, staring down into the gigantic fish's guts. "I knew they were prone to parasites, but I had no idea . . ."

Quinkley lifted a long, squirming wormlike thing with a pair of forceps. "Over forty varieties—in fact, it holds the world record for the most infested being on the planet. See this? Tapeworm that ordinarily lives in sharks. The fact that it's here means the sunfish is part of the tapeworm's life cycle—in order for the worm to reproduce, at some point the sunfish has to be eaten by a shark."

"That's fascinating—but I'm more interested in finding something that *doesn't* belong here."

"So far, I don't see anything out of place. The body has been previously cut into, but it doesn't look like any of the organs have been removed."

"Well, they must have had a reason to cut into it."

"Her." Quinkley pointed to a large, saclike organ. "That's her ovary, right there." He leaned over, inspecting it more closely. "Hmmm. It looks like there might be an incision in the top."

"Can you open it up?"

"I can."

Quinkley slit the organ open and pulled the flesh to either side. The interior was dotted with black, pearlescent spheres the size of a BB. "Looks like she recently laid her eggs."

"Isn't that what these are?"

Quinkley chuckled. "Yes, but these are only remnants. The mola mola has been known to carry as many as *three hundred million eggs*—another world record, by the way. By those standards, a few stragglers like these hardly count."

Delko thought for a moment. "It's a pretty roomy organ. Something could have been put in there through the incision, right?"

"It's possible—but if so, I see no evidence of it now."

Delko collected some samples from the inside of the ovary. "Maybe not, but I'm going to send this to our trace lab just the same—maybe they can find something on a chemical level."

Quinkley darted in with his forceps and pulled out another small, wriggling creature. "Ah-ha— amazing, isn't it? Their world has died, and yet they live on—for a time, anyway."

Delko put the samples he'd taken aside. "Wait a minute—how long?"

"It depends on the organism. Some of these parasites will survive as long as seventeen hours after the host has died."

"And since some of its hitchhikers are still clearly alive, that means this fish was caught less than seventeen hours ago."

Quinkley nodded. "I would agree."

"Can we narrow it down further? By looking at which parasites are dead, and which are still"—he glanced down at the creature squirming in Quinkley's forceps—"twitching?"

Quinkley considered the question. "It should be possible, yes."

"Great," said Delko. "Then let's go on a bug hunt."

"Thank you for coming in to talk with us, Ms. Dameo," said Natalia. She studied the woman sitting across from her intently, making no attempt to hide what she was doing. Cherise Dameo stared back, but after a moment she shifted her eyes to the side. "Yeah, whatever," she said. She tugged at a strand of her long blond hair nervously and said, "So, what's this all about?"

"Just trying to figure something out."

"What's that?"

"Why you'd agree to be Marssai Guardon's stand-in—sorry, sit-in—in an X-rated video."

Cherise tried to look defiant. "You can't prove that. And even if you could, it's not illegal."

"I'm a crime scene investigator—you'd be amazed at what I can prove. But you're right, what you did isn't illegal. Not the filming part, anyway."

Worry trumped her defiance. "What? What do you mean?"

"That video's been downloaded millions of times—somebody somewhere must be making money from it. If that's so, then your little prank becomes fraud. Maybe even a felony, depending on the amount of money involved."

Her worry was rapidly becoming misery. "But— Marssai said there was no way we could get in trouble. No *way*."

Natalia gave her a sympathetic smile. "Look, I'm just trying to understand. If all you did was appear in the video, you're probably fine—but I need to know the whole story."

"It was Marssai's idea. She said it would be great—like being a porn star but not. I mean, everybody thinks it's *her*, but it isn't—and I know it's *me*, but nobody else does. Does that make sense?"

"Actually, it kind of does. Weren't you worried the truth would eventually come out, though?"

"Not really. The only people who knew were me, Marssai, Delwyn, Gwen, and Jeremy. I trust all of them."

"How about Hiram Davey?"

"That writer guy? He was hanging around Marssai for a while, but she said he gave her the creeps. She's used to the press, though—she'd never tell him anything she didn't want him to know."

"Did he ever talk to you?"

"No, I never met him. Why?"

"How about the others? Did he talk to any of them?"

She shrugged. "I don't know. If he did, nobody ever mentioned it to me."

"Okay, Cherise, this next question is important: Who would stand to lose the most if the public found out the video was a fake?"

Cherise frowned. "I don't know. Me, I guess. I mean, my parents will freak *out* if they find out it was me."

"How about Jeremy or Delwyn or Gwen?"

"Ummmmm . . . no, I don't think so."

Natalia sighed. "All right. Thanks for your help, Cherise."

"Are—are you gonna tell everyone?"

Natalia smiled. "Well, it is my job to uncover the truth . . . but honestly, I think you've had *enough* uncovered."

*   *   *

Wolfe found Delko in the lab, studying a sample under the microscope. "Hey," said Wolfe. "Just finished talking to the ladies from the boat—both Faustino and Dragoslav lawyered up, said they won't say another word without counsel present."

Delko looked up. "Get anything useful?"

"Just that Dragoslav was celebrating some kind of business deal. How about you?"

"Don't think I'll be eating seafood for a while." Delko told him about the necropsy and the parasites they'd found. "We listed all the specimens we discovered, living and dead. Quinkley is going to cross-reference the data with how long each species can survive once the host is dead and email me the results. Should give us a time line on how long ago the fish was taken out of the water."

"So that's all you found? Dead or dying parasites?"

"More or less. A small chunk of flesh had been excised from one interior wall, and the ovary had been cut open—those seemed to be the signs the fish had been tampered with." Delko didn't look happy. "I was just checking some samples from the inside of the ovary. So far, every test I've run tells me the same thing: negative for drugs or any other foreign substance. If there was something stashed inside the fish, it didn't leave any traces behind."

"Maybe it's a dead end."

"What, you don't have any clever fish-related joke to make?"

Wolfe shrugged and grinned. "Hey, you spent the afternoon up to your elbows in fish guts and tapeworms. I figure you deserve a break."

"You're too kind."

"I know. It's a weakness."

"Okay, okay, you got me," said Marssai Guardon. She smiled brightly at Frank and Natalia on the other side of the interview table. "I did it, all right?"

"You killed Hiram Davey?" asked Natalia.

"What? No, of course not." Marssai rolled her eyes upward. "I mean I faked the video, okay? I was about to announce it, anyway."

Tripp didn't look impressed. "So the whole thing was a publicity stunt?"

"Publicity stunts are *so* nineteen-nineties. This is *viral marketing*, okay?"

Natalia shook her head. "*Not* okay. Explain it to me."

Marssai sighed. "These days, *everybody's* booty footage is being downloaded. Everybody I know is wiring their bedrooms with spycams and night vision. You want to get noticed, you have to give the public something different."

Natalia nodded. "Like a porn video that isn't what it appears."

"Sure. I mean, setting it in a pubic place like that got people's attention, but it's already old news. When people find out the whole thing was a hoax, it'll catch fire all over again—people will download it just to see if they can spot the mistakes."

Tripp crossed his arms. "And when your website launches, you'll be first in line to provide said downloads."

"Not just any downloads—the full DVD-with-extra-features version. People love a scandal, but they love a scam even more."

"So," said Natalia, "if Hiram Davey spilled the beans early, it would screw up your marketing plan."

Marssai laughed. "Are you kidding? He had no reason to do that, and he wasn't going to. I told him about the idea because I thought he'd appreciate it—and he did. He thought it was hilarious. He was going to work it into his book, which wasn't due to come out until next year. I figured the site might need another boost around then."

"I still don't get it," said Tripp. "You're an heiress. Aren't you worried about this affecting your inheritance?"

Marssai's grin faded. "Yeah, well . . . let's just say I *was* an heiress. My family isn't too thrilled with my lifestyle, and they laid down the law last year. No more partying, no more dating rock stars, no fun at *all*. So I said thanks, but no thanks."

"They cut you off?" said Natalia.

"Like Britney with an electric shaver. So I decided to turn a negative into a positive."

"Dragging your family's name through the gutter?" asked Tripp.

"It's *my* name," said Marssai coldly. "And I'll do whatever I damn well please with it."

It was Natalia's turn to sigh. "All right, Marssai—thanks for coming in. You're free to go."

"Any time. Hey, if you want, you could even arrest me—I'd love a shot of me in handcuffs for the site."

"Maybe later," Tripp growled.

After Marssai had left, Natalia scowled at Frank and said, "Well, one down."

"So to speak," said Frank.

Natalia raised her eyebrows at him, but she couldn't keep a straight face for long.

"Take a look at this," Delko said. Wolfe walked over to where Delko was sitting in front of a workstation. "Doctor Quinkley just sent over the parasite data from the necropsy."

Wolfe leaned forward and studied the screen. "So according to this, the sunfish was pulled out of the water around seven hours before the boat crashed into the pier."

"Yeah—which, according to the ship's log, was about three hours before the *Svetlana 2* initially left on its cruise."

Wolfe frowned. "So it wasn't caught on the ship; it must have been transferred to the boat while it was docked or at sea. Which, I have to admit, gives some credence to your theory about the fish being significant."

"Yeah. But we still don't know why."

6

"Horatio," said Calleigh, falling into step beside her boss. "How'd it go talking to Breakwash's employer?"

"Well, according to Mister Perrone, Timothy Breakwash was checking samples from his fish farm for an organism called *Pfiesteria piscicida*—also known as 'the cell from hell.'"

"Doesn't sound like something you'd want turning up in your tuna salad."

"No, definitely not . . . but Mister Perrone claimed he didn't know what Breakwash's findings were."

"Think Perrone was telling the truth?"

"I'm not sure. If Breakwash had found evidence of contamination and threatened to go to the authorities, it would have provided a strong motive for someone to shut him up."

"Even if Breakwash's findings were negative," Calleigh pointed out, "he could have lied or tampered with the results and tried to extort money from Perrone. Blackmail can lead to murder, too."

"True—but Perrone claimed Breakwash wasn't the type. Said he had big dreams but little follow-through."

"A dreamer, not a schemer?"

Horatio smiled. "Exactly. And after reviewing Mister Breakwash's files, I have to agree with that sentiment. It's possible he was using sensitive information to blackmail someone, but I don't think so. Still, maybe someone else was—Breakwash was subcontracting to a man named Lee Kwok, who works out of a University of Miami building downtown. I'm on my way to see him now."

She stopped outside the door to the layout room. "Wish I was doing as well. So far, all the evidence I've gathered seems to indicate Breakwash was definitely alive and by himself in the balloon while it was aloft. I'm going to see if I can locate the gun."

"Good luck."

"Thanks—I'll need it."

The Leonard M. Miller School of Medicine was the University of Miami's medical campus, located in downtown Miami. The medical complex had received a massive donation in 2004 of a hundred million dollars, a bequest so enormous it had caused the school to rename itself in honor of its benefactor. Lee Kwok worked in a fifteen-story highrise called the Clinical Research Building, where—not surprisingly—he had access to an SEM, a scanning electron microscope.

Horatio tracked him down just outside the main entrance, leaning against the glass wall and smoking a cigarette. Kwok was a young Korean in a white lab coat over a blue shirt, with a shaved head and a short, scraggly goatee that looked out of place on his round face.

"Mister Kwok?" Horatio said. "I'm Lieutenant Horatio Caine, Miami-Dade PD. Do you have a minute?"

Kwok dropped his cigarette on the ground and stepped on it. "Sure, I guess so. What can I do for you?"

"It's about a colleague of yours—Timothy Breakwash."

"Yes, I heard about that. Tragic."

"I understand you and Timothy were working together on a project?"

Kwok hesitated. "I was helping him out with some samples, yes. I wouldn't say it was anything as formal as a project."

"No, of course not. That would require more documentation than you could obtain, wouldn't it . . ."

Kwok frowned. "I don't know what you mean by that."

"What I mean, Mister Kwok, is that you were using the university's SEM to look for evidence of the *Pfiesteria* organism in samples provided by Timothy Breakwash—and you were doing so without the university's knowledge or consent."

"How did you—oh. You talked to my department head."

"Just a few preliminary questions. He doesn't know what you've been doing—yet."

"Look, it was harmless—just a favor for an old friend. I slipped them in as part of a research project I'm involved with."

Horatio studied him carefully. "And what did you find, Mister Kwok?"

"The samples he gave me weren't contaminated—not the ones from the fish farm, anyway."

"There were others?"

"He supplied me with some *Pfiesteria* cultures for comparison and practice. You have to strip off the outer coating to tell whether you have a genuine example of the organism or just a look-alike."

"Tell me, Mister Kwok—did any of the samples he gave you come from the Everglades?"

Kwok shook his head. "No. *Pfiesteria* usually shows up in river estuaries, not swamplands—it likes the combination of shallow water and high fish population you find there. I've never heard of it turning up in the 'Glades."

Horatio nodded. "You mentioned the fish farm. Timothy told you where the samples came from?"

"Sure, he explained the whole thing to me. He's a good guy; I thought I'd help him out."

"Very generous of you, Mister Kwok. Did you ever meet the man who hired Timothy?"

"No. Why would I?"

Horatio looked away, took his sunglasses out of his pocket. "That, Mister Kwok," he said, slipping them on, "is the question, isn't it . . ."

"Okay," said Calleigh. "Now, you understand we're not going up that high, right?"

She stood in the same field Timothy Breakwash had launched his final voyage from, talking to the owner of the bright yellow balloon that now towered above her. Liam Fellows was a tall, cheerful-looking man with long black hair pulled back in a ponytail.

"Not afraid of heights, are you?" he asked her.

"Oh, no. I just want to duplicate the flight path Timothy Breakwash took as closely as possible, and he never topped a few hundred feet."

"Well, I can't promise you we'll duplicate it—we're more or less at the mercy of the wind. But it's blowing in the same direction it was yesterday, and I'll keep it low."

Calleigh nodded. The balloon she'd rented was the same size as Breakwash's, holding a hundred thousand cubic feet of air and able to lift up to four people; she'd watched them inflate it, using a large, generator-driven fan to blow cold air into it first, then switching to a propane heater once the bag was almost full but lying on its side. It was early morning, the sun having just risen; it was the closest Calleigh could come to copying the conditions of Breakwash's flight.

"All aboard," said Fellows. She climbed into the basket, and a moment later they were off.

It wasn't quite what she imagined. The ascent was so smooth and gradual it didn't feel like they were going up at all; more like the Earth was dropping away. "How exactly do you control this thing?" asked Calleigh. They were approaching the edge of the 'Glades, but she still had a moment or two before she had to get to work.

"Look up."

She did, looking past the huge propane burner that perched over them like a giant Zippo, into the throat of the balloon itself. "What am I looking for?"

"See that little circle on the inside, at the very top? That's the parachute vent. I pull on this line here, and it pulls open. Hot air escapes, and we go down. I let go, and the outrushing air pushes the vent back in place."

"It's so—*basic*," said Calleigh. "Call me old-fashioned, but I'm used to having a whole aviation industry backing me up when I'm flying."

"That's what I love about ballooning—it's simple. No engines, no computers, no complicated flight protocols . . . just a gasbag, a basket, a big blue flame, and the sky."

She had to admit he had a point. Other than the occasional throaty hiss of the burner—it sounded to her like a giant, fire-breathing cat—it was eerily quiet. Since they were moving at the speed of the wind, even the air seemed still. Below them, the brilliant green edge of the Everglades was rapidly getting closer.

Calleigh dug into the satchel she'd brought with her and pulled out two bright orange plastic bricks. They were transponders, each one emitting a radio signal that she could track with a handheld unit. Her plan was to throw one to either side of the balloon at periodic intervals, giving her a broad trail that would, she hoped, provide the ground-based equivalent of Breakwash's flight path. The transponders were encased in tough, impact-resistant plastic—unless they fell directly onto a boulder, they should survive the fall.

She'd already placed two at the boundary of the field and the Everglades. She waited until they'd gone fifty or so feet past that point, then launched the first one over the edge.

"Bombs away!"

She was fortunate in that most of the terrain she was drifting over wasn't underwater; while there were many pools and streams, gleaming in the early-morning light, it was mostly mangroves and cypress below her. Of course, if the gun had gotten stuck in a tree she might never notice it . . .

She sighed, and kept chucking transponders over the edge at regular intervals.

The flight was over far too soon. They'd managed to stay more or less on course, though, touching down mere feet from the side of the road where Breakwash had ended up.

"Thanks for the lift," said Calleigh, climbing out of the basket. She could see her Hummer, right where she'd parked it earlier.

"You accomplish what you wanted?" Fellows asked.

"Oh, that was just preparation. Now comes the *real* work—and it's going to take me all day."

Two Miami-Dade Range Rovers pulled up, discharging groups of yawning police cadets clutching duffel bags and paper cups of coffee. "Fortunately," said Calleigh, "I'll have help."

Calleigh used one handheld unit, a cadet named Rosemary Montoyez another. Both of them had rolls of thin, bright pink plastic tape; one end was attached to a stake at its starting point, and the tape was paid out until they reached the first of the transponders. The transponder was picked up, the tape tied to a stake where it was found, and the process started all over again as they headed for the next signal. The other cadets walked behind them, spread out between the two bright pink lines, each sweeping a metal detector in a slow arc.

It wasn't a perfect system, Calleigh knew. The gun could easily lie to either side of her estimation of the balloon's footprint, or have gotten stuck in underbrush; the cadets were under instructions to pay close attention to such possibilities, but even so she was counting a great deal on luck.

Calleigh hated relying on luck. It made her irritable, and the rising heat of the day and the insect population—which seemed to treat her and her team as an all-you-can-eat buffet specially catered for their benefit—didn't help matters. Every inch of ground they covered made things worse; instead of feeling like they were accomplishing something, all Calleigh could think about was the fact that they might have already missed what they were searching for and were now getting farther away from it with every step. Her normally cheerful demeanor rapidly eroded to a simmering, intense silence that the cadets quickly learned to not disturb unless absolutely necessary.

And then, Calleigh abruptly found herself face-to-face with an armed man.

He stepped out of the brush directly in front of her, holding a shotgun in both hands. He was Hispanic, in his early twenties, and dressed in camouflage pants and a black hooded sweatshirt. The look on his face said he hadn't been expecting her any more than she'd been expecting him.

Calleigh's hand automatically went to the pistol on her hip. "Sir? I'm a Miami-Dade police officer. Please lower your weapon."

For a second she thought he was going to do the opposite, bring the gun to bear on her before she could clear her holster, but the moment passed. He made a visible effort to relax, pointing the barrel of the gun at the ground and raising his other hand in greeting.

"Hola," he said. "Caught me by surprise—thought I was all alone out here." At that moment a large bloodhound came crashing out of the brush, running up to stop at the man's legs. "Except for Hugo, here."

Calleigh didn't draw her weapon, but she kept her hand on the grip. "And you are?"

"Uh, Bolivar. Fredo Bolivar."

Calleigh could hear the cadets approaching behind her, and relaxed a little. "What are you doing out here, Mister Bolivar?"

"Just a little duck hunting. I've got a license."

"Can I see it, please?"

He dug in the pocket of his pants and pulled out a folded piece of paper. She took it from him and looked it over quickly. "This seems to be in order, Mister Bolivar." She handed it back. "Any luck?"

"Uh, no. Not my day, I guess. What's the deal with the tape?"

"We're trying to recover a piece of evidence in an investigation—a gun. You haven't run across one, have you?"

"What kind of gun?"

"Small-caliber—a twenty-two. Probably a handgun."

"Well, I haven't seen anything like that, but I'll keep my eyes open."

"Actually, sir, I'll have to ask you to leave the area." She hesitated, then dug in her own pocket for a business card. "But if you *do* find something like that, here or elsewhere, I'd appreciate a call."

He took the card from her and slipped it into his pocket without looking at it. "Sure. How long is this area off-limits? I mean, I only have a few days off and I'd really like to get in some hunting, but I don't want to break any rules or anything."

"The Everglades are a big place. I'm sure you can find another spot."

"It's just—well, this is kind of a tradition for me. Me and Hugo. We used to come here with my father to hunt, before he passed away."

"I'm sorry to hear that. We'll be done in a few days at the latest."

"Okay. Good luck."

"Thank you."

Bolivar headed back the way he'd come, until Calleigh stopped him with a loud, "Excuse me?"

He stopped. "What?"

"You're going to have to exit this way, staying between the lines of tape."

"Oh." He hesitated, seemed about to say something else, then changed his mind and walked back toward Calleigh. "Sorry about that."

"No problem."

It wasn't until after he was out of sight that Calleigh realized something—if he'd been out hunting ducks, he should have been carrying a bag to hold his kills. *Maybe he had one, made of plastic, folded up and stuck in a pocket,* she thought.

Somehow, she didn't quite believe it.

*   *   *

It was late afternoon by the time they emerged at the edge of the field, hot and sweaty and covered with insect bites. Horatio was waiting for her, leaning up against his Hummer with his arms crossed, looking composed and patient and as if his knowledge of the word *perspiration* was entirely theoretical.

Calleigh trudged up to him and said, "You know, I could cheerfully shoot you right now."

Horatio grinned, reached in through the open window of his Hummer, and pulled out a large, ice-cold bottle of water. "Not surprising. Maybe this will save my life."

She took it gratefully, opened it, and drank half of it before pausing. "Maybe not," she said, panting slightly, "but it's sure saving mine."

"How'd you do?"

"Didn't find it. Found beer cans, shotgun shells, an old lawn tractor, and too many bottle caps to count, but no gun." She finished the water and handed the empty plastic bottle back to Horatio. He tossed it into the Hummer, reached into the cooler on the driver's seat and got another one. She took it and said, "There was one thing, though. Met a guy out there that claimed he was hunting, but something was off about him. I got the feeling maybe he was looking for something, too."

"Did you get a name?"

"Fredo Bolivar."

Horatio nodded. "I'll run it, see what comes up."

He filled her in on what he'd found out talking to Lee Kwok.

"So," she said thoughtfully, "Kwok knew what was going on. If Breakwash wasn't the type to try extortion, you think Kwok might?"

"Possibly—but that still doesn't give him a motive for killing his partner."

"Maybe Breakwash was going to go to the police."

"Maybe. Or maybe Timothy Breakwash was a suicide, after all."

Calleigh shook her head. "I don't think so, H. I know the evidence is slim so far, but my gut is telling me we don't know the whole story yet."

Horatio smiled. "Then we follow your gut. Which, I'm thinking, could probably use a good meal about now."

"You got that right. After which I'm having the world's longest shower, and applying a gallon or so of calamine lotion."

"I'll give you a lift back to your vehicle."

Horatio wasn't quite ready to call it a night. He drove back to the lab, and checked Fredo Bolivar for priors. What he found prompted him to look harder.

The next morning, he was waiting for Calleigh in the layout room. "Good morning," he said as she walked in. "Feeling refreshed, I hope."

"A hundred and ten percent better. I'm thinking maybe I gave up too soon—I could expand the search parameters, widen the trail on either side."

"Not a bad idea. I did something similar, and made a very interesting discovery."

"Oh? You found something on Fredo Bolivar?"

"I did. He's been arrested a few times, but nothing major—assault, possession of stolen property. But his name sounded familiar . . . so I widened the trail. And I finally remembered where I'd heard it before."

Calleigh looked intrigued. "Where?"

"It was a case I heard about years ago, when I was on the bomb squad. Back in the nineteen-eighties, a woman named Consuela Bolivar was kidnapped and held for a considerable ransom—five million dollars, I believe."

"So she comes from money?"

"No. In fact, she's from a rather poor Colombian family. But at the time, she was rumored to be dating someone with access to a great deal of ready cash—a cocaine smuggler known only as Rodriguo. The kidnappers hoped Consuela meant enough to Rodriguo that he'd pay the money."

"What happened?"

"According to legend, Rodriguo paid the ransom in full—but he added a little bonus of his own. A thin sheet of C-4, hidden inside an interior wall of the suitcase with a very simple activator. The first time the case was opened it was primed; the second time it went off."

"He blew up the kidnappers *and* the cash?"

"Five million dollars apparently meant less to him than making a point."

Calleigh nodded. "So you think Fredo is related? Bolivar's not that unusual a name."

"No, but I called up the officer who arrested Fredo the first time; sure enough, he remembers the kid blustering on about 'you don't know who I am, who my father is.' Fredo was more than happy to tell him."

"So even if Fredo isn't Bolivar's son, he's certainly portraying himself as such."

"Yes. Which raises the question of what he was doing in the Everglades in close proximity to a crime scene."

"What he was doing," said Calleigh thoughtfully, "or what he was looking for."

"I've been going over the files on Rodriguo, but there isn't much; he was successful, he was feared, but nobody ever managed to bust him or even discover his real name. He vanished at the peak of his career, and it was widely assumed he'd been killed by a rival. I have a call in to a retired DEA agent named McCulver; he was in charge back then, and I'm hoping he can tell me more."

"Well, that's definitely food for thought. I guess I'll head back into the field and torment some more poor cadets."

"Don't forget your bug spray."

She sighed. "That stuff is worthless. I'm thinking maybe a thirty-eight; should take care of the smaller mosquitos, anyway . . ."

7

"So who's up next?" Tripp asked Natalia.

She was studying her laptop's screen as Tripp drove. "I thought we'd talk to Joshua St. George."

Tripp frowned. "Isn't he in his seventies? Seems unlikely, considering how violent the attack was."

"Maybe—but the character in the novel is in pretty good shape, so maybe the real St. George is, too. And he probably has the strongest motive."

"That's true. No statute of limitations on murder—and doing hard time at his age would be a death sentence. So where we headed to?"

She gave him an address in Liberty City, one of Miami's more crime-ridden neighborhoods. Named for the Liberty Square Housing Project of the nineteen-thirties, it was bounded by Northwest Twenty-seventh Avenue to the west, Interstate Ninety-five to the east, Northwest Seventy-ninth to the north and Northwest Forty-first Street to the south. Joshua St. George lived in an old three-story tenement on Twenty-seventh, an L-shaped concrete building that looked as if it hadn't had a fresh coat of paint since Nixon was in office—and the paint had been cheap and yellow then. St. George's apartment was a corner suite on the top floor, a prime location if you could ignore the area it looked out on. Across the street, piles of rubble crouched beside boarded-up public housing; the newest thing visible was a large wooden sign at the edge of a vacant lot proclaiming the exclusive condos soon to erupt from the ground like flowers sprouting on a grave.

Tripp nodded at the sign and said, "Gentrification. Why have six poor families living on a lot when one rich one will do?"

Natalia didn't say anything, but the look on her face told Tripp all he needed to know; somewhere between guilt and embarrassment, with just a touch of irritation.

"Hey, no offense," said Tripp as he parked.

"Why should I be offended?" asked Natalia.

"Beats me," said Tripp. "But you've got that look on your face—you know, the one Germans get when you mention World War II?"

"I just get tired of apologizing for having money sometimes. I mean, it's not like being well off automatically equates with being evil—but sometimes, that's the feeling I get from people."

"Not me, I hope."

"No, Frank, no. Let's just go talk to this guy, all right?"

"Fine by me."

They got out and climbed the wide cement steps that connected the floors. Half the iron railing was missing on the second story; what was left was rusting and twisted, looking more like decaying licorice than iron.

Natalia knocked on the door of the apartment. She could hear shuffling footsteps inside, then a raspy voice call out, "Hold on, hold on. I'll be there in a moment."

The door opened, revealing an old African-American man in a tattered gray bathrobe over a pair of new-looking blue pajamas. His hair was short and entirely gray, and he had a short, neatly trimmed gray beard. He was breathing in quick, wheezy gasps, as if he'd just run up a flight of stairs. "Yes?" he said.

"Mister St. George?" Natalia asked. "I'm Natalia Boa Vista of the Miami-Dade crime lab, and this is Detective Frank Tripp. I was wondering if we could ask you a few questions."

"About what?" he demanded.

"Hiram Davey."

"What about him?"

"He's dead," said Tripp.

"So? What's that got to do with me?"

"He interviewed you a few weeks ago," said

Natalia. "That's all we wanted to talk about. Please? It'll only take a few minutes."

He studied her suspiciously, then gave a resigned nod and beckoned them to come in. Inside, the apartment was sparse but neat, with an aging sofa and several overstuffed chairs. Posters of Malcolm X and Louis Farrakhan hung on the walls, as well as an ancient and frayed-looking Black Panthers flag. St. George took a seat in one of the chairs, and they sat on the sofa.

"So what do you want to know?" he asked. Between sentences, his breath was still coming and going in big, rasping gasps.

Natalia studied him for a moment before answering. From what she could see, St. George fit the description Davey had used in his book: angry, resentful, not willing to back down from anyone. "Davey was killed yesterday morning, Mister St. George. At the time of his death he was working on a book, and we think something in that book might have been the reason he was killed. He mentions you, but his notes on that part of the book are missing." It wasn't exactly a lie; the laptop that presumably contained a version of those notes had been stolen. "We were hoping you could tell us the same things you told Davey."

He mulled it over for a moment and then said grudgingly, "Well, I suppose. I heard about Davey getting killed on the news. Thought it was a shame;

he always gave me a chuckle when I read his column. He seemed nice enough in person, too—kind of quiet, but a good listener. Didn't expect that."

"What was it he talked to you about?"

"All kinds of things. Wanted to know about my life in the camps, mostly."

"The turpentine camps," said Tripp.

"That's right. I'm always amazed how many people—even Florida people—don't know about the camps. Friend of mine tried writing a book about it once, but nobody wanted to publish it. Guess nobody wants to hear that slavery was still alive and well in this state as late as nineteen-fifty."

Natalia nodded. She could tell by the tone of the old man's voice that he was getting warmed up for a story, and that was exactly what she'd hoped for.

"I was born in nineteen-thirty-six. My father was from Mobile, Georgia, and he'd come to Florida in thirty-five to get work. He found it in Cross City, at a turpentine camp, or so he thought. What he actually found was a living hell that eventually killed him.

"These days, mineral turps is what everybody uses for paint thinner and whatnot, and it's made from petroleum. But that wasn't always the case; used to be, turpentine came from pine trees—the longleaf, the loblolly, the ponderosa. You'd tap the tree and collect the sap, then boil it in vats."

"Like maple syrup," said Tripp.

St. George gave him a scornful look. "No, not like maple syrup. You had to debark a big chunk of the tree—a quarter or so of the circumference, and three or four feet up the trunk. You hacked a V-shaped cut into the exposed part and stuck a tin pipe at the bottom of the V. The resin flowed out the pipe into what was called a Hurty pot, which was dumped into the vat. But the biggest difference between the two is that collecting pancake topping won't burn your lungs out."

"That toxic, huh?" asked Tripp.

"You better believe it. And it wasn't just the turps—the Russians came up with this method of spraying sulphuric acid onto the bark to increase the sap flow, and pretty soon all the camps in the States were using it, too. Gave 'em an opportunity to sell us safety equipment—goggles, gloves, soda for acid burns. And that was how they got you, through the company store. Wouldn't sell you much but meal, flour, dried beans, or salt pork—but they'd charge you an arm and a leg, plus rent on the crappy little shack you were forced to live in. You found out real quick that the wages you were being paid weren't enough to cover living expenses, and that was just what the bosses liked."

Tripp frowned. "Sounds horrible—but this was the nineteen-forties, right? Couldn't people just leave?'

"You'd think so, wouldn't you?" St. George's voice was flat and cold. "But by the time you left, you already owed the store money—didn't matter how much. As far as they were concerned, that made you their property. Long as you stayed and worked, they didn't care how big your tab was; they knew you weren't ever going to work it off. But if you tried to leave, that bill came due—and anybody running out on a debt was treated exactly the same as a runaway slave. Local sheriff would block the roads, the boss would strap on a pistol and get out the bloodhounds. You'd be arrested and charged with deserting your debt, and the authorities would give you a choice; work it off on a chain gang, or go back to the camp. Some men picked prison, because at least they knew their debt would come to an end; back at the camp, it'd just get bigger."

Tripp shook his head. "Sounds like a helluva place to grow up."

"Hell is exactly right. No doctors or decent food, and they worked you from sunup to sundown. You complained or slacked off, you were beaten. They encouraged men to bring their families, because a man with a family was less likely to run off. Gave 'em hostages on top of everything else. I started working when I was nine years old, and by the time I was fourteen my father was gone. He lit out to get work in Kansas City, planned to pay off his debt from there. We never saw him again."

St. George paused, his eyes focused on a memory far away but still intense, like a burning house seen from a distance. "The bosses went out to hunt for him, and the dogs came back with blood on their muzzles. Tried to tell us he was no good, he'd just abandoned us, but I knew better. They killed him and buried his body in the woods—and he wasn't the first, either."

Natalia phrased her next question carefully. "How did you handle that?"

He met her eyes, let her see the fire still burning there. He took a few more sharp, wheezing breaths. "I let it go. I lit out myself, first chance I got, and they never caught me. Things changed around then—not as much as they should have, and damned slow at that—but enough that killing a black man became more trouble than it used to be. I went north, wound up in Chicago."

"That's where you got involved in the Civil Rights movement?" asked Natalia.

"That's right. Summer of nineteen-sixty-six— they called it the Chicago Freedom Summer after that. All kinds of things happening, from lawsuits to protests; it was us against Mayor Daley and his whole corrupt machine. Martin Luther King was our general, but he didn't want bloodshed; he just wanted what was right. I stood shoulder to shoulder with him at the second Marquette Park march, and I consider that one of the finest moments of my life."

"Weren't there riots that summer, too?" asked Tripp.

"There were streets full of angry people, yes. But a lot of the time, those people were white. When we marched from Marquette Park, there were five hundred of us, and we weren't there to make trouble; all we wanted was to be heard. The crowd that met us were made of white, middle-class Americans that were afraid we were going to move into their neighborhoods and drive prices down. There were four thousand of them."

He paused and shook his head. His breathing sounded like a machine badly in need of maintenance. "Four thousand. They threw rocks and bottles at us. They *spit* at us. They set ten of our cars on fire and pushed two more into the lake. And our so-called 'police escort' did nothing at all."

"Not our finest hour," said Tripp. Natalia didn't know if he was talking about members of his profession or his race.

"That's just how it was, back then," St. George said. "Two years later Doctor King was dead, but the movement went on. And I kept fighting, too."

"When did you move to Miami?" Natalia asked, keeping her tone neutral.

"Nineteen-seventy-seven. Got tired of those cold Chicago winters."

"You've lived here since then?" asked Tripp.

"In the neighborhood, yes. Moved around a bit, been in this place for the last fifteen years."

"Where were you living in nineteen-eighty?" asked Natalia.

The look on St. George's face changed, shifting from a contemplative nostalgia to a more focused suspicion. "Just around the corner from here, on Twenty-fifth Street. Not that it matters—that building's gone now."

"Was it damaged in the riot?" asked Natalia.

He gave her a long, appraising look before he answered. "The Liberty City riot, you mean? No, it was torn down a few years ago, after a fire."

"Were you here during the riot?" asked Tripp.

"I was here. Where else did I have to go?"

Natalia leaned forward, put her forearms on her knees. "Must have been terrible."

"Terrible? That's one word for it."

"How would you describe it?" asked Natalia.

"Necessary." He said the word coldly.

"Eighteen people died in that riot," said Tripp. "How can you call that necessary?"

"Because I'm not the one that made that decision." St. George's voice wasn't angry; if anything, it sounded sad. He got to his feet and shuffled into the small kitchen that abutted the living room. "I'm going to have a cup of tea," he said. "Chamomile. Can I offer you some?"

"No, thanks," said Tripp.

"I'll have a cup," said Natalia.

St. George kept talking as he moved around the kitchen, putting on a kettle and getting out the cups. "Either of you read the Ford Foundation's report that came out a year after the riot?"

They both admitted they hadn't.

"Well, that report said some very interesting things. I was actually there, in the middle of it, and it confirmed my own observations on the event.

"Wasn't the first riot I'd seen, but it wasn't like

any of the others. I was in Newark in sixty-seven, when a black cab driver got beaten by the police for illegally passing a double-parked patrol car. That was the kind of thing that would set it off; a black man would be shot or beaten or killed by the police, usually over some minor crime, and it would get people angry. Everybody'd be talking about it, and that talk would get louder and louder, until pretty soon people were hollering. And they weren't hollering at each other; they were hollering at the cops. I've seen fights between a man and his wife go the same way. And when the hollering ain't enough, it's time to start throwing things. Bottles, rocks, bricks. Windows get broken, and somebody decides to grab that TV or stereo that's just sitting there in a pile of broken glass. Once the looting starts, everything goes to hell right quick; it's like the signal that all the rules don't apply anymore. That's when people die, and buildings burn."

He shuffled out of the kitchen and set two cracked china cups on the coffee table, each with its own teabag. "That's what it was like in Newark, and according to some friends of mine, in Watts, too. But that's not how it was here."

He shuffled back into the kitchen as the kettle began to whistle. "What set things off here was the murder of a black man by the police, same as the others. Arthur McDuffie ran a red light on a motorcycle while driving on a suspended license, and when the cops tried to pull him over, he ran."

He emerged from the kitchen with the kettle and carefully poured the boiling water into both their cups. "Chase lasted eight minutes, until McDuffie slowed down and gave up. At which point, the four white officers that were chasing him pulled off his helmet and beat him to death with their night-sticks."

St. George paused, the kettle in one hand. He looked at Natalia, then at Tripp. Neither of them said anything. After a moment, St. George turned and shuffled back toward the kitchen.

"Then they tried to cover it up. Put his helmet back on and backed over his motorcycle with the police car. Tried to say he crashed his bike. Medical examiner said otherwise, and after making a deal for immunity, so did two cops who saw the whole thing."

St. George emerged from the kitchen and sank back into his chair. "Now, in Watts or Newark, angry crowds of black residents would have taken to the streets. But that didn't happen here, not at first. People were angry, people were upset, but the officers involved were arrested and fired. We took a 'wait and see' attitude, because there were some of us that actually believed justice would be done."

St. George picked up his cup of tea carefully. "We were wrong."

Natalia picked up her own cup. "They were found not guilty."

"That's right. Despite the fact that their own testified against them, despite the fact that the four officers charged had forty-seven complaints lodged against them during the six years previous—*and* had been involved in no less than thirteen internal affairs probes—an all-white jury acquitted them of all charges. They deliberated for less than three hours."

"Wow," said Natalia. "That's . . . unbelievable."

"Oh, we believed it," said St. George grimly. "What else could we do? We'd waited five months, we gave the system a chance to work the way it was supposed to. When it didn't, *that's* when we took to the streets. And by we, I don't mean the kind of people who naturally turn to violence as a solution; I mean middle-class, educated citizens. In Newark and Watts, seventy-four percent of the rioters arrested had criminal records; in the Liberty City riot, only thirty-four percent."

Tripp cleared his throat. "Yeah, that wasn't the only difference. A report by the Lembeck Center for the Study of Violence said that in previous race riots, the killing of whites was always a by-product; in Miami, it was the objective."

"We'd just been told it was acceptable for white police officers to murder a black man over a traffic ticket. We gave our response."

"Eighty million dollars in damage to your own neighborhood," said Tripp. "Eighteen dead, only eight of which were white. Doesn't sound like a real effective response to me."

St. George glared at him. "I didn't say it was effective. I said it was *necessary*."

"Mister St. George," said Natalia, "did you know any of the victims?"

"No. I'd seen one of them around the neighborhood, but the rest were strangers to me. Didn't know any of them personally."

"Did Hiram Davey ask you about the Liberty City riots?"

"It was one of the things we talked about, sure. He wanted to know what it was like, my own personal experience."

"And what was that experience?" asked Natalia.

"Not much to tell. I saw my share of looting, but no killings. Saw a few cars set on fire, and a U.S. mailbox get thrown through a plate-glass window, but I didn't see anyone die."

Natalia nodded. Until now, she and Tripp had just been trying to get St. George talking; now that they had, she wanted him to talk about something in particular. Hiram Davey's book had gone into a lot more detail about St. George's character than Natalia had implied, including the fact that St. George's fictional counterpart had been guilty of killing a young white man during the riot. Davey's notes hadn't made it clear if this was something he'd made up, or was based on fact. If it was more than just fantasy, it would establish that Joshua St. George was capable of murder . . . and would have had more than sufficient motive to kill again.

"Did you ever visit Mister Davey at his house?" asked Natalia.

"No. He came here."

"Can you tell me where you were, early yesterday morning?"

St. George turned his glare on her. "I was here, asleep. Didn't get up until around ten. And I think that's the last damn question I'm going to answer."

"Mister St. George—"

He got to his feet. "You think I don't know an interrogation when I hear one? You don't ask questions like that unless you're talking to a suspect. Well, I'm no damn suspect. You want to find out who killed some smart-ass white-boy writer, you're in the wrong place. Now I'll kindly ask you to leave."

Natalia and Tripp both got up. "All right, we're going," said Natalia. "But we may have more questions for you later."

"Questions," growled St. George. "Yeah, your kind always has questions. Don't want to listen to the answers, but lots of questions just the same."

Wolfe snapped his cell phone shut and grinned. "Hey, Eric," he said. "Time to stop flogging a dead fish. Just got word from the hospital—the guy that plowed the *Svetlana 2* into the dock is awake."

"Let's go see what he has to say," said Delko.

The survivor's name was Pace Birmingham, a stocky man in his twenties with stringy blond hair.

He was sitting up in his hospital bed when Delko and Wolfe arrived, looking groggy but oddly cheerful. His right wrist was attached to the railing of the bed by handcuffs, his left in a cast. "Hey," he said when they arrived, "I bet you guys are cops, right?"

"Good guess," said Delko.

"Aw, it's not a guess," said Birmingham. "I can spot you guys from a mile away." He sounded glad to see them.

Wolfe pulled Delko aside. "I think he's still pretty wasted," Wolfe said in a low voice. "How do you want to play this?"

"Well, anything we get won't be admissible in court—but we don't need him to incriminate himself, just give us an idea what was going on. Follow my lead—I have an idea."

Delko approached the hospital bed with a smile on his face. "Hope you don't mind us bothering you again, Pace—we just have a few follow-up questions."

Birmingham's smile stayed in place, but his eyes clouded over with confusion. "Follow-up? To what?"

"The interview we conducted this morning with you," said Delko.

"Right," added Wolfe. "You were very helpful—we want to thank you again for that."

Birmingham put a hand to his bandaged forehead. "I—I don't remember that."

"No?" asked Delko. "Well, some memory loss is

common in cases like this. Don't worry, I'm sure that answering a few questions will bring it all back."

"Oh. Okay."

"Let's see . . ." said Delko, pulling a notebook from his pocket and pretending to consult his notes. "You told us about the gun battle, and how you got shot. You talked about feeling seasick before it all started . . . there's just a few details I'd like to clear up. For instance, you told me who was the first person to board the *Svetlana 2,* but not who was last."

"I didn't? Well . . ."

"Oh, hang on—here it is. Sorry, my notes are kind of messy." Delko gave him a big grin. "Let's see . . . we concentrated on the attack itself, not on what happened before that. Can you give me a more detailed description of the start of the whole incident? Starting with you and your friends in the other boat?"

"I . . . I guess so. Like I said, I was feeling kind of seasick. I was up top, waving to the boat with my shirt. I was supposed to be in trouble. Ernesto, he figured they'd be more likely to trust me 'cause I was white. Everybody else was down below, where they couldn't be seen."

"Sure," said Wolfe. "So they saw you and approached. Then what?"

"Everything went okay at first. I tied up alongside, and they helped me aboard. I told them I was having engine trouble and my radio was busted.

Those big Russian guys weren't happy to see me, but they said I could use their radio. I was up in the wheelhouse when it all went down."

"What happened first?"

"Well, Ernesto and Jorge jumped out and used the boarding plank. It was this thing Jorge built, with two big locking clamps on the end, attached on our end with chains. They practiced with a fake railing and everything, and it worked every time. They got so they could clamp onto the practice railing in less than ten seconds. Then everybody was supposed to just swarm on board and take the crew by surprise."

"But it didn't go as planned," said Delko.

Birmingham blinked slowly. "Welllll, no. You could say that."

Wolfe turned away so Birmingham wouldn't see his grin.

After a moment, Pace continued. "They were a lot tougher than we thought. The whole all-out attack thing was supposed to overwhelm them, but I think it just made them *mad*."

Delko hesitated. He knew they'd arrived at a critical point, and he had to be careful. "Well, that's understandable—considering what they were protecting."

"Yeah, I guess. But I don't think that was it. Those guys were just *mean*." He sounded as if he'd been wounded by more than mere bullets. "You know, I don't think I'm in the right line of work."

"No?" asked Wolfe.

"No. I was considering giving it up when you guys showed up—I must have *already* decided to but I forgot." He yawned. "Sorry. Having a hard time keeping my eyes open."

"Just a few more questions," said Delko quickly. "So when did Ernesto take off with the boat?"

"What? No, Ernesto didn't stay behind on the boat—that was Jorge. He waited until all the shooting stopped, then I guess he got scared because nobody came to tell him what happened. I was in the wheelhouse with the captain, but he got shot early on. Not by me—I was the decoy, so I wasn't armed. Anyway, I was crouched down, and then I heard the boat take off. That's when I went downstairs to see what was happening."

"And that's when you got shot?"

"Not right away. Everybody was dead—that's what I thought, anyway. So I started searching."

"What did you find?" asked Wolfe. Delko shot him a warning glance, but Pace seemed oblivious to the directness of the question.

"Lot of bodies. That was about it." Pace shook his head slowly, as if his head wasn't securely attached and he was afraid it would fall off. "Nothing. No drugs, no guns, no diamonds."

"Which one were you looking for?" asked Delko.

Now Birmingham turned petulant. "Come on—I *told* you, we didn't know. We had solid information that Dragoslav was out there to pick up this big illegal shipment—something worth millions—but we didn't know what it was. Could have been drugs, could have been weapons, could have been all kinds of things. Just 'cause we didn't know what it *was* didn't mean we were going to let this kinda opportunity pass us *by*."

"No, of course not," said Wolfe. "So how'd you get shot?"

Pace looked embarrassed. "One of the Russians. He wasn't as dead as I thought. He got one shot off at me, and then I shot him. *Then* he was dead."

"One shot, huh?" said Wolfe. "Funny. They pulled three bullets out of you."

Pace looked even more embarrassed. "Well, maybe. It was self-defense, anyway. I knew I was going to die if I didn't make it back to shore, and the radio got all shot up in the battle. So I just pointed the boat in the right direction and tried not to pass . . ." He yawned again. " . . . pass out."

"Okay, Pace," said Delko. "We'll let you get some rest. Thanks for your cooperation."

"Sure. I guess . . ."

Out in the hospital corridor, Wolfe turned to Delko and said, "So we know there's at least one other survivor—Jorge."

"Yeah. But we still *don't* know what kind of contraband the *Svetlana 2* was supposed to be carrying."

"Well, according to your buddy Pace, Jorge took off without it, and he couldn't find it. Which means either Dragoslav's crew managed to dump it overboard in the middle of a firefight—"

"—or it's still on board." Delko shook his head. "I guess we go back to the boat, really rip it apart. Maybe there's a false compartment or something we missed."

"I'm going to see if I can track down this Jorge, first. Maybe he knows more than Pace." Wolfe grinned. "Though that wouldn't take much. Hey, how did you know about him getting seasick?"

"Took a look through what was in his pockets when he was brought in. Found dimenhydrinate."

"Motion sickness pills? That's thinking ahead."

"Not far enough . . ."

8

HORATIO HAD DEALT with all kinds of cops in the course of his career, from ambitious rookies eager to make the jump to the next pay grade to street-weary veterans just hanging on until they could make retirement. He had encountered a broad governmental spectrum as well, from the U.S. Treasury to the FBI; the higher up the Federal Ladder, the less polite they tended to be.

During the nineteen-eighties, the Drug Enforcement Agency was in a class by themselves—and they knew it. Tasked with winning an unwinnable war against druglords who had more money than some countries, their job was high profile and never-ending. It even spawned a TV show, though most cops winced when it was brought up.

But the glory days of large-scale busts and screaming headlines were over; these days, people were more interested in the latest Baghdad car-bombing than a cigarette boat caught smuggling a few keys of cocaine. The press and the public had acknowledged long ago that the drug war was a losing proposition, and more than one cop had said the same thing publicly.

A cop who had done more than just talk was Garrett McCulver. He'd quit the DEA in disgust just three years shy of his pension, and according to Horatio's sources he hadn't gone quietly, either. Some stories had him breaking his superior's nose; others had him actually pulling a gun on the man. Whatever the details, he was obviously a man with deeply held convictions.

McCulver had retired to a small bungalow in Surfside, no more than a few steps from the beach. He was out on his small deck when Horatio walked up, lounging on a lawn chair in a pair of denim cut-offs, an old gray sweatshirt, and a Detroit Tigers baseball cap. McCulver looked to be in his fifties, tall and broad-shouldered, obviously still in good condition. He wore no shoes, and his skin had the leathery look of a man who spent a lot of time in the sun.

"Garrett McCulver?" asked Horatio.

"At your service. You Caine?"

Horatio smiled. "You still have good sources."

"A few." McCulver's voice was surprisingly soft. "They told me you'd been asking around about me."

"Mind if I sit down?"

"Not at all." McCulver reached out with one long

arm and dragged another lawn chair over. Horatio sat, and nodded his thanks.

"It's not so much about you," said Horatio, "as one of your old cases."

"I don't know if you've heard, Lieutenant, but I'm not much of a team player." McCulver's soft voice held just a trace of bitterness.

"That's not what I heard at all."

"No?"

"No. What I heard is that you were a good cop with a lousy boss. Happens to all of us, sooner or later."

"But most of us don't quit." It was somewhere between a question and an accusation.

"Sometimes the only option is to walk away. I think it takes more guts to do that than ignore the facts."

"In that case, I've got plenty." McCulver paused, then shook his head. "I'm sorry, Lieutenant. You're still on the job, and I'm busting your balls for it. Go ahead, tell me what you need."

"First of all, call me Horatio. And second—I need to know whatever you can tell me about a man named Rodriguo."

McCulver took his own sunglasses off and squinted at Horatio with ice-blue eyes. "Rodriguo. You're talking about the smuggler?"

"I am."

"You're sure the guys at the Agency didn't send you down here to yank my chain?"

"No sir, they did not."

"Huh. Well, all right then, Horatio—let me tell you about Rodriguo. He was my big fish, the one that got away. Until he vanished, Rodriguo was one of the biggest players in the cocaine trade, both on the East Coast of the U.S. and in Colombia. He was something of a legend in the eighties, and at one point I headed a task force put together for the sole purpose of stopping him. We failed. At the time of his disappearance, Rodriguo was at the top of his game—maybe that's why people still talk about him today. There are even occasional reports that he's still alive, living the rich life on the French Riviera or on some tropical island."

"You think it might be true?"

"Nah. Just the drugrunners' version of Elvis sightings. I may have never met the man—or even seen his face—but over the years I got to know him. And if there's one thing I can tell you about Rodriguo, it's that he was fearless. There's no way he would go into hiding. Go out in a blaze of glory, sure, but stay out of the limelight for the last two decades? No way. He's dead."

Horatio nodded. "Tell me about what he did while he was alive."

"He moved coke. No heroin, no marijuana, no speed. He took it from Colombia to the U.S., and he used some of the ballsiest methods I've ever seen."

"Such as?"

"There was one time—we heard about this after

the fact, you understand—he swapped a cargo container full of furniture for one full of nose candy; the container was being used to ship the belongings of an Air Force colonel from a base in Panama to one stateside. Another time, he used an old Army bomber to airlift a hundred keys into Florida—or should I say carpet-bomb Florida. He dropped fifty crates, all of 'em with parachutes, forty-nine filled with baking powder. Left us running around half the state trying to find the right one."

"Sounds like a gambling man."

"He was what we called a cocaine cowboy. Live fast and hard, always go for the big score, never back down from a challenge." McCulver shook his head and chuckled. "I even heard rumors he was negotiating with the Soviets for a decommissioned submarine before the Wall fell. Hell, for all I know he actually managed to buy one. Maybe that's where he is—he went from being a cowboy to Captain Nemo."

Horatio smiled. "I sincerely hope not."

McCulver glanced at him. "So what's this all about, Horatio? Has Rodriguo resurfaced after all this time?"

"Not exactly . . ." Horatio told him about Fredo and Consuela Bolivar.

McCulver looked thoughtful. "Yeah, I can vouch for the accuracy of the kidnap story; we knew about it and so did the FBI, but nobody ever got charged. That was the thing about Rodriguo—he had this ability to be famous and invisible at the same time. Everybody heard the stories, but only after he was already gone. The guy lived in the wind."

"Well, he must have come down to earth now and then—or he wouldn't have a son."

"*If* it's his son, you mean. In certain circles, saying you're related to Rodriguo is like claiming to be descended from Julius Caesar—easy to say, hard to disprove."

"You don't think there's any credence to it?"

McCulver shrugged. "Hard to say. If he is Rodriguo's son, you'd think he would have come forward before now."

"To claim his father's empire?"

"Not so much an empire anymore. What Rodriguo had was a network, and that was pretty much carved up right away. Rodriguo didn't seem to believe in the kind of opulent mansions the other druglords lived in—or if he did, he kept their location so secret we could never locate them. He only trusted a very small circle of associates with his secrets, and they all knew better than to talk. Sometimes I think there must be a gigantic mansion in the middle of the Colombian jungle, overrun with vines and creepers, spider monkeys swinging from the chandeliers, one lone skeleton sitting in a rotting armchair with a snake crawling through its eye sockets . . ."

"You have quite the imagination."

"I have a whole lot of time on my hands."

Horatio hunched forward, clasped his hands together. "So what happened to all the money?"

"Ah. Now *there's* the question. Nobody knows exactly how big that mountain of cash was, but it had to have been in the hundreds of millions. Most people assume he stashed it in some secret offshore account we've never been able to locate; a few think it's still in hard currency, boxed up in some old warehouse like the Ark of the Covenant at the end of *Raiders of the Lost Ark*. And then there's the old cranks, like me."

"And what," said Horatio, "do the old cranks think?"

"Oh, there's all kinds of crazy theories. I think my second favorite is the one that he secretly bought Disneyland and lives in the basement of the Haunted Mansion."

"And your favorite?"

McCulver didn't answer right away. He stared out at the ocean instead, watched two gulls fighting over the remains of a discarded hamburger. "That would be mine," he said at last. "See, I probably know more about Rodriguo than anybody in law enforcement, and I think I finally figured out what Rodriguo wanted out of all this."

Horatio waited.

"He wanted his own country," said McCulver. "One where he wouldn't be hunted, where he'd have respect and power and wealth. He couldn't get that in the U.S., he couldn't get it in Colombia. But I think he found a place where he could."

"Where?"

"Cuba."

"A communist dictatorship?"

"I told you it was crazy. But hear me out. You're a CSI—if my theory is flawed, you should be able to spot the holes."

"Go ahead."

"Okay. The only way he could pull this off is with Castro's approval and help. It's the one country the U.S. is guaranteed not to be able to extradite him from. As long as he's under Castro's wing, he can live the high life, in a climate and a culture he's used to. Hell, Rodriguo might even have been Cuban in the first place; from what I hear, *Scarface* was his favorite movie. There's an apocryphal story that after it came out, Rodriguo liked it so much he had a kilo of his best Peruvian flake delivered to Pacino's front door.

"Anyway, none of this makes sense unless Castro's on board. And what can an obscenely wealthy druglord offer to a head of state?"

"An extremely large check?"

"No. A flat-out bribe would make for disastrous publicity. Castro would have required something to give the whole thing a veneer of respectability—at least, that's what Rodriguo would have figured. The answer he came up with was *art*.

"Specifically, Cuban art. When Castro's revolutionary party took power in nineteen-fifty-nine, hundreds of thousands of people fled. They took what they could with them, but a lot of things got left behind. In some cases, relatives were asked to look after such things—the assumption being that the revolution wouldn't last and the family could come back to reclaim their property. That didn't work out so well—almost five decades later, they're still waiting."

"But not everyone was so patient?" asked Horatio.

"No. Between Castro's socialist policies and the U.S. trade embargo, life in Cuba became a lot harder. And if you're sitting on a pile of paintings you know are worth thousands, maybe millions, while your second cousin is living in a condo in Miami Beach . . . well, the temptation to maybe smuggle them out of the country and to an auction house gets stronger every year. Cuban art has been hemorrhaging off the island ever since."

McCulver took a long swallow of iced tea. "Even a lot of the stuff the original exiles took with them has wound up on the market—starting a new life in a new country isn't cheap, and the quickest way to get some ready cash is to hock a few heirlooms. I figure Rodriguo had no problem building an extensive collection."

"So you think he was buying Cuban art? To what end?"

"Eventual repatriation. See, he figured Castro wouldn't be able to resist the public relations opportunity—wealthy South American philanthro-pist donates a hundred million dollars in lost na-tional treasures to the Havana National Museum, and *el presidente* welcomes him with open arms. Ro-driguo retires with three or four hundred million to spare, never to be heard from again."

Horatio nodded. "An intriguing theory. Do you have anything to back it up?"

"A little. Back in eighty-five, I was tracking an anonymous collector who was paying top dollar for Cuban and Spanish-American art—I was sure it was Rodriguo, but I could never prove it. Spent around a hundred million, give or take. I still have the docu-mentation, if you'd like to take a look at it."

"I would."

"Give me a minute to dig it out, okay?" McCul-ver got to his feet.

"Sure."

McCulver stepped into the house through the open patio door. While he was gone, Horatio took in the view; a few lazy sailboats on the water, a sin-gle jet skier buzzing along in the distance like an angry mosquito too waterlogged to get airborne. It was a peaceful, sedate environment, the kind that many cops dreamed of retiring to; no pressures, no worries, no responsibility except keeping the cooler stocked and maybe walking the dog.

He was pretty sure McCulver hated it.

The ex-agent returned, a beige file folder in one hand. Horatio guessed McCulver hadn't had to do much digging to find it; he suspected that, in fact, it was never too far from reach. McCulver may not have been drawing a salary, but he was still a cop.

"You want to know something funny?" said McCulver, retaking his seat. "Even if Rodriguo's plan had worked out, a bunch of the stuff he bought might have been resold, anyway. A lot of the Cuban art that surfaced in the nineties was supposedly stolen and put on the market by Castro's own government—they needed some hard currency after the Wall fell and the Soviets couldn't subsidize them anymore."

He offered the folder and Horatio took it. "Let's say you're right," Horatio said. "Rodriguo put a large portion of his fortune into art, with plans of trading it for a new home in Cuba. What went wrong?"

"Who knows? My best guess is that all that treasure sitting in one place was too big a temptation for someone. Maybe one of Rodriguo's own men betrayed him. Maybe Castro pulled a double cross. Maybe the scheme even worked, and Rodriguo is living the high life in Havana while Castro decided to keep the whole collection in his basement."

"I thought you said you were sure Rodriguo was dead."

McCulver laughed. "I did, didn't I? Well, you know how it is with old cases—one day you're sure of one thing, the next you're convinced you had it all wrong for years. Like I said, Rodriguo's the one that got away. If you think you can figure out what happened to him, I'm glad to help. Maybe it'll help me sleep a little better."

"Tell me," said Horatio, "can you think of any reason Fredo Bolivar might be involved in the murder of a hot-air balloonist?"

"A balloonist? Well, Rodriguo used all kinds of methods to move his product—but I can't say I ever found any evidence he used a balloon. Too slow, hard to control, not much of a payload—plus, they're visible as all hell. Not much good to a smuggler."

"Maybe not," said Horatio. "But one might prove useful to a treasure hunter . . ."

McCulver told Horatio he could take the file with him, as long as he promised to keep him updated. Horatio thanked him and left, leaving the retired cop where he'd found him: sitting in a lawn chair and drinking another bottle of iced tea, watching the gulls argue and soar.

Horatio couldn't help but think of what he would do when he retired—assuming, of course, that he survived to do so. Would he wind up like McCulver, alone and bored, baking like an aging lizard in the sun while obsessing over old cases?

The thought brought up the memory of Marisol, and the constant, dull ache that accompanied her memory. She'd been young, vibrant, and so *alive;*

she was like a clear river that had run, oh so briefly, through the dark landscape of his life. Being with her made him forget the pain so deeply rooted in his own heart, made him see you could draw strength from something other than suffering.

And then she had died.

It amazed him, still, how much it hurt. It was as if all the previous pain in his life had just been shadows, and Marisol's death was a solar eclipse. And lurking behind the blackness, obscured but still visible, the blaze of his rage.

But he hadn't let it consume him. That would have dishonored her memory, would have been disrespectful and wrong. He and Eric had done what had to be done, had avenged the death of a wife and a sister, and now Horatio could only hope she was at peace. He knew peace was what she wanted for him, too—but not the peace of the grave. No, she wanted him to live, to enjoy life the way she had, to savor the fine taste of wine in the evening, to revel in all the spice and subtlety that a good meal could offer. He could almost hear her voice, sometimes, telling him it was all right to be happy, and it was that voice that kept him going. That voice, and his sense of duty.

He sympathized with McCulver's problems with the higher-ups. Horatio had endured his own problems with interdepartmental politics, and had come close to quitting more than once. Not over wounded pride or stubbornness—he refused to let personal feelings get in the way of doing his job. But sometimes you had to take a stand, simply to make those who would abuse their power reconsider; to let them know they were in for a fight, that you wouldn't back down no matter what the consequences. It was important.

So maybe that was his fate. Maybe he'd wind up all alone, just him and his memories on a beach, wondering if he'd made a wrong choice somewhere along the line.

Horatio turned on the radio. He found a station playing an old jazz standard—one Marisol would have liked—and softly hummed along, all the way back to the lab.

Horatio spent the afternoon in his office, looking through the file and cross-checking references. Calleigh showed up around three, looking just as frustrated as she had the day before.

"Still no luck?" Horatio asked, leaning back in his chair.

"No. Either my calculations of the flight path are off, or we've just missed it. Either way, it's got to be out there."

"Unless Fredo Bolivar got to it first."

She frowned. "You talk to that DEA agent?"

"I did. He had some interesting tales to tell."

She sank into a chair. "Well, I *love* a good story . . ."

He told her everything McCulver had told him.

"So," said Horatio, "It could be that Bolivar was out there hunting more than ducks."

"Or discarded firearms," said Calleigh thoughtfully. "And a hundred million dollars in art would certainly be motive for murder."

"Just what I was thinking. And hunting for it is also exactly the kind of endeavor that Timothy Breakwash would be attracted to."

"Well, hunting for buried treasure is practically Florida's official sport. You think Breakwash got the bug and was using the balloon to search from the air?"

"It makes sense. Especially if he was looking for an aircraft that went down in the Everglades twenty years ago."

Calleigh nodded. "So Bolivar and Breakwash might have been competitors."

"Or partners that had a falling out. If Breakwash actually found Rodriguo's stash, he might have gotten greedy, held out for a bigger cut."

"Which means Bolivar knows where it is, too; he wouldn't kill Breakwash otherwise. But if that's the case—"

"—why was he out searching the Everglades when he should be hauling away treasure?" Horatio shrugged. "I don't know. Logistics, maybe. He might need heavy equipment or diving gear or even explosives. He was probably scoping out the situation when you scared him off."

"Maybe. Or maybe he still doesn't know where it

is—which means Breakwash could have been killed by someone else."

"True. But whatever the case," said Horatio, getting up from his chair, "I think one thing is obvious. It's time to have a little talk with Fredo Bolivar . . ."

Fredo Bolivar stared at Horatio with flat black eyes. He wore what Horatio thought of as generic gang-wear: baggy jeans with boxers showing over the waist, oversize basketball jersey, baseball hat with the brim at a forty-five-degree angle away from the forehead, expensive sneakers. And the sneer, of course; that was mandatory.

"Fredo," said Horatio. "Thanks for coming in to talk to us." Horatio was on his feet, holding a beige file folder in one hand; Calleigh sat across from Fredo, who was trying to look as though he were lounging casually in a chair designed to make that impossible.

"Yes," added Calleigh. She leaned forward, putting her elbows on the interview table, and gave Fredo her warmest smile. "We appreciate it. Can I get you a soda or something?"

Fredo lowered his gaze about a foot, from Calleigh's eyes to her cleavage. "You don't have to go anywhere," he said with a grin. "*He* can go get me a cold one, though."

Horatio smiled himself, but didn't rise to the bait. "Fredo. Do you know a man named Timothy Breakwash?"

"Never heard of him."

"You sure?" said Calleigh. "Maybe you and he ran into each other while you were out duck hunting. You know—with your father."

That got a flicker of his attention. "My father. That's what this is all about?"

"That depends, Fredo," said Horatio. "It depends on exactly who your father is."

"My father's dead."

"You know that for sure?" asked Calleigh.

"I know it in my heart. He was a great man—if he was still alive, he would have let me know."

"And what," asked Horatio, "was this great man's name?"

"His real name doesn't matter. He was my father, and that's what is important."

"Maybe you don't know what his real name was," said Horatio. "Maybe you don't care. Maybe what's important isn't his name . . . but what he left behind."

The smile was gone from Fredo's face, replaced by a cold glare. "What's this all about? If you have something to ask me, just ask."

"All right, Fredo," said Horatio. "Where were you yesterday morning, around sunrise?"

"Out hunting. In the 'Glades."

"Alone?" asked Calleigh.

"Just me and my dog."

"Kill anything?" asked Horatio.

"No."

"Guess you're not much of a shot," said Calleigh.

"Didn't even fire my gun."

"Did you notice anything unusual in the air that morning?" asked Horatio.

"Sure. Saw a big balloon go right overhead."

Calleigh nodded. "Is that all you saw?"

"That's it."

"So," said Horatio, "if I were to dust Timothy Breakwash's house for prints, I wouldn't find yours—because you've never been there, correct?"

"That's right. I told you, I never heard of him."

"You want to know what I think, Fredo?" asked Horatio. "I think you did know Timothy Breakwash. I think the two of you were looking for your father's legacy in the Everglades—you on the ground, him in the air. I think your relationship soured, and Timothy Breakwash wound up dead."

Fredo shook his head in disgust. "That's a crazy story, man. This Breakwash guy was in that balloon? What, you think I shot him from the ground, or something? Well, I haven't fired my gun in weeks—go ahead, check it out. And as for my father's so-called 'legacy,' the only thing he left me was a bunch of stories my mother told me. I guess him and Breakwash have that in common—I never met either of them."

"We *will* check that out, Fredo," said Horatio. "You can count on it."

*   *   *

Six hours later, they were back to square one. Calleigh had gone back to the Breakwash residence and scoured it for prints, epithelials, any kind of trace that could put Fredo there; Rodriguo's purported son had even voluntarily given them a DNA sample. She found nothing. Even though his gun wasn't the make they were looking for, Calleigh tested it anyway; Bolivar had been telling the truth. The gun hadn't been fired recently.

Calleigh met Horatio in the layout room and told him the news.

"Well, at least we accomplished one thing," said Horatio. "If Fredo does know where the art is, he won't move on it now; he knows we're watching him."

"Do you really think it's out there, H? A hundred million in missing art?"

"It's possible. I've been going over the files in Breakwash's computer and the files McCulver gave me; there's a lot of overlap."

"Breakwash had files on missing art?"

"Breakwash had files on all sorts of things. The art didn't jump out at me until McCulver brought it up—take a look."

Horatio sat down in front of a monitor and tapped a few keys. "According to McCulver, Rodriguo concentrated on two things: paintings and pearls."

"Ooh," said Calleigh. "Diamonds may be a girl's best friend, but pearls are definitely number two on my speed dial."

"They're highly prized as gems, but they're also pieces of history. McCulver seems to think Rodriguo was the one that bought a pearl called *La Pellegrina* in 1987, just before he vanished. It has a fascinating past; supposedly discovered off South America, it was originally called *La Reine de Pearl*, and was part of the Spanish crown jewels. It was given to Philip the Fourth's daughter when she married Louis XIV, and became part of the French crown jewels. In 1792, it was stolen; it resurfaced in India, then was brought to Russia where it was renamed the Zozima pearl. It became the property of Russian royalty and disappeared until the eighties, where it was sold at auction to an unknown buyer."

"How much did it go for?"

"Just shy of half a million dollars."

"Born in South America, hung around with criminals and royalty, known for changing its identity and disappearing—sounds like Rodriguo might have found it irresistible."

"Maybe so. Another possibility is a pearl called *La Huerfana*—the Orphan. It was briefly owned by Isabel de Bobadilla, the first female governor of Cuba."

Calleigh nodded. "That would fit, all right. What's it worth?"

"Hard to say. It weighed in at thirty-one carats, was part of the Spanish crown jewels, and was said to be nearly flawless—but it was also supposedly destroyed when the Spanish palace in Madrid went up in flames in 1734. However, it wasn't the only artistic treasure on display there; the Spanish court had many masterpieces hanging on the walls. According to historical accounts, when monks from a neighboring monastery noticed the fire, they rushed into the burning castle, ripped as many canvases off the walls as they could, and threw them out the windows in order to save them."

"You think one of the monks saved a little something for himself?"

"Anything's possible. But if such an item came up on the market, someone like Rodriguo would have found it extremely tempting."

"Assuming that Rodriguo really was collecting art. And while we're making assumptions, let's not forget we're assuming that Fredo is really Rodriguo's son. Oh, and that Timothy Breakwash's death was a murder and not a suicide." Calleigh sighed. "You know, so far this case is just a big old briar patch of assumptions. I would give a week of vacation days for some good, solid *evidence.*"

"Find me some," said Horatio, "and you can have mine."

9

DR. ALEXX WOODS looked around her autopsy theater and sighed. She was tired, having worked almost nonstop for the last twenty hours, but that wasn't what was bothering her. She *hated* it when people died in large groups.

Not because of the inconvenience or the pressure, but because she felt that every body that passed through her care deserved her full attention, and when there were a lot of them all at once she had to make compromises.

And apologies.

"Okay," she said to the corpse on the stainless-steel table. "Sorry, sweetie, but somebody has to be last. Looks like that's you."

The body on the table was that of a man in his thirties. He had a prominent gut, with the kind of flabby arms and chest she'd seen on too many desk jockeys. The body had no gunshot wounds, unlike all the others from the yacht shooting; she noted again that his lips looked cyanotic and his skin pale. "What did you in, honey?" she murmured. "No visible signs of trauma—did you have a coronary in the middle of all the shooting? Too much excitement for a heart that needed more exercise and less time as a couch potato? Only one way to find out . . ."

She picked up a scalpel and made the first incision.

"What are you looking at?" asked Wolfe, walking into the layout room. "I thought you were going to go back and reexamine the boat." Delko had a dozen different stacks of paper spread out on the surface of the light table.

"Thought I'd take a look at what we have on the shooting victims first. We've IDed every body, and all of them have priors. The Cubans are low-level gangbangers, while the Eastern European types have links to the Russian mob. All of them except this guy." Delko picked up a piece of paper and handed it to Wolfe.

"Stanley Wolchkowski," read Wolfe. "No priors, no known criminal connections—until now, I guess. Who is he?"

"He owns a chain of high-end supermarkets," said Delko. "The kind that cater to people who don't do their own cooking. This really doesn't seem like his kind of crowd."

"Maybe he provided the food. I seem to recall that buffet looked pretty pricy."

"You don't usually invite the caterer along on a private cruise."

"True," Wolfe admitted. "But you *do* invite someone you're trying to negotiate a business deal with. Someone, say, who owns a trucking firm and has ties to the Italian mob."

Delko frowned. "Who are you talking about?"

"Valerie Faustino. She owns a trucking company that distributes merchandise up and down the East Coast—and she has ties to the Luccini family."

"Okay, that makes a certain amount of sense. It looks like whatever Dragoslav was planning, an alliance with the Luccinis was part of it."

"Yeah—but how does Wolchkowski fit in?"

"Well," said Delko, "for one thing, Wolchkowski was the only one who wasn't shot. He was the vic in the stateroom, on the bed."

"We have a COD, yet?"

"Alexx is working on it. She's got a lot of bodies to process, though."

"Don't let her hear you talk like that," said Wolfe. "I called a vic a stiff in front of her once. Not going to do *that* again."

"The alimentary tract," Alexx said into the microphone of her recorder, "is extremely distended. There are also signs of hypersecretion, suggesting a possible cholinergic crisis leading to respiratory failure."

She collected the stomach contents, noting the color and consistency, then took a blood sample for tox screening. She already had a theory about what killed him, but she wouldn't know for sure until certain tests were performed; she sent a sample of the stomach contents to the lab for gas chromatography.

She looked down at the body and shook her head. "Poor baby. You really liked your food, huh? From the condition of your liver and your heart, you liked a few drinks to go with it, too. If you didn't cut back on the fat and alcohol, a heart attack probably would have got you in a few years, anyway."

She started closing him up. "But you don't have to worry about any of that now. No stairmaster for you, no low-fat yogurt or early-morning jogging or diet soda. All you have ahead of you is a little embroidery, and then a nice, long rest . . ."

"What's next?" asked Delko. He took a long sip of his coffee.

Wolfe took a last bite of his sandwich and swallowed before answering. "I'm going to try to track down Jorge and the boat. I have a hunch that the guys who planned the robbery might have a better idea of what they were looking for than Pace Birmingham did."

Delko nodded and signaled the waitress for the check. "Yeah, I get the feeling they didn't trust him with any more information than they had to."

"If I get something useful, I might be able to use it as a lever to pry something about the deal out of Valerie Faustino. Right now, her lawyer's got her mouth locked up like Fort Knox. How about you?"

Delko finished his coffee and got to his feet. "Alexx sent me the stomach contents of Stanley Wolchkowski. I'm going to run some tests."

"Well, whatever he ate," said Wolfe, looking down at his half-eaten sandwich, "I'll bet it was better than this."

"Don't be too sure."

The tests Delko ran came back positive for the presence of a chemical known as TTX. Delko studied the results, nodded, and put in a call to a local ESL school the police department occasionally used. He was going to need a translator—his Russian was pretty good, but he only knew a few words of Japanese.

The translator's name was Michiko Kotosaya. She was a shy, slightly plump woman in her twenties, whose English was flawless. She wore jeans and a pink T-shirt with a cartoon robot on it, and sat next to Delko in the interview room.

On the other side of the table sat Yamada Osamu, the cook from the *Svetlana 2*. He was dressed in more casual clothes now, but he still looked as nervous as he had when Delko had first seen him huddling in the ship's freezer.

"Mister Osamu," said Delko. "How long have you worked for Mister Dragoslav?"

Michiko translated and listened to Yamada's reply. "He says he's never worked for him before. This was a favor he was doing for Mister Dragoslav."

"I see. Who do you normally work for, Mister Osamu?"

"I work for a restaurant in Manhattan, *Fujikawas*."

"I've heard of that place. Very expensive. You must make a good living."

"I studied the preparation of *sashimi* for many years in Japan. I am licensed to prepare *tessa*, as few chefs in America are."

"Tessa? What's that?"

"It is also known as *fugu sashi*."

"Fugu? The poisonous fish?"

"Yes. Prepared correctly, it is not dangerous."

Delko knew about fugu. Considered a delicacy in Japan, it was made from the flesh of the pufferfish and contained a chemical called tetrodotoxin. Fugu poisoning caused total muscular paralysis; voodoo priests in Haiti used it to immobilize people so thoroughly they appeared to be dead, which inspired stories of zombiehood when the victim was later seen alive.

Not all of those poisoned with tetrodotoxin survived, though. If the paralysis was severe enough to affect the respiratory system it would cause asphyxiation. Chefs who prepared the food had to be specially licensed, and serving certain parts of the fish was illegal.

Delko nodded. "Mister Osamu, we found a chemical called TTX in the stomach of a man named Stanley Wolchkowski on the *Svetlana 2*. You might know it better as tetrodotoxin—and it was what killed him."

When Michiko had finished telling him, Osamu bowed his head, a look of immense shame on his face. When he spoke, it was haltingly, his voice breaking.

"Yes. It was my fault. When I saw the moonfish, I could not resist telling Mister Dragoslav that it belongs to the same family as the pufferfish, and is sometimes eaten as a delicacy also. He was amused, and told one of his passengers, who was knowledgeable about food and considered himself a gourmet. The passenger asked that I prepare some for him. Foolishly, I agreed, though I have never prepared moonfish before. Now, I am responsible for his death."

Delko sighed. *An accident*, he thought. If Osamu's intention was to murder Wolchkowski, he wouldn't have used a thousand-pound moonfish to do it—a chef like Osamu had access to real fugu, which would have proved more tempting to a sophisticated palate than a parasite-riddled bonefish. And if Dragoslav had wanted Wolchkowski dead, simply shooting him and dumping him over the side would have been quick and easy.

Looking at the anguish on Osamu's face, Delko knew it was sincere. The man had risked his professional reputation and another's life on his skill, and he had lost. Even if he didn't spend time in jail, his career was over and he would live with guilt and shame for the rest of his life. He honestly felt sorry for the man.

Which made what he had to do next that much harder.

He put a harshness he didn't feel into his next words. "That's quite a coincidence, Mister Osamu. One man just happens to die of an accidental poisoning while fourteen others are shot on the same boat? The boat of a known gangster?"

"I know nothing of that. My dishonor is my own."

"No, Mister Osamu. What will be your own is the needle they'll put in your arm when you're executed for murder."

Michiko hesitated before translating, clearly disturbed.

"Say it," Delko told her tersely.

She did. His reaction was what he'd hoped; stark disbelief and fear.

"But I did not mean to. It was not murder."

"Tell it to a jury, Yamada. You think they'll believe you, or what I put in my report?"

"Why would you say this? I had no reason to kill this man."

"I say this because you're not telling me the

whole truth, Yamada. You know what kind of man Dragoslav is, and you know why he was out on that boat. You tell me that, and maybe my report won't make you sound like a cold-blooded killer."

There was a long silence while Osamu considered Delko's words. Delko waited. The look Michiko gave him made him feel like dirt, but Delko's job was to solve cases; right now, his best chance of doing that was to put pressure on Yamada Osamu. Of all the survivors of the shootout—all the nondrugged ones, anyway—he was the one most likely to talk.

Finally, Osamu began to speak. His voice was soft, and he was obviously choosing his words carefully.

"It is true that I know of Mister Dragoslav's reputation. There are others of his kind in Japan, and it is to them that a member of my family owes a favor. By doing this favor, I am canceling a debt. However, the debt is now satisfied. I will tell you what I can, but I know very little."

"Do you know what the purpose of the meeting was?"

"I do not."

Of course he wouldn't. He's just a specialized chef, brought in for show. Delko tried another approach. "Did you see anything odd or unusual aboard the ship?"

"I saw that many of the men carried guns. I believe several of the young women were prostitutes.

Until the shooting began, I saw nothing out of the ordinary."

"How about the moonfish? Were you there when it was brought aboard?"

"Yes. It was brought aboard once we were a considerable distance out at sea, transferred from another boat. I assumed it had been caught by them."

"So the other boat was a fishing boat?"

Osamu frowned before replying. "No. It was a freighter of some kind."

"Do you remember the name of the ship?'

"I'm sorry. I do not."

"How was the fish brought on board?"

"They used a crane—there is a hatch that opens directly into the galley. The fish was lowered, then taken to the refrigerated area. I was told to leave the galley, and was not allowed back for half an hour."

"Mister Osamu, this next question is important. Did you notice anything on the ship that hadn't been there before the fish was brought on board? Anything new, anything you noticed for the first time?"

Osamu gave the question careful consideration, his brow wrinkled in thought. At last, he spoke.

"There was one thing. There were a number of large, square white buckets with lids—the kind that can hold around five gallons of water. They were stacked together, one nested inside another. They were present at the beginning of the journey, but later they had vanished, along with their lids. A small detail, but a careful chef knows the location and use of every item in his kitchen."

So if something was hidden in the fish, it might have been transferred to the buckets. We didn't find anything like that on the ship—so what happened to them? He shook his head. It looked like the only option he had left was to tear apart the *Svetlana 2*, piece by piece.

"Thank you, Mister Osamu. You've been very helpful. I'll do my best to stress the fact that the poisoning was accidental."

This time when Osamu spoke, Michiko hesitated before translating.

"He says," she said at last, "that for someone in his profession, it might be better to be seen as a murderer than as incompetent."

Wolfe had only a first name to work with: Jorge. He tried going back to talk to Pace Birmingham, but the drugs had worn off by then and Pace refused to say a word without a lawyer present. Undaunted, Wolfe checked Pace's arrest record and came up with the name "Jorge Sonoma" under known associates. Sonoma belonged to a gang called the Habaneros, who operated out of Little Havana and mostly stuck to drug-dealing. He checked the priors of the other Cubano shooting victims, and all of them belonged to the gang, too.

He tried the Florida State DHSMV database,

checking boat registrations; sure enough, Jorge Sonoma was the registered owner of a motor launch. Wolfe noted his address and took out his cell phone.

Sonoma lived in a five-story apartment building in Little Havana, a brick structure that looked as if it had recently been renovated; Wolfe knew that the forces of gentrification were slowly making their way through the neighborhood, driving up prices and displacing the older residents with younger, more affluent buyers. The lobby of the building had been completely redone, a new red-brown granite floor installed, chromed Art Deco light sconces on the walls. The elevator door looked as if it was made of hammered tin, like the ceilings of some of the older restaurants in the area. Wolfe wasn't sure if he liked the idea of a tin elevator, even if it were only an illusion created for the sake of style; he preferred his mechanical conveyances to be made of something a little sturdier.

Sonoma's place was on the top floor. Wolfe knocked on the door, and a few seconds later heard a voice say, "Who's there?"

"Mister Sonoma?" said Wolfe. "My name is Ryan Wolfe. I'm with the Miami-Dade crime lab."

"What do you want?"

"Just to ask you a few questions."

"Yeah, yeah, okay. Just a second."

The door unlocked and swung open. Jorge Sonoma stood there, wearing only a pair of baggy surfing shorts. He had a machine pistol pointed straight at Wolfe's chest.

"Crime lab, huh?" Sonoma said. "You don't fool me. You're here to arrest me. What, you thought you'd get all the glory by making the bust by yourself? Not too smart, *hermano*."

Wolfe studied him calmly, his hands held at his sides. "Well, you're absolutely right about one thing. I did come here to arrest you. But—"

The sound a riot shotgun makes being cocked is a very distinctive one. Sonoma's eyes widened as he heard it directly behind him.

"—what makes you think I came alone?"

The Gang Unit officers on either side of the door stepped into view, guns aimed at Sonoma's heart. On the fire escape, the officer with the shotgun said, "Put your weapon down. *Now.*"

Sonoma swallowed and lowered his gun. Seconds later, he was facedown on the floor and cuffed.

"Now, Mister Sonoma," said Wolfe, getting down on his haunches and pulling a piece of paper out of his pocket, "this is a search warrant for your apartment *and* your boat. You don't really look like you have the space to store it here—unless you've got a really outstanding walk-in closet—so it would really help me out if you'd just tell me where it is."

"Vete para la pinga, cabrón," Sonoma muttered.

"Well, that's not very nice. Guess I'll just have to do this the hard way."

At least, Wolfe thought to himself as they took Sonoma away, *his apartment has air-conditioning.*

Wolfe smiled. On the other side of the interview table, Jorge Sonoma looked back sullenly.

"You know how long it took to find your boat?" asked Wolfe. "About thirty seconds. Marina slip stuck to your fridge with a magnet. I could have done it even quicker, but the slip was half hidden by a pizza menu."

"So you found my boat. So what?"

"So we *searched* your boat, Jorge. Know what we found?"

"No."

"A very unusual device. Looks kind of like the offspring of a pair of vise grips and a grappling hook—ingenious, really."

"That? It's just something I made to help with mooring. Latches on when there's nothing good to tie up to."

"Like a convenient yacht, for instance?"

"Huh?"

"Very convincing. But what's even *more* convincing are these photos." Wolfe slapped two pictures down on the table in front of Sonoma. "See, these are the tool marks your little invention made on a metal rod in my lab. And *these* are the tool marks left on the outside railing of the *Svetlana 2*—the yacht you tried to rob."

Sonoma studied the photos for a moment, then

shook his head. "Someone must have taken my boat."

"Come on, Jorge. We got you. We have your prints on the clamping device, we have the tool marks on the railing, we have paint trace from the side of the yacht that's going to match the paint on your boat—and we have an eyewitness. How do you think we found you in the first place? Pace Birmingham may not be too bright, but he managed to survive the gun battle—and he was smart enough to give you up instead of being the only person left alive to pin piracy charges on."

"Son of a *bitch*," snarled Jorge. "That worthless . . . he was the only one that lived?"

"The only one on your crew. The owner of the boat and a few others managed to hide out until it was all over."

"Figures it would be that *maricón*. We only took him along as a decoy—we didn't even give him a gun. All my brothers are dead and he's still drawing breath. For now, anyway."

"I wouldn't be too hard on Pace if I were you, Jorge. After all, he stuck around—you were the one who took off."

From the look in Jorge's eyes Wolfe knew he'd struck a nerve. He decided to strike it a little harder. "Was it worth it, Jorge? Leaving all your brothers behind to die, just so you could live?"

"I didn't have a choice," Jorge spat. "Those Russians—it was like fighting a goddamn *war*, okay? We thought we had the element of surprise, but they reacted so fast it didn't make any difference. They knew what they were doing, and they had better cover than us. They cut us to pieces. If I hadn't left they would have killed me, too."

"Really? I don't think you heard me right, Jorge. I said the owner of the boat and a few others survived—none of the Russians did. Your guys didn't give up. They got cut to pieces, yeah . . . but they took every one of the Russians down with them. Kind of makes you wonder what would have happened if your guys had just one more man on their side . . ."

Wolfe let that sink in, waited until he saw the rage on Jorge's face start to crumple into shame. "You should consider yourself lucky," Wolfe said. "The getaway driver usually does less time than the other members of the crew. In your case, you can probably shift the blame for the whole mess onto someone who's already dead—who's going to contradict you, Pace? He's a go-along-to-get-along type. Play this right and you can probably avoid a death sentence."

Jorge sighed. "What do you want?"

"Information. I want to know what you were hoping to take from that ship, and who you were planning to sell it to." Wolfe didn't actually care about how they planned on getting rid of their haul—he just knew it was better to ask for more than you expected to get.

"Didn't Pace tell you? We didn't know, not for sure. We just heard that a couple of people from New York were coming in to make a deal, and the meet was going to take place on this yacht. Then somebody else told us that a shipment was coming in at sea, and it was going to be transferred to the *Svetlana 2*. We figured it had to be drugs—cocaine, maybe heroin. One of the guys thought it was a bunch of Ecstasy pills from some European lab. Something worth at least a million dollars, anyway."

Wolfe scowled. "Come on. You expect me to believe that? You and your crew take on a whole boatload of heavily armed ex-KGB types for a rumor? For something you don't even know the name of, let alone if you can sell it? What would you have done if it were illegal computer parts—try and cut a deal with Circuit City?"

"Hey, there's always someone willing to buy. No matter what it is."

"Well, the next people you're going to have to sell that to is a jury. Good luck."

Wolfe stood up. Jorge hesitated, then said, "Hey. Tell me something."

"What?"

"What *was* it? The shipment?"

"When I figure that out," said Wolfe, "I'll let you know."

10

HORATIO KNEW SOMETHING was wrong as soon as he pulled up to the house.

He'd driven out to the Breakwash place to talk to Randilyn Breakwash, hoping to get her reaction to McCulver's theory. Though Timothy Breakwash hadn't left anything definitive on his computer, he might have confided in his wife that Rodriguo's treasure was what he was searching for. And if Randilyn knew about her husband's treasure hunt, she hadn't mentioned anything about it to Horatio—which meant he might be able to catch her in a lie now.

But it appeared that someone had visited her first.

The front door of her house was ajar. The same car that had been parked beside it the last time Horatio had talked to her was still there, but its driver's side door was open; Horatio could see that the seats had been ripped apart with a blade. Someone had been conducting a search of their own.

He radioed for backup immediately, then jumped out of his Hummer and drew his Glock. The lack of any other vehicle told him the perp was probably long gone, but he didn't intend to take any chances.

"Mrs. Breakwash?" he called out as he stepped through the front door, his pistol held in front of him. "Randilyn? It's Horatio Caine. Are you all right?"

The kitchen was thoroughly trashed: cupboard doors ripped off, their contents pulled out and scattered everywhere; the sink full of food that had been dumped into it and sifted through; the refrigerator on its back like an open coffin. Spilled pasta crunched underfoot as Horatio stalked across the floor and into the next room.

The rest of the house was just as torn up. Horatio stepped carefully through the wreckage of the living room and spotted a blood trail leading to the hall. He followed it.

The body of the bulldog pup lay just outside the bedroom door, blood soaking its fur. He found Randilyn Breakwash inside.

She'd been tied spread-eagled to the bed, naked, and a rag stuffed in her mouth. Her body was covered in small, perfectly circular burns.

She was still alive.

Horatio moved quickly, stepping to her side and

pulling the gag out of her mouth. "Randilyn? Listen to me—*is he still here?*"

"N-no. I don't think so . . ." She began to cry, terrible little whimpering noises that sounded like she was afraid to acknowledge how badly she was hurt. Horatio holstered his gun and worked on freeing her wrists.

"It's okay," he said. "It's all right. You're all right now . . ."

Somehow, he didn't think she believed him.

Calleigh stood beside Horatio with her arms crossed, watching the ambulance take Randilyn Breakwash away.

"Paramedics say she'll make it," said Horatio. "She's in shock, but they've given her drugs for the pain."

"Too bad they can't give her drugs for the scars," said Calleigh.

"At least she's still alive."

"Did she say anything to you about who did this?"

Horatio shook his head. "No, she was too traumatized to make any sense. But I can think of only one reason someone would do this to her."

Calleigh nodded, her face grim. "A hundred million reasons, you mean."

"Yes. And I don't think he got what he was after, either. If he had, he wouldn't have left her alive."

"You think it was Fredo Bolivar?"

"I don't know," said Horatio, slipping on his sunglasses, "but I'm going to find out."

Calleigh started in the bedroom. She collected the ropes used to bind Randilyn, the sheets she lay on and the gag, documenting everything thoroughly with pictures. It wasn't hard to tell what he'd used to burn her; a soldering iron with a round tip lay on the dresser, small flakes of charred skin still stuck to the end.

She lifted prints from every available surface, including the frame of the bed, the surface of the dresser, and the doorknob. Then she moved into the hall, kneeling beside the body of the dog. "Poor girl," she sighed. "Looks like he tried working on you first, trying to get your owner to talk." *And when that didn't work, he tried a more direct method . . .*

She took samples from under the dog's claws, hoping that maybe the bulldog had managed to scratch her tormentor, and collected blood from the hallway runner. The living room was next, and it was a big job; Randilyn's attacker had used a chainsaw to rip apart the walls themselves in his search. The chainsaw lay discarded in a corner. Calleigh bagged it, intending to take a closer look at it in the lab.

The home's fairly isolated, Calleigh thought. *No one close enough to hear home renovation being done at three* A.M., *anyway. Or screaming . . .*

If it was Fredo Bolivar, he's pretty sure of himself. He

knows we've gone over this place looking for his DNA or prints, and found nothing—but to spend a whole night here and not worry about leaving a single trace?

Or maybe it's not Bolivar at all. Maybe there's a third partner we don't know about.

She wondered if the searcher had found what he or she was looking for. Somehow, she doubted it; the extensive burns on Randilyn Breakwash's body and the state of the house seemed to indicate a long interrogation followed by a thorough search. And, as Horatio had pointed out, Randilyn was still alive. That suggested her attacker still believed she knew something valuable.

Now it was Calleigh's turn to search. Her methods were more subtle—but they almost always produced results.

The first thing Horatio did was put out a BOLO for Fredo Bolivar—he wanted the man off the street and in an interview room as soon as possible. He headed for the address listed on Bolivar's driver's license, but it was a false lead; a Nicaraguan family lived there now, and had for the last six months.

Horatio mulled over the case as he drove to the hospital to check on Randilyn. The brutality of the attack indicated either a cold-blooded determination or an innate tendency toward sadism. He tried to decide which profile was a better fit for Fredo Bolivar and couldn't; he didn't know the man well enough to make that sort of judgment. Bolivar had seemed to him like many gang members he'd encountered: angry, arrogant, with a calculated coldness underneath that was supposed to communicate that he was capable of anything.

Maybe he is, maybe he isn't. Maybe he's trying to live up to his father's reputation—or maybe someone else is.

A hundred million dollars, Horatio knew, could bring out a lot more in people than just greed. He'd seen horrendous acts committed for far smaller amounts, by the kind of upright citizens who normally would swerve if a cat ran in front of their car.

He considered the other potential suspects. Joel Greer? As Timothy Breakwash's ground crew, he would be the one most likely to know what Timothy was hunting for, and he was familiar with the house.

Lee Kwok? It was possible Breakwash had confided in his old college buddy, maybe even approached him for assistance in some way; Kwok had access to lab facilities Timothy didn't.

Sylvester Perrone? Horatio couldn't see any apparent connection, but that didn't mean there wasn't one. If recovering the treasure required an outlay of cash—perhaps for equipment—maybe Breakwash had approached Perrone as an investor.

Horatio didn't know. What he did know was that someone had tied up and tortured Timothy Breakwash's widow and torn apart her house.

And he was going to find them.

*　　　*　　　*

Randilyn Breakwash's eyes were closed as Horatio approached the bed.

"Mrs. Breakwash?" he asked softly.

Her eyes fluttered open. The doctor on duty told him she'd calmed down a lot since they sedated her for the pain, but had remained conscious; her eyes focused on Horatio immediately and she said, "Lieutenant Caine?"

"It's Horatio," he said. "How are you doing?"

"I'm—" Tears welled up in her eyes, but she tried to smile. "I've been better." Her voice was hoarse but firm.

"I know you've been through a lot, but it would help our investigation a great deal if I could speak to you for just a moment."

"He didn't rape me," she said. "That's—that's not what he was there for."

"Who, Mrs. Breakwash?"

"I don't know. He wore a mask the whole time— a surgical mask, one of those blue ones. And one of those paper suits painters use, the kind with the hoods. I think he had something over his feet, too."

Horatio nodded. "How about height, build, race?"

"Around five-ten, a hundred and fifty pounds. I think he was Hispanic. His eyes were black, so black . . ."

Horatio decided to take a chance. "I know what he was after, Mrs. Breakwash."

"What?"

"I know about what your husband was searching for in the Everglades. I know about Rodriguo's plane."

She stared at him for a moment. He could see the immense weariness in her eyes, and it wasn't just from the medication. "Rodriguo's plane. God, I hope I never hear that phrase again."

"Then you know what I'm talking about."

"Of course I do. It was his latest obsession. Just the kind of thing Tim loved: an epic story, with larger-than-life characters and a big payoff at the end. It might as well have been about pirates and a treasure chest full of gold." Randilyn's voice held both anger and a kind of wry amusement. "I never could understand how a scientist could be such a dreamer at the same time."

"An interest in how the world works doesn't mean you don't have ideas about how it *should* work," said Horatio. "But Mrs. Breakwash—you didn't mention this project of Tim's before."

"Can you blame me? It was just another of his crazy schemes. I was embarrassed, frankly—I didn't want people remembering my husband as some kind of wacko." Her gaze slid away from Horatio's; whether it was because of the drugs or something else, he couldn't tell.

"So you're saying Tim didn't find what he was looking for."

"What? Of course not. It was just a wild, pie-in-the-sky fantasy. Millions of dollars worth of art, in the hold of a plane that crashed in the Everglades twenty years ago? Come on, Lieutenant—how believable does that sound to you?"

"As a very smart man once said," said Horatio, "the credibility of a proposition has nothing to do with its truth. Even the most far-fetched theories, Mrs. Breakwash, sometimes prove to hold water."

"Not this one."

"Somebody obviously believed otherwise. That's what your attacker was after, wasn't it?"

She looked down, but didn't reply.

"We know this was no random attack, Randilyn. Your house was ransacked and you were systematically interrogated. No one goes to those lengths without a very good reason."

"All right, yes," she said quietly. "That's what he was after. The location of the plane. But there *is* no damn plane! It was all just another of Tim's stupid, pointless treasure hunts, looking for the pot of gold at the end of the rainbow. And now—now look at what it's done to me." She lifted up her left arm, the one with the IV in it. Angry red circles covered it like an oddly symmetrical rash. "If Tim had found the plane, he would have told me. And if I knew where it was, I would have told the man who did *this.*" Fresh tears flowed down her face. "I would have told him after the very first burn. But he didn't believe me. And he didn't stop . . ."

She began to sob, in the exhausted, hopeless way only deep trauma could produce.

"I'm sorry," Horatio said. "Try to get some rest. I promise you, we'll find the man who did this."

Her sobs were already slowing into a more regular kind of breathing. In a few seconds, she was fast asleep, the drugs finally overpowering her system.

Horatio's cell phone rang as he was getting into the Hummer. Fredo Bolivar had been picked up in a bar in Miami Beach, and was on his way to a holding cell.

Timothy Breakwash's garage was set up as a combination lab and office. Calleigh had already been there twice—first to pick up Breakwash's computer and printer, then to try to find Fredo Bolivar's DNA or fingerprints.

It had been in considerably better shape the last time. Now papers and books were scattered over the floor, drawers had been ripped out of filing cabinets and upended, the few pieces of equipment Breakwash had owned taken apart. An acrid, rotten-fish odor hung in the air; it looked as though the searcher had gone as far as dumping containers of chemicals down the stainless-steel sink.

"Lucky you didn't cause an explosion," Calleigh murmured to herself. "Or maybe it wasn't luck at all . . ." She examined the empty containers beside the sink, then looked around and spotted a large green plastic bucket in one corner, half full of a pale blue liquid. A quick sniff confirmed her suspicions: hydrogen peroxide.

She went back out to her Hummer and got a hazardous materials mask, came back and finished processing the garage, then did the vehicle. When she was done, she loaded up everything she'd collected and headed back to the lab.

"Hello, Fredo," said Horatio. "You look a little tired. Busy night?"

Fredo Bolivar was dressed the same way he'd been the last time he and Horatio had talked. His attitude hadn't changed, either; he still looked at Horatio with a combination of arrogance and uncaring.

"You know," he said. "Same old same old. Just chilling with some friends."

"Uh-huh. And I suppose those friends would be willing to verify your presence?"

"Every one."

"And where did this get-together take place?"

"Nice little house on Key Largo. Got a big-screen TV, pool table, hot tub—all the necessities of life. No reason to go anyplace else, you know?"

"So you weren't anywhere near the Breakwash residence in the last eight hours?"

"I told you, man—I don't even know where that is."

"Right. Of course. And you've never met Randilyn Breakwash, either."

"Name doesn't ring a bell."

Horatio studied him for a moment. He got to his feet and walked around the table to where Bolivar sat. Bolivar watched him approach, flicking his eyes to the side but refusing to turn his head. Horatio leaned in close, inches away from his ear.

"Listen to me, Fredo. There's a woman in the hospital right now, with injuries that are going to scar her for life. She's lost her husband and any sense of safety she might have had. *She's not going to lose anything else.*"

Fredo stared straight ahead. "You sure about that, Lieutenant?"

"Yes, Fredo. I'm sure. Because I'm going to find the human garbage that did that to her, and I'm going to put them someplace where they can't ever hurt her again. That's a promise."

Now Fredo turned his head, met Horatio's eyes. "Me, I don't believe in promises," he said softly. "They break too easy."

"That depends," said Horatio, "on who makes them."

Calleigh ran into Wolfe in the elevator. "Oh, hey, Ryan. How's your case going?"

Wolfe shook his head. "Don't ask. We made an arrest on piracy charges, but there's a hole in the evidence the size of a fish. An extremely big fish."

"You mean that huge thing in Alexx's autopsy room? Did you misplace it or something?"

The elevator doors opened on the foyer and they both got out, continuing their conversation as they walked down the hall. "No, it's still there. That's the problem—we don't know *why* it's there. A guy with ties to the Russian mob went to a great deal of time and trouble to obtain this thing, which appears to have virtually no value except as an entry in the Guinness Book of World Records. That, and accidently poisoning supermarket executives." He told her about Stanley Wolchkowski.

Calleigh smiled. "So what's next? Are you going to grill your prime suspect—maybe with a little tartar sauce on the side?"

Wolfe smiled back. "That's good. Mind if I pass it along?"

"It's all yours."

"How about you? I hear the balloon case turned ugly."

Calleigh's smile faded. "Yeah. Randilyn Breakwash is in the hospital with burns over thirty percent of her body. I just got back from processing the scene."

"Find anything?"

"Too early to tell. Have to see what AFIS and CODIS tell me—but I did find one interesting thing in Breakwash's lab."

"What's that?"

"Nothing blown up," said Calleigh. They reached the Trace lab and she waved good-bye as she went in. Wolfe grinned and kept going.

Calleigh fumed the chainsaw for fingerprints, lifted some epithelials from the ropes used to bind Randilyn, ran the blood from the hallway. She examined every set of prints she'd lifted, checked them against Fredo Bolivar's. If he'd been in the house, he had to have left *something* behind; she'd even taken off the pipe traps in the bathroom, kitchen, and lab, in the hopes they might contain something useful.

The results were frustrating. None of the prints matched Bolivar. The epithelials belonged to one donor, the woman they'd been used to tie up. The blood was canine.

There was one thing she hadn't taken a close look at yet, and there was a good reason for that. She'd found a clear glass specimen flask with a murky fluid inside and a biohazard decal, labeled *Pfiest. Pisc.* She was studying it when Horatio walked in.

"Any luck?" he asked.

"Not so far. If Fredo Bolivar was in that house, he was careful."

"According to Randilyn Breakwash, her attacker wore a surgical mask, a painter's suit and possibly some kind of protection on his feet. The physical description she gave is a rough match to Bolivar, but hardly conclusive."

"What else did she say?"

Horatio put his hands on his hips. "Well, we're on the right track with the McCulver theory. Randilyn confirmed that her husband was looking for the treasure, supposedly the cargo of a downed plane.

Her attacker thought Tim had found it and had passed that information along to his wife."

"Information she didn't have."

"Correct. If she had, she would have talked and saved herself a lot of suffering . . . but she couldn't give him what she didn't possess."

Calleigh frowned. "So either Timothy Breakwash didn't find the plane, or he found it and kept it a secret from Randilyn."

"It looks that way. I just finished talking to Fredo Bolivar."

"And?"

"He has an alibi, but not the kind I put any faith in. Friends claim he spent the night with them, in a private home."

"How cozy. I'm guessing those friends have some experience in providing this kind of alibi."

"That's not a guess, it's a fact . . . is this the so-called 'cell from hell'?" Horatio indicated the flask.

"I think so. Found it in Breakwash's lab—he must have kept some samples around, even though he didn't have the equipment to test them. What was even more interesting, though, was what I found in the sink." She told him about the emptied containers and the bucket of hydrogen peroxide. "I tested samples from the trap. The rotten-fish odor told me they were probably volatile amines, and I was right. One of the chemicals was aniline."

"Used in making dye, correct?"

"Among other things. But mixing it with a

strong oxidizer like hydrogen peroxide could likely lead to an explosion or fire—and apparently, that's something our intruder knew."

"So he's educated, maybe has a scientific background. At the very least, he knows enough to not mix certain classes of chemicals . . ."

"What are you thinking, H?"

"I'm thinking," said Horatio, "that considering the amount of stress she was under and the fact that she only saw his eyes, Randilyn Breakwash could have mistaken Asian features for Hispanic."

"Mister Kwok," said Horatio. "Please, have a seat."

Lee Kwok sat down across from Horatio. He glanced around the interview room. "Anything I can do to help?"

"Let's start with where you were last night, between the hours of ten P.M. and eight A.M."

"I was working late at the lab."

"Pulling an all-nighter? I thought only undergrads did that sort of thing."

"I had a grant proposal to finish. Deadline was this morning."

"I understand. Was there anybody with you?"

"No."

"Night watchman, maybe a janitor? Anyone that could vouch for your presence?"

"It was just me. But I guess the security cameras would have me on them when I arrived and left—I ducked out for a bite to eat around three."

Horatio nodded. "We'll check that. Mister Kwok—did you know Timothy Breakwash's wife?"

"Randilyn? Sure, I met her a few times. Tim had me over for dinner once, took me up in the balloon another time. We didn't hang out on a regular basis, but I guess I saw him more often once I was running those samples for him. I think he felt like he owed me."

"Is that what you think, Mister Kwok? That he owed you?"

"For doing a little side work on the university's dime? No. I was happy to do it."

"Really? Even though it could cost you your job? From what I understand, research positions aren't that easy to come by. And academia is a close-knit world; get fired from one institution and all the others hear about it. That could seriously upset the career track of an ambitious man."

Kwok shook his head and leaned forward, his face intent. "Look, what is this all about? I don't understand why the Miami police are so concerned about me doing a little off-the-books research for a friend. You're acting like I'm some kind of bioterrorist."

"That's because somebody was terrorized, Mister Kwok. Randilyn Breakwash was assaulted in her own home, and the person who did it was after some very specific information. Information he was willing to use torture to get."

Kwok's eyes widened. "Torture? Is she—is she all right?"

"Traumatized but still breathing. Her attacker didn't get what he came for, but not for lack of trying . . . tell me, Mister Kwok, did Tim ever talk to you about someone named Rodriguo?"

"No, I don't think so—is that who's responsible? What did they want?"

Horatio studied the man carefully before answering. Lee Kwok appeared genuinely shocked, but that could be an act. "What they were after, Mister Kwok, was the location of a downed plane filled with extremely valuable artifacts. Timothy Breakwash was also looking for this plane . . . and someone, at least, believes he found it."

"A plane?" Kwok frowned while he processed this. "So this—this doesn't have anything to do with his research."

"What it has to do with, Mister Kwok, is who else knew what Timothy had found. The person that attacked Mrs. Breakwash also ransacked her home, including her husband's lab. The intruder even emptied containers of volatile chemicals into a sink, in case something had been hidden inside them . . . but he knew enough about chemistry to not mix incompatible compounds with one another."

"Oh, hey, hang on. If you think I had anything to do with this, you're wrong. Tim told me about a few of his moneymaking ideas, but he never mentioned anything about searching for a plane. Besides, like I said, I was in the lab all night—just check the security cameras."

Horatio met the man's eyes. "We'll do that, Mister Kwok. We'll do that . . ."

Calleigh caught Horatio just as he was walking out the front door of the lab building. "Bad news, H," said Calleigh. "I just looked over the security footage from the university. Lee Kwok was telling the truth—he was there all night, except for about an hour between three and four. No way he could have been the one that attacked Randilyn Breakwash."

Horatio nodded. "Cut him loose. I've been doing a little checking on some of our other suspects, looking for a possible background in chemistry. Sylvester Perrone has an MBA, but nothing science-related. One of our other players, though, took three years of chemistry before dropping out."

"Who?"

"Our old friend, Fredo Bolivar."

"So you think it was him, after all?"

"I do. Right now, our best chance is to break his alibi—and that means breaking one of his friends."

"That's where you're heading right now?"

"I am. Care to accompany me?"

"You hum the tune," said Calleigh, "and I'll play along."

11

NATALIA PARKED the Hummer and she and Tripp got out. Tripp stopped on the sidewalk, hands on his hips, and looked up. "On a Roll Bowl," he said. "Twenty-four-hour bowling. Nice sign."

Natalia had to admit it was. Miami was home to a lot of neon and a lot of Art Deco—but even so, On a Roll Bowl's storefront was impressive. Electric-blue neon wings radiated from the backs of chrome angels, one on either side of the door, their wingtips touching in the center. The sign above them spelled out the name of the place in bright red, race-track logo letters, while a yellow bowling ball spitting lighting blazed from one end of the sign to the other, over and over.

"Looks like the entrance to Heaven for people who rent their shoes," said Tripp.

"I don't think the words *Heaven* and *rented shoes* belong in the same sentence."

She pulled open the large wooden door and stepped inside. The interior was a little more run-down than the exterior; while the bowling alley had clearly once been an impressive establishment, its glory had faded. The walls, painted a rich purple, were cracked and peeling; only three-quarters of the chromed light sconces on the walls were working; and the thick pile carpet underfoot was badly worn and scarred by decades of dropped cigarettes and spilled drinks. Like most bowling alleys, it was simply a very large, single room, with a diner-style counter that ran along one back wall. Twenty-five lanes filled most of the space, stretching from one wall to another, although only five of them were being used at the moment. A country station played over the PA system, the signal just weak enough to add a layer of static to the steel guitar. The singer seemed to be saying something about buying her Lexus in Texas, though that didn't make a lot of sense to Natalia.

"Hey," said Tripp. "Check this out." He jerked his thumb at a poster on the wall.

The poster advertised a bowling tournament, hosted by On a Roll Bowl, with a two-million-dollar first prize. "Pretty high stakes," said Natalia. "You think it might have something to do with the case?"

"Could be. Especially if what Davey's files said about this guy are true."

Natalia approached the woman behind the

counter, who was listlessly spraying disinfectant into a pair of shoes. "Excuse me. I'm looking for the owner—is he around?"

The woman, a bleached blonde in her sixties with a tired, pinched face, said, "Gord? Yeah, he's over on lane twelve. The big guy with the gray hair."

"Thank you."

Lane twelve was in use, but it didn't look as if they were keeping score; the area above the lane where the scorecard was usually projected was blank. A tall, rangy man with sideburns and a trucker's hat was poised to bowl, the ball held in front of him and his eyes fixed on the pins. He launched the ball as Natalia and Tripp walked up, his delivery careful and much slower than Natalia expected. The ball—an iridescent gold in color, not black—almost seemed to creep toward its targets. When it finally reached them, though, its accuracy made up for its velocity; every pin fell down.

"Good roll, Leroy," said the man sitting in the booth behind the lane. He had a shock of curly gray hair, and a wide, smiling face.

"Mister Dettweiler?" said Natalia.

The man turned to her and said, "I surely am. What can I do for you?" He had a low, deep voice that seemed to merge naturally with the basso thrum of ten-pin balls rolling across polished wood.

"I'm Natalia Boa Vista with the Miami-Dade crime lab, and this is Detective Frank Tripp. We'd like to talk to you about Hiram Davey."

If the fact they were police officers bothered Dettweiler, it didn't show on his face. He levered himself out of the booth, revealing a prodigious gut on a heavy, short frame. His smile got even wider, and he stuck out his hand to Natalia. "Call me Gord, everybody does. I'd be happy to help in any way I could. Leroy, take a break."

Leroy nodded and slipped off to the counter without saying a word. Dettweiler shook Natalia's hand, and then insisted on shaking hands with Tripp, too.

"Now, what's this about Hiram Davey?"

"Excuse me, Natalia," Tripp said abruptly. "I haven't eaten all day, and I would just about kill for a chili dog. You mind if I grab a quick bite while you two talk?"

"Uh—not at all. Go ahead."

Frank nodded. "Thanks." He turned and walked back toward the counter.

"So, Gord. I understand you knew Mister Davey."

"Well, I wouldn't say I really knew him. He dropped by to bowl a few now and then. I recognized him from his column, said hello. Even bought a round of beers for him and his friends."

"I see. So there were no hard feelings between you two?"

Gord shook his head. "Oh, no, no. Very sad, him passing. City'll be a little darker without him."

"Yes, it will. Tell me, Gord, did Davey ever mention anything to you about a book he was writing?"

Dettweiler's forehead corrugated in thought. "No . . . no, I don't believe he did. Not that I can recall, anyway."

"Okay. Just one more question, all right?"

"Shoot."

"Does everyone fall for your folksy act, or do some people tell you just how full of crap you are?"

The smile on his face never wavered. "Well, I suppose some people don't cotton to me right off—"

"No? How about Francisco Girelli? They 'cotton' to you when your hair is dyed black and you're wearing an Italian suit instead of a snap-button cowboy shirt?"

The smile stayed in place, but he stopped talking.

"Or how about Olaf Kirkenstein? Little blonder, bushy mustache, real hearty type. Said he was a real estate developer to an investment group in Oklahoma and disappeared with a bunch of their money. You did time for that one, Gord."

"All right, all right. No need to raise your voice. True, I've made mistakes in my past, but that's all behind me. I run an honest business here, have for years. You wouldn't hold a few youthful indiscretions against me, would you?"

Natalia wasn't smiling. "Stop trying to con me, Gord. You knew Hiram Davey a lot better than what you've admitted to, and you knew all about the book."

Dettweiler sighed, a man with the undeserved

weight of the world on his shoulders. "I suppose I did. I didn't want to say anything, because I knew how it would look."

"How's that, Gord?"

"Like I hadn't changed. See, I'm something of a talker, and Hi was a real good listener. Plus, I admit I was a little starstruck—I was a big fan of his. So when we started swapping tales after a few beers— and Hi knew how to spin a yarn—I guess I tried to impress him. Told him a few stories from my bad old days, some of the scams I used to pull. He asked me if he could use them in his book, and I said no; I told him they were strictly off the record."

"I see. Were you aware that he was planning on using them anyway?"

Dettweiler frowned. "I very much doubt that. I talked to a lawyer, and he said any unauthorized use of my name in a work of fiction was grounds for a lawsuit. Hi may have liked my stories—hell, I think he was even a little jealous—but he wasn't stupid."

"No, he wasn't. He was a journalist, and he knew the rules." Natalia reached into her bag and pulled out a sheet of paper. She handed it to Dettweiler. "He also knew how to do research. He had a copy of your arrest record and corroborating details from several of your victims. You can't sue someone for telling the truth, Gord—even if it makes you look like a scumbag."

Dettweiler glanced at the piece of paper, then

handed it back. "Is that so? Well, my lawyer was of a different opinion. According to him, even the hint of a lawsuit is enough to scare off a publisher. He seemed to feel he could make Davey see reason."

"Uh-huh. And if Davey insisted on being unreasonable? What were you going to do then?"

"Let the court decide, of course."

"Mister Dettweiler, where were you the morning Hiram Davey was killed?"

"Out doing a little bass fishing. Nice and quiet early in the morning."

"You have a way of proving that?"

Dettweiler chuckled. "Well, I've got a couple of big-mouth bass in my freezer, but despite their name they don't talk much. Leroy was with me, though."

"I'll get him to confirm that."

"You go right ahead. This whole thing is all moot now, anyway; Davey's dead, and I don't think he ever got around to finishing that book."

"Now, how would you know that, Gord?"

He smiled at her, just a good old boy shootin' the breeze. "Oh, Hi told me he wasn't that fast a writer. Last time we spoke was a few weeks ago, and he'd barely got the thing off the ground. Unless he was hit by one heckuva burst of inspiration, I doubt there's much more to his novel than a few notes and an outline."

Natalia nodded. "If I were you, Gord," she said, "I wouldn't worry about Hiram Davey's abilities. I'd worry about *mine*."

*   *   *

"So," Natalia asked Tripp once they were back in the Hummer, "what's up with the sudden urge for a chili dog?"

"Sometimes you have a better shot at a wingman," said Tripp. "Guy like Dettweiler always surrounds himself with people he can easily manipulate—reinforces the idea that he's smarter than everyone else. Seen it a hundred times. Building a fence around you made of idiots might be all right if you need cannon fodder, but it's not a great way to protect your secrets."

"So—a chain-link fence? With Leroy being the weak link?"

"Exactly. He looked to me like the kind of guy you could sit next to and have a conversation with—second banana to second banana, you know?"

Natalia pretended to be shocked. "Why, Frank—is that how I treat you? Like a—a piece of *fruit*?"

"'Course not. But Leroy doesn't know that, and playing the 'I have a bitch for a boss' card usually works with jokers like him. Just two guys commiserating in the trenches, you know?"

"Right. How'd it work?"

"So-so. He's not the sharpest tool in the shed, but he's not much of a talker, either. I got him going about bowling, though, and managed to move the conversation toward the tournament."

"What's the story with that?"

Tripp shifted in his seat. "All Dettweiler's idea. He's got a few local merchants to put up part of the prize money, figures on using participation fees from competitors for the rest."

"Really? That seems like a lot of money to raise."

"Lot of money to lose, too. Davey telling the world the tournament's being run by a professional con man might have killed the whole deal."

"Except he got killed first—and two million dollars is definitely motivation."

Tripp nodded. "What did you get from Dettweiler?"

"A lot of down-home-flavored manure, mostly." She filled him in. "And you heard what Leroy said when I asked him about the fishing trip."

"Yeah. Backed up everything his buddy told you. Thought it sounded a little too rehearsed, myself."

"So did I. But you know what?"

"What?"

Natalia smiled, holding the steering wheel in one hand, staring straight ahead. "I may not be much with a rod and reel myself, but I'm pretty good with a net."

Wolfe met Delko at the entrance to the MDPD impound yard, both of them dressed in blue coveralls and carrying aluminum equipment cases.

"You ready to do this?" asked Delko.

"Aye-aye," said Wolfe.

They walked in. Their objective wasn't hard to

find; it sat in the middle of the yard, taking up thirty parking spots. The *Svetlana 2*, resting now on a drydock trailer.

"I'll take inside, you take outside," said Delko. "False bulkheads, hidden compartments, anything at all."

"Whatever happened to X marks the spot?"

"At least you can stop worrying the boat is going to sink."

"No. Now all I have to worry about is heat-stroke."

They'd already searched the ship once, but this time they concentrated more on the structure of the craft itself. Wolfe used a smaller version of the ground-penetrating radar used to locate buried bodies to scan the hull; Delko did the same for the bulkheads, floors, and ceilings inside. If there were any hidden cavities or compartments, they'd find them.

They found nothing.

They sat outside on the GPR cases, using the bulk of an impounded camper for shade. Delko took a long slug of water from a plastic bottle. "Man, it's hot in there," he said. "A boat turns into a big heat sink when it's not in the water."

Wolfe wiped the sweat off his forehead with the sleeve of his coverall. "It's no picnic out here, either. Working on black asphalt is like standing in a frying pan."

Delko put a hand to his head and winced.

"Hey, you okay?" asked Wolfe. Ever since Delko had gotten shot, Wolfe had been hyperaware of his colleague's health; he tried not to let it show, but he worried about Eric. Delko had been the one who'd raced Wolfe to the hospital when he'd taken a four-inch spike from a nailgun in the eye, and Wolfe had never forgotten it.

"Fine. Just a little dehydrated." Delko gulped down the rest of the bottle of water. Wolfe uncapped his own bottle and joined him.

"So," Wolfe said. "Whatever happened between you and that dancer? Haven't seen her around in a while."

"Marie? We're not together anymore. Being taken hostage shook her up bad—she never really got over it."

"That's too bad. She seemed nice."

"She was." Delko shook his head slowly, his eyes fixed on some point in the distance. "Being with a cop, it's not easy. You go to sleep every night thinking about getting that knock on the door, opening it up to find an officer on your doorstep with that look on his or her face."

"I know. I dated a girl once, she used to get nightmares just like that. She'd hear a doorbell, open it to find a beat cop in dress uniform—formal blues, white gloves."

Delko nodded. "The outfit they wear to funerals."

"Yeah. Except this cop, he doesn't have a face at

all—just a skull. That's when she'd wake up." Wolfe paused. "We didn't go out that long."

"Well, once she got to know you, that was inevitable." Delko grinned.

"Yeah, yeah. So says the guy who spends half his life underwater. I think I've figured out why you're so obsessed with that sunfish—it's because you have a *crush* on it."

"Well, it is female. But from the condition of her ovary, she's already met the sunfish of her dreams."

"That's a shame," said Wolfe, getting to his feet. "But you know what they say: plenty of other fish in the sea . . ."

"Okay," sighed Delko. "I admit it."

"What, that you're in love with a fish?"

"No, smart-ass. I admit I can't locate whatever Dragoslav had aboard the ship—but only because it's not there anymore. I went over the entire interior, and I couldn't locate those white buckets the sushi chef mentioned. Dragoslav or one of the crew must have thrown them overboard when the shooting started."

"Then there's only one way left to find out what was on board."

Delko nodded. "Ask someone who knows."

"Ms. Faustino," said Delko. "Thank you for agreeing to talk with me."

Valerie Faustino fixed him with a cold look that spoke volumes about her opinion on the meeting.

Her lawyer sat beside her, a bullish young man named Bronz with close-cropped black hair.

"Let's just get this over with," said Faustino. "I have to get back to New York. I have a business to run."

"Of course," said Delko. "Business is exactly what I'd like to discuss. Specifically, the business you had with Jovan Dragoslav."

Bronz spoke first. "Ms. Faustino has no professional relationship with Mister Dragoslav."

"Then why was she on his yacht?"

"It was for purely recreational purposes. Mister Dragoslav and Ms. Faustino were introduced by mutual friends who thought they would get along. Mister Dragoslav invited Ms. Faustino to enjoy his hospitality aboard his boat, and she accepted."

"Sure. Tell me, who were these mutual friends of theirs?"

"I don't see how that's relevant."

"Would these mutual friends be members of the Luccini family?"

"Ms. Faustino has no intention of incriminating herself—"

Faustino held up a hand. "Paul, please. It's no crime to admit you know someone. Yes, we were introduced by Giovanni Luccini—he's an old friend. So what?"

"So we know that was more than a pleasure cruise, Ms. Faustino. It was a business meeting. And it took place where it did so that all parties concerned could take a good look at the merchandise."

"Really," said Faustino, her face impassive. "And what merchandise would that be?"

"I don't think you understand how much trouble this could make for you," said Delko. "Hiding it in the fish was clever, but that doesn't mean it didn't leave behind traces of its presence. You can forget about whether we found your shipment; what we're deciding now is who to charge. Stanley Wolchkowski is dead, which leaves Dragoslav or you. Guess who my partner is talking to right now?"

Faustino's eyes narrowed. "Oh, please. You think either Jovan or myself are amateurs? You think you can pull this play-one-against-the-other crap and see which one of us folds like a teenager caught shoplifting? Tell you what, Mister CSI; I'll show you mine if you show me yours."

"Meaning?"

"Meaning you tell me exactly what you found on that boat, and I'll tell you who it belongs to. How about that?"

Delko glared at her. She'd called his bluff, but he still had one more card to play. "What we found, Ms. Faustino, was one of the men who robbed you—and the boat they used. You think a Miami gangster wannabe who's stupid enough to take on the Russian mob *and* the Luccini family will be as tough to crack as you? The rest of his crew is dead and he's looking at homicide and piracy charges—he doesn't have a lot of bridges left to burn. So far he hasn't said much, but that's more out of stubbornness than smarts. Believe me, sooner or later he's going to realize where his best interests lie—and that means that the next conversation you and I have? You're going to be wearing handcuffs."

Bronz held up a hand. "Okay, we're done. Ms. Faustino is not going to sit here and listen to these groundless accusations—"

His client interrupted him. "No, Paul, hang on. I've got something I want to say."

Bronz frowned. "I don't think that's a good idea."

"You think what I pay you to think. Right now, I'm paying you to shut up."

Faustino crossed her arms. "Okay, Detective or Doctor or whatever the hell your title is, you want some information? I'll give you something just to get you off my back. You obviously think this is all about drugs, and you're hoping you can scare me with a trafficking rap. But you're barking up the wrong tree, which is why I'm annoyed instead of scared. I *know* you didn't find any drugs or any traces of drugs, because there *were* no drugs. You want to rattle Dragoslav's cage, go ahead—but you're not going to make him any more nervous than you are me. *Capiche?*"

She got to her feet. "Okay, Paul, let's go. *Now* we're done."

After she left, Delko sat and thought about what Faustino had said, trying to decide exactly what it meant. *No drugs. Either she's lying to try to throw me off the scent, or telling the truth because she thinks I have no chance of finding what was actually being smuggled. Which is it?*

Faustino seemed pretty sure of herself. It was more likely she'd deny any involvement at all than tell him the shipment wasn't drugs—which she'd managed to do without actually admitting there *was* a shipment. He thought she was telling the truth.

So, then what had been transferred from the moon-fish's guts to the buckets? Something liquid, or maybe stored in liquid? Something worth, in Jorge's words, "at least a million dollars." *But what?*

"Pearls," said Calleigh.

"Excuse me?" asked Wolfe.

Calleigh looked up from the eyepiece of the comparison microscope. "Oh, I'm sorry—didn't hear you come in. Sometimes I talk to myself when no one else is around. Anyway, that's what I'm looking at."

Wolfe walked over. "You mind?"

"Not at all."

Wolfe peered into the eyepiece. "So what exactly is this?"

"It's from Timothy Breakwash's lab. It was already mounted on a slide, but not labeled. Know what it is?"

"Structure's crystalline. . . . calcium carbonate?" He looked up for confirmation.

Calleigh favored him with a smile. "Close. It's called aragonite—found in caves sometimes, but more often inside the shells of bivalves. It's a polymorph of calcium carbonate, more commonly known as mother-of-pearl."

"He was a biologist, right? Maybe this was part of his research."

"Maybe. But H thinks Breakwash knew about a stash of lost art—and some of that art was in the form of pearls."

"Don't think I've ever heard pearls referred to as art before."

Calleigh frowned in mock disapproval. "That's because you've never worn a necklace worth more than your house. When a single pearl can list "part of the crown jewels" more than once on their resume, it's definitely closer to art than decoration. Pearls have even done duty as a cocktail."

"I don't follow."

"There's an apocryphal story about Cleopatra betting Marc Antony she could provide a more expensive banquet than he could. When it came time to eat, she had a single glass of sour wine placed in front of her, then took off one of her earrings—pearl, of course—crushed it, and dumped it in the wine. She drank hers and offered the other earring to her guest."

Wolfe grinned. "Sour wine equals vinegar—

around six percent acetic acid. Strong enough to dissolve calcium carbonate. Cleopatra knew her chemistry."

"She won the bet, too."

"You think this sample is proof Breakwash found what he was looking for?"

"I don't know. It's definitely mother-of-pearl, but its provenance is a mystery."

Wolfe shook his head. "At least you know what you're looking for. According to Delko, about the only thing we know is what we're *not* looking for—drugs. And even that's not confirmed."

"Still no luck, huh? You talk to the owner of the yacht, yet?"

"Yeah, he's in interview room two. Just letting him cool his heels for a while."

"Think you can get anything from him?"

Wolfe sighed. "The guy's Red Mafiya, so he's not going to be easy to crack. All we have for ammunition is a big, dead fish—which is just what this case is starting to remind me of."

12

Jovan Dragoslav looked as relaxed and at ease in the interview room as someone lounging at poolside. He wore a simple blue polo shirt and jeans, with white deck shoes. He had even told his lawyer to go home, a sign Wolfe didn't like at all.

Wolfe sat down across from him without saying a word. Instead, he flipped open a file folder and studied what was inside.

Dragoslav said nothing, either. Wolfe finished reading the first page, flipped to another.

A few minutes passed.

"You know," Dragoslav finally said in an amused tone, "if you think you can outwait a Russian, you are bound to be disappointed."

I think that's what I just did, though. Wolfe looked up from his reading. "But you're not Russian, Jovan. You're Serbian. You just like *playing* with the big boys."

"I suppose that is my file?"

"It's *our* file, Jovan—you're just the subject."

"Interesting reading?"

"Disappointing, actually." Wolfe closed the folder and tossed it down on the table in front of him. "See, I've been laboring under a misconception, Jovan. I thought you were a player. Big yacht, lots of security, meeting with a member of the Luccini family? I was sure you were up to something big. So were the crew that hit you. But you fooled us all, didn't you?"

Jovan's easy smile stayed in place, but he raised his eyebrows in a question.

Wolfe nodded. "None of it holds up once you take a close look. And that's what I do, Jovan—I look at things very, very closely. And the closer I looked at you, the more I realized what it was I was looking at."

Wolfe spread his hands. "Nothing."

"Pardon me?"

"It's all there in your record. Petty thefts. Dealing in stolen merchandise. A little penny-ante loan-sharking with cheap, dumb muscle backing you up. You're not a player, Jovan; you're a wannabe." Wolfe put as much amused contempt into his voice as he could. "That yacht isn't yours—it's leased. The so-called member of the Luccini family is a grandmother who inherited her son's trucking business."

Wolfe crossed his arms and leaned forward. "You know, we searched that boat from top to bottom.

Even X-rayed the superstructure. We were sure you were smuggling in something illegal and expensive—probably narcotics, but we wouldn't have been surprised to find guns, gemstones, even counterfeit money. But—of course—we found exactly what I just told you: nothing."

"So you admit that—"

Wolfe talked right over him. "None of those things are in your league, are they? You're more a bootleg–blue jeans kind of guy, right? Made a little cash in the black market back home, thought you could move up in the world? But this isn't the old country, Jovan. This is America. You can only play at being a gangster so long before you get in over your head—and that's just what happened."

"You Americans," Jovan said. He was still smiling, but there was an edge in his voice. "So arrogant, so self-righteous. You think you rule the world, and we should all be grateful. You think Miami is a dangerous city? You wouldn't last a week in Sarajevo."

Wolfe smiled back. He hated playing the Ugly American, but his only hope was to get Dragoslav angry enough to say something revealing. He knew it was a long shot, but Dragoslav was plainly feeling cocky; attacking his ego now might get an unguarded response. "Yeah, right. What did you do there, peddle illegal DVDs of *Desperate Housewives*?"

Dragoslav's smile had faded. "I did what I had to in order to survive. As I do here."

"Sure. You're all talk, Jovan. Am I supposed to be impressed by the fact that you had Stanley Wolchkowski on your rented boat? A guy who buys and sells produce for a living? Hey, that must be it—you were bringing in a big load of illicit lettuce, right?"

Jovan's smile returned. "Yes, that's it. You are so clever, Mister Wolfe. You have cracked this case wide open. Please, handcuff me and take me to prison."

The anger had mutated into mockery. For just a moment, Wolfe had been sure Dragoslav was going to let something slip . . . but the moment had passed, and the man's self-assured façade was firmly back in place.

Dragoslav nodded. "I understand why you are treating me this way. You are frustrated. You seek to blame your failings on someone else. Perhaps I should simply accept your jealousy and accusations as a sad but inevitable consequence of my own success—but I feel you need a lesson in courtesy more than my pity."

"Really."

"Really. The reason your search was fruitless has nothing to do with me. It is the fault of your own stupidity, your own preconceptions, your own prejudices. You say your business is to examine things closely, but to me you are a blind fool."

Dragoslav got to his feet. "I have nothing further to say. Since you obviously have nothing to charge me with, I will be leaving. I sincerely hope I do not suffer your company again, Mister Wolfe. If I do, it will be in a courtroom, and you will be the one facing charges—for harassment, for false arrest, for anything else my lawyer can find."

"Looking forward to it," said Wolfe.

If Fredo Bolivar is lying, Horatio thought, *he has at least three friends willing to lie along with him*. It reminded him of an old saying: lie down with dogs, get up with fleas. But Horatio intended to deliver a lot more discomfort than a little itching.

The three were Kevin Laza, Domingo Rivas, and Michael Gomez. Horatio had all of them waiting in interview rooms, but he wasn't ready to talk to them yet. He was in his office, studying their files.

There was an art to breaking an alibi based on a lying witness. Fortunately, Bolivar had already made his first mistake; the best alibi was the simplest, and the fact that Fredo thought three eyewitnesses were better than one was a serious error on his part. An alibi was like a diamond; if it was real, it provided a hard, impenetrable surface that reflected truth like a gem refracted light. If it was fake it could be shattered, either by pressure or one well-placed blow. Success depended on knowing exactly where to apply that pressure, exactly how and where to strike.

Fredo Bolivar had provided Horatio with three possible targets. He considered each carefully, looking for a flaw to exploit, an angle to attack.

Kevin Laza. Youngest of the three. Arrested for assault, drunk and disorderly, possession of a controlled substance. A hothead, prone to acting without thinking. Probably has less status than the others, may be trying to prove himself to them. He looked at the mug shot, studied the heavy jaw of the boy, the sullenness in his eyes. Laza radiated resentment, a barely concealed rage at the unfairness of the world and what it had done to him. Black stubble bristled on his skull, and a pink scar ran from his forehead into the hairline.

Domingo Rivas. Arrested for illegal possession of a firearm, multiple counts of assault, possession of a controlled substance for the purpose of trafficking. Older than Laza by a decade. Obviously more experienced. Drug dealer, carries a gun, not afraid to use it. Knows the system, won't be easy to intimidate. The photo showed a heavyset man in his late twenties, with a shaved head and tattoos on his neck. His lips were thick, his eyes almost sleepy. Horatio wasn't fooled.

The last one was Michael Gomez. *Arrested only once, for possession of a controlled substance. Younger than Domingo, about the same age as Bolivar himself.* Gomez was skinny, with a sallow, bony face and longer hair, worn slicked back and close to his skull. There was something in his eyes, too, something none of the others had, and Horatio smiled when he recognized it.

Fear.

*   *   *

"Hello, Domingo," Horatio said.

The man sitting opposite him shifted his bulk in his chair, leaning back and sticking his legs out. "Hey," Rivas said.

"I'd just like to go over a few points of your statement, if that's all right."

"Sure. Whatever."

Horatio smiled at him. It was a soft smile, a gentle smile, the kind of smile a pastor would bestow on a member of his congregation. "I understand you spent the evening in question in the company of your friends?"

"That's right. All night."

"Uh-huh. And what did you do to pass the time?"

"Not much. Y'know, drank a little gin and juice, listened t'some music, watched some DVDs. Shot some pool."

"You do anything else? Take a dip in the hot tub, maybe?"

"Yeah. So?"

"Just trying to get things straight, Domingo. What did you watch on DVD?"

"I don' remember."

"Really? Well, lucky for you I have a list of all the DVDs in your house right here. Nice of you to have them all labeled and in plain view like that." Horatio pushed a sheet of paper across the table. "Take a look. It was less than twenty-four hours ago—it would certainly look odd if you couldn't remember something that easy."

Domingo picked up the list, read it carefully. "Know what?" he said when he was finished. "I know why I'm havin' such a hard time rememberin'. See, I had a little too much t'drink. Think I passed out right aroun' when the other guys started talkin' bout watchin' somethin'."

"Was the movie over by the time you woke up?"

"Musta been."

"So there was a period of at least an hour and a half when you couldn't account for your friends' whereabouts."

"What? No. No, they was there the whole time."

"Really? How would you know?"

"I didn't sleep that long. Maybe twenty minutes. I remember looking at my watch."

"At what time?"

"Two A.M."

"Sure. So the movie was still playing?"

"No. I mean, yeah, I guess it was, but it was on in the background. I didn't pay no attention to it—that's why I can't remember."

"Right. How many games of pool did you play?"

"I don't know—three or four. Maybe five."

"Did you win any of them?"

"What?"

Horatio leaned forward, his smile still gentle. "Did you *win* any of them, Domingo? If you were sober enough to play, you must have been sober enough to remember something like that, right?"

"Yeah, of course. No, I didn't win any of 'em."

"Not your night, I guess. Who else played?"

"Everyone. We all did."

"So everyone else beat you at least once."

"I guess so."

Horatio nodded. "Did everyone go in the hot tub?"

"Yeah."

"How long were you in there?"

"I don't know."

"An hour? Two hours?"

Domingo shrugged. "I don't remember."

"Okay, Domingo. Thank you for cooperating—you've been very helpful."

"That's it? I can go?"

Horatio stood up, and his smile got a little brighter. "Not just yet."

He'd been careful with Domingo, but he approached Kevin Laza with even more caution. The boy was only nineteen, and had the odd combination of cockiness and suspicion that life on the street often produced. Horatio treated him as gently as he would a ticking bomb, probing for answers without setting him off. An emotional explosion would produce nothing but a retreat into sullen silence; he knew he'd get better results by playing on the boy's insecurities, making him prove his worth to his friends. He talked to Laza for over an hour, and when he was done he was finally ready to tackle Michael Gomez.

*   *   *

Gomez had been waiting longer than any of the others. When Horatio finally walked in the door, Gomez looked more grateful than irritated. "Hey, about time," said Gomez. He was dressed a little better than the others, wearing a designer basketball shirt with gold chains dangling over the oversize number on the front. "Can we make this fast? I got places to be."

"No, you don't," said Horatio. His voice was neutral, his expression the same. He didn't sit, but instead stood beside Gomez and looked down. Horatio opened the folder in his hand and took an eight-by-ten photo out. He held it in his hands, studying it, but didn't show it to Gomez.

"Do you know why you're here, Mister Gomez?"

"Yeah. You want me to confirm that Fredo was with me, Dom, and Kev all night—"

"No. That's incorrect." Horatio's voice got a little colder. "You're here because Fredo asked you to lie to me."

"No, man—"

"I don't like being lied to, Michael, but I'm used to it. It takes a certain kind of lie these days to get under my skin . . . but when one does, it makes me a little crazy. Do I seem a little crazy, Michael?" Horatio's voice was completely calm, but he stared into Gomez's eyes without blinking.

Gomez swallowed. "No."

"Good. I can't always tell . . . tell me about that night, Michael. What did you do?"

"We had a few drinks. We listened to some music, watched some movies. We played some pool."

"How many games?"

"I'm—not sure."

"Guess."

"A couple."

"Two?"

"Yeah."

"Who won?"

"Uh—I did."

"Are you sure about that?"

"What? Yeah, of course. Why wouldn't I be?"

"So you won both games. Domingo didn't win any?"

"Uh—maybe he did. Yeah, he won one and I won one."

"Okay. What movies did you watch?"

Gomez coughed into his fist. "I think . . . some war movie."

"Which one?"

"I don't remember."

"But you watched the whole thing."

"Yeah."

"Funny how you can watch a whole movie and not remember what it was. Your friend Kevin didn't have that problem—he remembered the movie in detail. He remembered all sorts of things, in fact. Tell me—how long has the hot tub been out of order?"

"How the hell would I know?" Gomez tried to make it sound confrontational, but it came out more like a plea. "It's not my damn hot tub."

"Did that make you angry? Were you planning on a nice soak in your friend Domingo's Jacuzzi?"

"Hey, I don't give a damn about the Jacuzzi. It was broken, so what. We played some music, watched some movies—"

"—shot some pool. I know." Horatio still held the photo in his hand, and now he studied it again as he spoke. "But here's the thing, Michael. Your story has more holes in it than a drug dealer after a drive-by. According to Domingo, he played four or five games of pool and never won a single one. According to Kevin, you watched a frat-boy comedy and a horror film. And both Domingo and Kevin enjoyed their dip in the hot tub. So you, my friend, are lying through your teeth."

Gomez looked rattled but stubborn. "So maybe I'm a little confused on the details, so what—"

"So what? Do you even know why Fredo asked you to lie?"

"I'm—I'm not lying."

"I'm sure he promised you money—probably a great deal of money—but that's not what I mean. I mean the reason he needed an alibi. The crime he was committing while you and your friends drank and played pool and pretended he was there."

"I don't—"

Horatio thrust the photo in Gomez's face. It was

a close-up of Randilyn Breakwash's upper chest and arms, the burns covering her skin like some hideous exotic disease. "This is what your friend Fredo was up to, Michael. He was torturing an innocent woman. Burning her with a red-hot soldering iron, over and over again. Did he tell you that?"

Gomez's face had paled, and he looked like he was about to throw up. "Get that away from me," he said weakly.

Horatio kept the picture right where it was. "Look at it, Michael. You helped make this happen. Aren't you proud of yourself? Doesn't this make you feel that you're just like your friends?"

"I'm not like that. I would never do that."

"But you are, Michael. In the eyes of the law, you're an accessory after the fact. You may as well have been in the same room, with her screams in your ears and the smell of burning skin in your nostrils. And if you feel sick now, how do you think a jury is going to feel when they see this picture? How do you think they're going to look at you when you're up in the witness box, trying to sell them this story while the prosecutor rips it apart?"

Horatio leaned in close. "They're going to look at you like you were a piece of garbage, Michael. And they'll be right."

Gomez sagged in his chair, and Horatio knew he'd won. Gomez's weak point was his own need for respect, the simple human desire to be seen as worthwhile. That couldn't stand in the face of the evidence Horatio had shown him; it couldn't stand in the face of how Gomez saw himself.

"All right," Gomez said quietly. "He wasn't there. It was just the three of us. I don't know where he went or what he did, okay? I didn't have anything to do with—with that picture."

Horatio straightened up, placed the photo back in the folder.

"I know, Michael," he said. "I know."

"Your alibi is gone, Fredo," said Horatio. "And soon, you will be, too . . ."

Fredo Bolivar stared back at him insolently. "How's that?"

"None of your friends can agree on the details of your night together."

Fredo stared out the honeycomb-gridded window of the interview room, seeming particularly interested in a bird on a tree branch outside. "Yeah? Shouldn't you be asking me those questions?"

"Maybe I should—but I think I already know what you're going to say."

"Oh, you're a mind reader, too?"

Horatio smiled. "You'd be amazed at what I can find out, Fredo. But I'll indulge you . . . tell me, what movies did you watch with your friends?"

"I don't remember."

"What were you drinking?"

"Whatever it was, I must have drank a lot of it— 'cause I don't remember that, either."

"Did you use the hot tub?"

"You know—I don't remember that, either."

Horatio nodded. "What a surprise. Quite the case of amnesia you have, Fredo. Similar to what happened to an officer I know. It's a terrible sensation, losing something so thoroughly you're not even aware of what it is you've lost. But I'm sure that won't be a problem for you."

Abruptly, Horatio was inches away from Bolivar's face. "You won't have that problem for a long, long time. You'll be locked up in a cage with nothing to do but think about all the things you've lost: your freedom, your dignity, your ability to choose where to go or what to do. No more women, no more wine, no more sunny beaches or all-night parties. All you're going to have is time, and it's going to steal even the memories of those things from you eventually. And this is what you'll be saying about all those good times, so long ago." Horatio took a slim piece of paper out of his pocket and tossed it onto the table, then turned around and left the room.

Bolivar stared at it for a moment, then picked it up and unfolded it. The piece of paper had one sentence written on it.

I DON'T REMEMBER.

"Oh, honey," said Alexx to Calleigh.

"I know, I know," said Calleigh. "I'm sorry I have to ask you to do this—but I need the bullet."

Both of them looked down sadly at the small, still body of the bulldog pup on the autopsy table. "First Delko and Wolfe bring me a two-ton fish," said Alexx. "Now you show up with a dead puppy. What's the matter, don't *people* die anymore?"

"That's a little harsh, don't you think?"

Alexx sighed. "I'm sorry. It's been a rough week, you know? All those victims from the yacht— young men full of bullet holes instead of dreams. Now this. What was her name?"

"Chiba. The man who killed her also tortured Randilyn Breakwash. Horatio broke his alibi, but we still don't have any evidence to actually charge him with the attack; I'm hoping the bullet might do that."

"If it's in there, I'll find it." Alexx picked up her scalpel.

The necropsy proceeded mostly in silence; Alexx didn't have to perform her usual thorough analysis of the victim. It didn't take long before Alexx pulled a misshapen piece of metal out of the body. "Entered through the skull, traveled the length of the body, and lodged in the base of the spine," said Alexx. "Poor thing. Didn't suffer, though—the shot would have killed her instantly."

"Alexx—what are those?" Calleigh pointed to some small, pink, misshapen lumps on the underside of the tongue. "They look almost like tumors."

"Yes, they do. That's odd—a dog this young shouldn't have anything like that growing in her.

Not unless she was raised in an extremely toxic environment."

"No," said Calleigh thoughtfully. "Actually, she was raised in a very controlled environment—Randilyn told Horatio the dog was never allowed out of the house."

"Then unless this is some kind of genetic defect, this dog was exposed to something in that house she shouldn't have. Something nasty."

"Well, Timothy Breakwash was an environmental consultant—he had a lab set up in his garage. I suppose the dog could have gotten into something carcinogenic."

"Tell you what—I'll take a closer look at those tumors, do a cellular analysis. I might be able to tell what caused them."

"Thanks, Alexx."

"Hope it helps. Whoever did this," said Alexx, "gives our whole species a bad name."

"This is a warrant to search your premises, Mister Bolivar," said Calleigh. She handed the man the paper. "I'll have to ask you to wait outside with this officer."

Bolivar's place wasn't much; just a single-wide trailer in a park outside of Hialeah, with a weed-threaded gravel patch for a lawn. His hound was tied up with a thick rope to the front porch, but all Calleigh saw of him was his snout; he was lying in the dirt beneath the trailer, trying to beat the heat.

Bolivar took the paper from her with a grin. "Go ahead, beautiful. *Mi casa es su casa*."

"Thank you," said Calleigh coldly, and stepped past him.

The interior matched the outside: Dingy walls, dirty windows, and thrift-store furniture that didn't match. Posters of rap artists and sports cars were apparently Bolivar's idea of art.

At least that's what Calleigh thought—until she saw the thick book on the coffee table. *"Treasures of Cuban Art,"* she murmured. She picked the book up and leafed through it; certain pages were bookmarked with yellow Post-it notes.

She put it down and moved on to the bedroom. The bed was messy and unmade, the air dank and stale. A box of condoms sat on the bedside table beside an empty bottle of gin, and dirty clothes lay heaped on the floor.

Calleigh got to work. Her warrant specifically listed one thing she was looking for, and it didn't take her long to find it: a loaded .22 caliber pistol in the drawer of the bedside table.

She slipped it into an evidence bag and smiled. "Well, Mister Bolivar," she said to herself, "it looks like your *pistolero* is also *mi pistolero*."

Horatio found Calleigh in the ballistics lab. "Is that the new Bullettrax 3D unit?"

"Yes it is," said Calleigh. She was fitting a spent bullet into an adjustable vise beneath the confocal sensor. "It'll give us a three-dimensional image down to the nanometer level. Every striation, perfectly captured and digitized." She turned the machine on and the bullet slowly rotated. A graphic came up on the screen set up beside the optical unit. "I've already input the bullet Alexx pulled out of Breakwash's dog. This is one I just test-fired from the gun I found at Fredo Bolivar's trailer."

When the scan finished, Calleigh called up the file on the first bullet. Both three-dimensional images rotated slowly, side by side, then merged into a single overlapping image. NO MATCH flashed on the screen beneath them.

"Not fired from the same gun." Calleigh sighed. "So maybe Fredo isn't our shooter."

"Or he's smart enough not to use his own gun," said Horatio. "Run the bullet through IBIS, see if we get any hits on previous cases."

Calleigh did so. "Nothing's coming up, H."

"So the gun's clean. I'm still sure Mister Bolivar is not."

"Something doesn't add up, Horatio." Calleigh shook her head. "If Timothy Breakwash was hunting for Rodriguo's treasure, the only reason for anyone to murder him is because he found it, and somebody wanted it all for themselves. But if that were the case, why would Fredo Bolivar torture Randilyn Breakwash? That tells us that Fredo doesn't know where the treasure is."

"And if he doesn't know, he wouldn't risk killing

Timothy. So either Fredo didn't kill Timothy, or Fredo didn't torture Randilyn. Right now, we don't know which of those statements is true . . . but we do know one thing for sure. Someone is convinced that Randilyn Breakwash knows more than she's letting on."

Calleigh nodded. "Maybe she does. She didn't tell us about her husband's treasure hunt the first time we talked to her. You think maybe she wasn't entirely forthcoming the last time, either?"

"Maybe not with us. But considering what her interrogator put her through, I'm betting she was considerably more honest with him."

"So the question is: Exactly how much does Randilyn Breakwash know?"

"I think," said Horatio, "that it's time to find that out."

13

"TWO MORE SUSPECTS left to go," said Tripp. "Who do you want to look at next?"

Natalia studied the screen of her laptop, shifting her position in the passenger seat to minimize the glare coming in through the Hummer's windshield. "I thought we'd take a crack at Adano Bermudez."

"The carjacker? Like to live dangerously, huh?" Tripp grinned.

Natalia grinned back. "Oh, I think we'll be okay. We might have to bring along a bottle of No-Doz, though."

Adano Bermudez had had his fifteen minutes of fame in Miami a few years ago. He and a friend had tired of watching the endless parade of tourists through the city, especially when it seemed that each and every visitor had far more money than he or she actually needed—and *definitely* more money than either of them. Adano's friend—Natalia couldn't recall his name—had claimed to be somewhat experienced in relieving tourists of such financial burdens, and offered to share his expertise with Adano. Adano, though initially reluctant, had agreed. He was a new resident of Miami, having just moved from Georgia, and didn't know many people. As it turned out, he didn't know his new friend very well, either.

The plan—such as it was—was simple. They picked an intersection close enough to Ocean Drive that it was sure to attract potential targets, but also near enough to the freeway that they could make a quick getaway. When their victim was stopped at the intersection's traffic light, they would jump into the car. A toy gun, waved in the motorist's face, would be all they needed to ensure compliance. They would pick a car with only one person in it and the windows rolled down.

Everything went fine at first. They watched and waited for just the right opportunity, scrutinizing every passing vehicle carefully. Finally, they saw what seemed to be the perfect target: a woman in her fifties, alone, driving a convertible.

When she stopped at the red light, they ran over and jumped in—Adano in back, his friend in front. The woman, according to Adano, "made a sound like a chicken having a heart attack." This sound—no doubt coupled with the stress of the situation—produced a burst of inappropriate laughter from both of them.

The woman, however, proved to be tougher than she sounded. She gave up her purse easily enough, but refused to part with the car. Adano's partner, unable to intimidate the driver, decided to cut his losses and run. He jumped out of the car and took off, expecting Adano to follow suit.

Adano didn't. He was slumped in the backseat, fast asleep.

"The narcoleptic carjacker," said Tripp. "Man, I wouldn't have liked to be that guy in prison. A cross-dressing ex-cop would have gotten more respect."

The victim, with Adano peacefully snoring behind her, had driven to the nearest police station. She'd double-parked and run inside to report what had happened to her, and when an officer had followed her outside to verify her statement, Adano was still in dreamland. He was snoring, his mouth open, and drooling ever so slightly.

The officer had gone back inside and gotten a camera.

"Every cop I know had that picture pinned up somewhere," said Tripp. "Talk about a relaxed approach to crime."

"He didn't fall asleep because he was relaxed," said Natalia. "Narcolepsy is a sleep disorder with a specific set of triggers. Laughter is one of them."

"I'll remember not to tell any jokes while we're talking to him."

Tripp pulled over and parked. Adano Bermudez

had done two years for his role in the crime, and since he'd gotten out he'd kept a low profile. He was working at a shoe store in North Miami, and hadn't been arrested since; Natalia had tracked him down with the help of his parole officer.

The shoe store specialized in high-end sneakers, the kind with designer labels and a pricetag to match. Tripp and Natalia walked in the front door and looked around. The store was a long rectangle, shoes displayed on either wall all the way to the back, where a small counter with a till on it blocked access to the stockroom. Back-to-back yellow leather couches ran down the center of the store, with a young woman in a tank top and miniskirt perched in the middle of one with her shoes off.

"Check this out," said Tripp. He picked up a shoe colored electric blue, with a translucent orange plastic heel. "When I was a kid they called 'em runners, because that's what you did in them. This one looks like it belongs on an astronaut."

"Style never sleeps," said Natalia. She eyed Tripp's suit and smiled. "Though in some cases, it has been known to hibernate."

A black man in his twenties came out of the back with a shoebox in his hands. He was dressed in a short-sleeved white shirt with the store's logo on the breast, black pants, and a pair of bright white sneakers he had probably gotten at a store discount. He'd grown a mustache and his hair was in dreads, but it was definitely Adano Bermudez.

Bermudez walked up to the young woman and opened the box. "Try these," he said. He sounded less than enthusiastic.

"Hey, Adano," said Tripp. "Miami PD. Got a minute?"

Adano looked at Tripp with dull eyes. "I'm with a customer."

"Not anymore," said Natalia. She pulled out her ID. "Now you're talking with us."

Adano nodded. "Sure. Excuse me, Miss." He led them to the back and leaned up against the counter with his arms crossed. "So. What can I do for you?" He didn't sound angry, just resigned.

"We'd like to talk to you about Hiram Davey," said Natalia. "We understand he interviewed you?"

"Davey? *That* jerk? Look, there was no interview. I don't care what he said, I didn't agree he could put me in his book."

"But you did talk?" asked Natalia.

"Well, yeah. But what he put in his column, that wasn't true. I mean, okay, I said those things, but not the *way* he said I did. And all that stuff about sleep-whacking was just made up."

"Sleep-whacking?" Natalia raised an eyebrow.

"One of the columns Davey did," said Tripp. "Right after Adano was sentenced. Sort of riffed on the idea of Adano developing a career as a hit-man. Suggested using a pillow as his signature weapon."

"Sorry I missed that," said Natalia. "I'm not talking about back then, Adano. I mean recently, since you've been out of jail."

"Yeah, I talked to him. He called me up last week, wanted to talk to me about this book he was writing. He said it was going to be based on real life. Thought I would make an interesting character."

"And you agreed to that?" asked Natalia. "Even after what he said about you in the paper?"

Adano shook his head. "I thought he was going to write about the real me, not the made-up stuff in his column. Give me a chance to explain my side of the story. But that wasn't it at all."

"How so?" asked Tripp.

"He just wanted to make more jokes. It wasn't a real-life story, it was some kind of mash-up of real and pretend. He called it a Roman cliff or something."

"*Roman à clef,*" said Natalia. "It means a story based on actual people and events, but the names and some of the details have been fictionalized."

"Whatever. He was going to call my character Sleepy Bermuda, and have him fall asleep in all kinds of stupid places—on the toilet, in court, in the middle of having sex—and I told him no. No way. Maybe I nodded off in court that one time, but I wasn't on the witness stand like he said. And I ain't *never* fallen asleep while having sex."

"I'm sure all your fans will be happy to know that," said Tripp. "Did you meet with Davey, or just talk on the phone?"

"We talked first, then I went over to his house."

Natalia frowned. "Why? If you told him you weren't interested, why would you go over to his house?"

"It wasn't like that. He was real friendly on the phone, and I thought maybe his book would help me get some dignity back. He didn't tell me what he was really going to do."

Tripp gave him a hard stare. "Then how'd you find out?"

"He was working on his laptop. When he got up to go to the kitchen for something, I took a look at his notes."

"Bet you weren't too happy, huh?"

Adano looked away. "No. He wanted to make me look like an even bigger fool. I told him he could forget it."

"That all you told him?" asked Natalia. "You tell him what would happen if he went ahead and did it anyway?"

Adano shook his head. "Is that what Davey said? Okay, so we argued. I was upset. But I didn't touch him, and I didn't make no threats. I'm still on probation—I'm not stupid, no matter what Davey says. Not my fault I got this damn disease."

"No," said Tripp, "But it *was* your fault you tried to terrorize and rob an old lady. People laughing at you is the least you deserve."

"I have to get back to work."

"Really?" Natalia looked around. The customer

Adano had been talking to when they arrived had left, and no one else was in the store. "You don't look too busy to me. Tell me, Adano, where were you yesterday morning, between five and six A.M.?"

"Asleep at home."

"Can anyone verify that?"

"No. I was alone. Why?"

"Because that's when Hiram Davey was murdered," said Tripp.

Adano's eyes widened. "What? Hey, I didn't have nothing to do with that. I didn't even know."

"Doesn't look good, Adano," said Tripp. "You've got a motive, a criminal record, and no alibi."

"Am I under arrest?"

"We're just gathering information," said Natalia. "I wouldn't lose any sleep over it."

"Mrs. Breakwash," said Horatio softly. "Randilyn?"

The woman in the hospital bed opened her eyes slowly. The painkillers she'd been given for her burns had finally caught up with her, and now she looked barely conscious. "Mister . . . Lieutenant," she said, her voice thick and heavy. She coughed, raising a hand to her mouth and wincing at the movement of her injured arm.

"Horatio. I'm sorry to bother you again so soon, Mrs. Breakwash, but there's a few more things we need to go over."

"My—my head's all muzzy, Horatio. Can't we do it later?"

"No, Mrs. Breakwash, we can't. We need to talk about Timothy."

"Tim." Randilyn's eyes filled with tears. "Tim's dead."

"Yes. I'm sorry about that. He was a real dreamer, wasn't he?"

"Uh-huh. Head in the clouds."

"But you stood by him. You believed in him. And he believed in you. He was a romantic, and even though you sometimes found that infuriating, it's the reason you stayed with him."

"Tim. My Tim."

"I understand the kind of man he was, Mrs. Breakwash. And after all those years of failure, the one thing I *can't* believe . . . is that he wouldn't share his biggest triumph with his wife."

Horatio put his hands on his hips and waited.

"Okay," said Randilyn softly. "It's true. I thought the whole thing was just a waste of time, at first. Another crazy dream. But then he found it . . . he really did."

"Where, Mrs. Breakwash?"

"No," she said, her voice stronger. "You think I'll tell you, just like that? I didn't tell the person who did *this*"—she said, holding out her arms—"you think I'll tell *you*?"

Horatio studied her face for a moment before replying. "No, Mrs. Breakwash, I don't think that. Because you can't *tell* what you don't *know*."

The look in her eyes was all the confirmation he

needed. "Your husband had a partner. Someone he needed but didn't trust—so he kept you in the dark for your own protection."

"Some protection," she whispered. "Look at me. I loved him, but he never thought anything through. Never thought what he might be putting *me* through—not ever."

"What did you tell the man who assaulted you, Mrs. Breakwash?"

"The only thing I knew. That Tim made a map, but I don't know where he hid it." She closed her eyes. "Now, please. I want to be alone."

"Down to the final suspect," said Tripp. "Any special reason you saved this one for last?"

"Honestly?" said Natalia. "I sort of hoped we'd have someone locked up by now. If this suspect is anything like the character Davey described in his book, she's definitely a long shot."

"If she's anything like the character in Davey's book, she's a looney tune."

"Let's not make any judgments just yet, okay?"

They parked beside the building and got out, their vehicle the only one in the parking lot. It looked as if the place wasn't quite ready to open, but the sign was already in place over the entrance: huge, neon-green letters that spelled out FROG WORLD.

Natalia pulled open the unlocked door and they stepped inside. The interior was cool, dark, and cavernous; it gave the immediate impression of a large, damp cave. Fake stars twinkled in the high ceiling, and the walls were edged with tropical plants. The floor was rough concrete, littered with lengths of white PVC piping and scraps of wire.

"Looks like they're still under construction," said Natalia.

"Yeah, but no workmen."

"They've gone home for the day." A tall, stout woman in coveralls and hiking boots stepped out of the shadows at the back of the room. "I'm the owner. Can I help you?"

"Sheila Smithwick?" asked Natalia. "I'm Natalia Boa Vista, with the Miami-Dade crime lab. This is Detective Frank Tripp."

"Hello." The woman strode forward and shook both their hands, her grip firm and her smile wide. She was in her forties, her skin tanned, her salt-and-pepper hair cropped short. "What does the crime lab want with me?"

"We'd like to ask you a few questions about Hiram Davey," said Natalia.

"Ah. I see. Am I a suspect?"

"We're just collecting information, ma'am," said Tripp.

Smithwick nodded. "All right. It was a real shame what happened to Mister Davey."

"You two got along all right?" asked Natalia.

"Oh, yes. I was hesitant to talk to Mister Davey at first—he's a humorist, after all, and I take my work very seriously. He told me he was interviewing people for a murder mystery he was writing, and he promised he'd be scientifically accurate when discussing my field of expertise. He was quite intrigued by my efforts."

"And your efforts have to do with . . . frogs?" asked Natalia.

Smithwick beamed. "That's right. Would you like me to show you around? All the exhibits aren't finished yet, but the main pond is ready and stocked and I just installed a bunch of exotic specimens today."

"Sure," said Natalia.

Smithwick motioned for them to follow her. She led them to the back of the room and through an arched doorway to an even bigger space beyond, lit in the same way. The room was dominated by a large, artificial pool, with a maze of walkways suspended just above it, hanging from the ceiling on steel cables. The outer walls were lined with glass terrariums. "I got the idea for the space at Disney World," said Smithwick. "You know, the *Pirates of the Caribbean* ride that empties out into a Louisiana bayou at dusk? It's a beautiful illusion—the stars are just coming out, there's the faintest glow of the sunset still lingering on the horizon, you can hear the crickets and nightbirds. And the frogs, of course."

"Sure," said Tripp. "Been there with my wife. They make a mean mint julep—long as you don't mind the absence of booze."

Smithwick marched down the walkways. "You can see the basic framework of the viewing areas already."

Behind her, Natalia said, "Framework? They look pretty well ready to go, to me."

"Oh, no. All the walkways are going to be completely enclosed in Plexiglas. Suspended and enclosed, to prevent actual physical contact between the amphibians and the public."

"Sounds a little sterile," said Tripp.

Smithwick turned and faced him. "That's the point. Did you know frogs are one of the fastest-vanishing species on Earth? Over sixty species in Latin America have completely disappeared in the last decade."

"I know," said Natalia. Tripp gave her an inquiring look, which she ignored. "Some scientists think higher global temperatures are promoting the growth of a fungus that's preying on amphibians."

"That's one theory. More recent data imply that global warming is doing a lot more than just encouraging a fungus—it's changing whole ecosystems. Frogs are the first ones to suffer because they rely on two environments to thrive and reproduce—water and land. Disturb the balance of either one and their population suffers. Factor in skin made of a permeable membrane that'll absorb any toxins present and you have a species in a very precarious position. You know about canaries and coal mines?"

"Sure," said Tripp. "Miners used to take one in a cage underground with them. If there were any poisonous gases, the canary would be the first to keel over."

"Exactly. Frogs are the canaries of the global ecology—in fact, they were the first animals to develop a true voice. And we're all stuck in this coal mine together."

"So that's what the Plexiglas is for?" Tripp asked. "To protect them?"

"Yes. I want people to see them in their natural habitat, but I want the impact on the frogs themselves to be minimal."

"So," said Natalia, "Hiram Davey shared your views on ecology?"

"I think so. He seemed very interested and asked lots of questions—especially about the more bizarre types of frogs. Like this one." She walked over to the wall and pointed at one of the terrariums. "It's called Darwin's Frog, because that's who discovered it. The male guards the eggs for around two weeks after the female has laid them, then scoops them up in its mouth. The tadpoles live in the male's vocal sac until they've shed their tails and grown limbs. I wanted to get a gastric brooding frog—they actually gestate their tadpoles in their stomach—but there were only two species discovered, and they both went extinct in the mid-nineteen-eighties."

Tripp nodded. "Yeah, I can see Davey getting a kick out of either of those ideas—not the extinction, the tadpoles-in-the-mouth-or-stomach part."

"Or this one," Smithwick said, indicating the next terrarium. "A microhylid of the genus *Kaloula*."

"Chubby little guy," said Tripp.

Smithwick chuckled. "He sure is. He has stubby little arms, too—both of which cause him major problems when it comes to mating. Difficult for him to get in position and then stay there—but he has an ingenious solution."

"Which is?" asked Natalia.

"Glue. He secretes a biological adhesive from his belly that attaches him to the female so securely he can't be removed until the glue breaks down or the female sheds her skin."

"Now that's sticking to the job," said Tripp.

"Speaking of which . . ." said Natalia. "I hate to ask, Miss Smithwick, but can you tell me where you were yesterday morning between five and six A.M.?"

"Of course. I was just getting out of bed—work on this place starts early. And to answer your next question—no, I don't have anyone that can corroborate that. I didn't get here until about seven-thirty."

Natalia nodded. "Did Davey ever show you any of the book?"

"Oh, no. He said he never showed anyone what he was working on until he was finished. It's too bad—I was quite curious."

Natalia glanced around. "This is all very impressive—but it must be expensive. Do you have a lot of investors?"

"Nope. It's all me." Smithwick grinned. "I got lucky last year in the Powerball draw. Twelve point four million dollars. That's how I'm doing all this."

"Congratulations," said Natalia. "Culmination of a lifelong dream?"

"No, not really," Smithwick said, her grin fading abruptly. "Actually, I only got interested in frogs about six months ago. I have a lot of interests."

"Oh. Well, I'm sure Frog World will be a big success. Good luck."

"Thank you. I'll show you out."

On the drive back to the lab, Natalia asked, "Well, what do you think?"

Tripp glanced over, one hand on the steering wheel and the other tapping his thigh. "Florida's got a history of roadside wildlife attractions. I think she could make a go of it."

Natalia rolled her eyes. "Not Frog World, Frank. Smithwick."

"Her? If she's crazy, she did a pretty good job of hiding it."

"Yeah. Right up until the end, anyway."

"How long did she spend in that institution?"

"Four years. We don't have access to her medical records, of course, but we know why she was there." Sheila Smithwick had been arrested for attacking a man with a machete in broad daylight, screaming about demons and talking toadstools. She was judged not responsible for her actions, and wasn't allowed to re-enter society until she'd spent a long stint in a mental health facility.

Tripp adjusted the air-conditioning. "You think she got a look at what Davey was actually writing?"

"Maybe. Sheila managed it, and she seems a lot brighter than him."

"Sure. Which means she's a psycho with brains—*and* twelve million dollars."

Natalia sighed. "Not to mention a whole lot of frogs."

"I don't know—maybe she's got a sense of humor about the whole thing. What Davey wrote about her wasn't *that* bad."

"Not that bad? Frank, let me refresh your memory." Natalia opened up her laptop and called up the file, then read aloud: "Professor Cheryl Smashwack regarded the swimming pool full of frogs with undisguised glee and just a touch of arousal. 'Swim, my slimy army, swim! Soon it will be mating season, and you will be in the throes of amplexus! You will fill my pool with ova and spermatozoa, and I will soak in the glorious batrachian soup and be *renewed*!'???"

Natalia looked up and raised an eyebrow.

"So? You've read the notes—it's a beauty treatment she's trying to peddle."

"Frank, Davey has her swimming in frog eggs. While they're being fertilized."

"Hey, all beauty treatments sound weird to me. I stopped trying to understand 'em around the time women started washing their hair with beer—and what the hell's amplexus, anyway?"

"Frog sex."

"That's what I figured, but I thought I'd make sure . . . okay, let's say she's crazy as a sackful of skunks. Maybe she'd take the whole amplexus-swimming thing as a compliment."

Natalia tapped a few keys, then read from a different section: "Smashwack was a loon. Not just your average, everyday loon, but the kind of loon other loons crossed the street to avoid. Even her imaginary friends thought she was crazy. She worshipped the Egyptian goddess Heket, who had the head of a frog and was married to a guy with the head of a goat. Smashwack had tried a trial marriage to an actual goat once, in the spirit of ecumenical solidarity, but it hadn't worked out. The goat's parents couldn't stand her."

Tripp grinned despite himself. "Okay, let's assume she read that and didn't take it in a good-natured way. You think she's capable of planning and executing a murder?"

"She's capable of planning a full-scale theme park, Frank." Natalia had done some checking before they visited Smithwick building they'd seen was only the tip of an amphibian iceberg. Smithwick had applied for permission to build an entire park around her current obsession, including a roller coaster and a restaurant. Approval was still pending.

"Well, she doesn't have an alibi," Tripp conceded. "Then again, neither do Adano Bermudez or Joshua St. George—and Gordon Dettweiler's is more than a little shaky."

"Then I guess it's time to shake all their stories a little harder," said Natalia, "and see what falls apart."

14

"SO NOW WE KNOW FOR SURE," said Calleigh. She and Horatio were in the layout room, going over everything they had on the Breakwash case. "Timothy Breakwash *did* find Rodriguo's treasure."

"According to his widow, yes. But we still have no hard evidence of that."

"I know—hard evidence is in short supply on this case. She said there's a map?"

"Yes. She said she doesn't know where her husband hid it, and I believe her."

Calleigh shook her head. "If there's a map, it's not at the Breakwash house. It's been searched three times, twice by professionals. He must have hid it somewhere else."

"I agree. But let's not lose sight of one very important thing."

"What's that, H?"

"That finding Rodriguo's treasure isn't our job. Finding Timothy Breakwash's killer is."

Calleigh blinked. "Of course. Afraid I've been bitten by the treasure bug, Horatio?"

Horatio smiled. "You wouldn't be the first. Just a reminder to stay focused."

"Oh, don't worry about me. When I watch pirate movies, I'm always rooting for the people getting robbed. Once a cop, always a cop, I guess."

"No guessing about it," said Horatio.

Calleigh's cell rang. "Calleigh Duquesne. Oh, hi, Alexx."

"I took a closer look at those tumors I found in the bulldog," said Alexx. "They're something called Sticker's sarcoma."

Calleigh listened to what Alexx had to say for a few minutes, interjecting only once with a question. "Okay, Alexx, thanks. I'll talk to you later."

"What's up?" asked Horatio.

"That hard evidence we were looking for?" Calleigh said, slipping her phone back in her pocket. "I think some just sat up and begged."

"You know," Fredo Bolivar said, "I'm getting real tired of this. First you take my gun, now you want my dog? What's next, my underwear?"

"That won't be necessary," said Calleigh. Horatio sat to her right, Fredo across from her. "Not unless you raped Randilyn Breakwash as well as tortured her."

"But you didn't do that," said Horatio. "Did you, Fredo? No, you were focused on longer-range plans."

"I still don't see what my dog has to do with this."

"Your dog has a small cauliflower-shaped tumor growing on his nose," said Calleigh. "I noticed it when we met in the Everglades."

"Yeah, so?"

"So we also found tumors in the body of the Breakwash's young bulldog. It's a disease called canine transmissible venereal tumor, which usually manifests on the genitalia. In some cases—such as yours—CTVT can show up on the nose or in the mouth."

Fredo waved his hand dismissively. "You must think I'm some kind of moron. So both dogs had cancer, so what? Cancer's not contagious."

"In this instance," said Calleigh, "it is." She pushed two pieces of paper across the table at Bolivar. "See, Sticker's sarcoma is unique. In human beings, the papilloma virus can be spread through sexual contact and *cause* cancer, but that's not what's happening here. This is a case of the cancer *itself* jumping from one host to another—like a parasite."

"And because of that," said Horatio, "we can prove exactly where it came from. Your dog infected Breakwash's dog, Fredo—and DNA tests will confirm that."

"You're saying my dog had sex with another dog? That'd be tough—I had that hound fixed years ago."

"CTVT can be spread by saliva," said Horatio. "The bulldog was notorious for licking anything and anybody—but she wasn't allowed out of the house. The only way she could have been infected was if your dog was in the Breakwash residence. We've got you, Fredo." Horatio leaned forward. "Your alibi's no good, and we can put you inside the house."

Fredo stared out the window as he considered Horatio's words.

"Okay, so I was in the house," he said at last. "But I had a good reason to be there, and it didn't have anything to do with Mrs. Breakwash. Her husband and I were working together."

"That's not exactly news to us, Fredo," said Horatio. "We know you two were partners, and we know what you were looking for: a stockpile of art put together by your father. That's why you killed Timothy Breakwash, and why you tortured his wife."

"You don't know as much as you think you do, *esse*. For one thing, I didn't kill Tim. Why would I? He knew where the plane went down, but he didn't tell me. If he had, don't you think I'd be out there right now, getting paid?"

"So Timothy *did* find the plane?" asked Calleigh.

"So he said. Wouldn't make much sense for me

to kill the one guy who knows where it is, would it?"

"Maybe not," said Horatio. "But it would give you plenty of motive to interrogate the one other person who might know."

"Tim's wife? Like I said, I never met her. The only time I was even in the house, she wasn't there. But let me tell you something, Caine; that treasure is *mine*. My father didn't steal it, he bought it, and I'm his only living heir. I *own* it."

"That's debatable," said Calleigh. "First, that art was paid for with profits from drug dealing—if it belongs to anyone, it probably belongs to the DEA. Second, Rodriguo did a really good job of staying under the radar; no known photo of him exists, let alone a DNA sample. Good luck proving you're related."

"I don't need luck. I know Tim made a map, and I'm going to find it."

"I don't think so, Fredo," said Horatio. "We both know it's not at the house. Randilyn Breakwash doesn't know where it is, either. I may not have the evidence to charge you with breaking into her home and brutalizing her, but I can make sure you never go near her again."

"You do whatever you have to," said Fredo coldly. "I always do."

Natalia took Tripp out for ice cream.

They got large double-scoop cones at a place on

Ocean Drive, then strolled down the sidewalk across from the beach.

"You know, I'm not really used to discussing cases in this kind of environment," said Tripp. He'd gone for pistachio and strawberry and had already gotten some on his tie.

"I suppose you'd prefer some dark and grungy cop bar." Natalia took a satisfying lick of her moccachino and chocolate--chocolate chip. "Mmm. Come on, Frank, loosen up. What's the use of living in Miami if you don't take advantage of it once in a while?"

"You ever see a bald man with a sunburned scalp? It's not a pretty sight. Besides, there are too many . . . distractions out here." Tripp eyed a blond amazon in a bikini as she rollerbladed past, eyes veiled by sunglasses and ears plugged with an iPod, exposed to and insulated from the world at the same time.

Natalia laughed. "Deal with it, tough guy. I have faith in you."

"All right, all right. Let's run down where we are."

"Okay. I think we can forget about Marssai Guardon; Davey's book would have given her exactly the kind of publicity she wants."

"Which is any kind at all. I don't think she could spell shame without a dictionary."

"One down. Then there's Joshua St. George."

"He's angry enough, that's for sure. Been arrested a few times, too—assault, disturbing the

peace. If Davey had proof St. George killed someone during the Liberty City riots, Joshua might
have killed him to keep it quiet."

Natalia took a meditative lick of her cone. "Well,
we didn't find anything like that on Davey's duplicate files. I guess he could have hidden them someplace else, though."

"Yeah—like on his missing laptop. But if he went
to the trouble to hide a backup copy of his files, I
can't believe he wouldn't make a copy of something that important, too."

"True," Natalia admitted. She stopped to pet a
small dog on a leash, while the owner, a gray-
haired man in a yellow tracksuit, waited with a patient smile on his face. "So maybe," she continued,
"we need to take a closer look at Davey's house.
See if we missed anything."

"That's your department. Just make sure you finish your cone first."

"Very funny. Who's next? Oh, Adano Bermudez."

"Mister Sleepy? I think he's our best bet so far."

She stopped, surprised. "Really, Frank? Why's
that?"

"Adano may seem like a joke, but I saw the look
in his eye. Frustration leads to rage, Natalia. There's
only so much a man can take before he snaps, and
Adano's had more than his fair share of humilia-
tion. Whoever punched Davey's ticket was more
than a little ticked off."

"Knife attacks do tend to be personal—and Davey was stabbed multiple times."

Tripp nodded. He'd finished off the pistachio and was halfway through the strawberry. "It may be a cliché, but it really is the quiet ones you have to watch out for. Half the time they're wrapped so tight that when they finally cut loose, it's like a bomb going off."

"And then there's Gordon Dettweiler. The only one with an alibi."

"An alibi that smells worse than the bowling alley he runs. He definitely bears checking out—I'm guessing his story won't hold water once we poke it a few times."

"Okay. Poking is your department."

Tripp raised an eyebrow, and Natalia laughed. "Sorry. That came out wrong."

"I'll let it go. Anyway, I don't trust Dettweiler any more than I trust his buddy—they've got *something* going on that's not on the level. I'll see what I can dig up."

"And lastly, Sheila Smithwick. The Frog Queen."

"Maybe—but I get the feeling that if she wanted to murder someone, she'd use some kind of poisonous pond-hopper to do the deed."

"That's not a very scientific approach, Frank."

"Neither is pistachio ice cream, but I'm warming up to the idea."

*   *   *

"Alexx," said Natalia. "Got a minute?"

Alexx looked up from the body she was working on. "Just finishing up—give me a sec." She tied off the last stitch in the chest incision and cut away the loose thread. "All done. What do you need?"

"Some advice."

"I was just going to grab a cup of tea—all right if we do this in the break room?"

"Fine with me."

A few minutes later they were both seated in the break room. A lab tech who'd apparently had a late night was slumped over a table in the corner, head in his arms, fast asleep. "Reminds me of med school," said Alexx. She blew on her tea carefully.

"Reminds me of a suspect in the case I'm working," said Natalia. "But that's not what I wanted to talk to you about. What do you know about long-term exposure to a combination of turpentine fumes and aerosolized sulphuric acid?"

"That's a pretty specific combination," said Alexx. "You're talking about someone who worked in a turpentine camp, right?"

"Yes, for at least five years. He claimed his lungs were damaged—they certainly sounded like they were—but I wanted a doctor's opinion."

Alexx put down her cup. "Did he wheeze? Take big, raspy-sounding breaths?"

"He did. We talked to him for at least fifteen, twenty minutes, and he never stopped. I just wanted to know if he could breathe normally if he had to."

"If his symptoms are the result of his time in the camps, the answer is no. It's a condition called metabolic acidosis, when the body's pH balance is upset. The deep, rapid breathing is Kussmaul respiration; by exhaling more carbon dioxide, the body causes the alkalinity of its blood serum levels to increase, partially counteracting the acid. If he stopped breathing like that, his entire metabolism would be affected—he could have seizures or go into a coma."

Natalia nodded. "So you know about the turpentine camps?"

"Sure. It's part of Florida's history, honey—and a couple of other states, too. I'm always amazed by all the people who *don't* know about them."

Natalia shook her head. "It's just—this was going on in the forties? It sounds like something out of the Civil War."

"Nothing civil about it," said Alexx. She picked up her cup of tea and took a sip. "They may have changed the rules and called it something else, but it was still slavery. Right down to runaways being dragged back in chains. Who's your suspect?"

"Guy named Joshua St. George. I don't think he's a suspect anymore, though—what you just told me clears him."

"How so?"

"The victim's digital recorder picked up the

sound of the killer breathing. No way it could have been St. George."

"Glad I could help. If he spent time in one of those camps and he's still alive, he must be one tough old bird."

"Yeah, it sounds like he's had quite the life. Marched beside Martin Luther King in Chicago, saw the Liberty City riots. A real survivor."

Alexx's eyes saddened. "Yeah. No offense, Natalia—but every time I hear that phrase, it just about breaks my heart."

"What? I'm sorry—what did I say?"

Alexx finished her tea and stood up. "It's not your fault. But an entire life lived—*anyone's* life— deserves more than just the description *survivor*. All that really means is that their life was hard, and they managed to hang on. And in the end, even that definition isn't true. We're *all* survivors, Natalia . . . until someone or something takes that title away."

While there were always certain crimes that provoked a universal response from police officers— cop killers, for instance, or child molesters—many cops also had that one class of criminal they despised above all others. For Frank Tripp, that meant con artists.

He hated even using the term—as far as he was concerned, calling it an art was like calling assassination a sport. He didn't care how much skill was involved, or how clever the con was; what it all boiled down to for him was that someone had taken that most fragile of human emotions—trust—and turned it into a knife he could stick in someone's back. Practitioners of the con often claimed the victim's own greed was to blame, that "you can't con an honest man."

"Right," Tripp would growl. "Guess you can't rape a virgin either, huh?"

Any further discussion would usually end badly.

Most people assumed that Tripp's attitude on the subject was because of personal experience, that either he or someone close to him had been taken by a grifter. That wasn't exactly the case; while Tripp had investigated many cases of fraud, he didn't know any of the victims involved himself.

It didn't matter. It wasn't a personal grudge for Tripp, it was something closer to patriotism. Florida seemed to attract scammers the way rotting meat attracted gators, and it was their sheer number and variety that provoked Tripp's disgust. Real estate swindlers, lotto ticket telemarketer cons, phony psychics, door-to-door collectors for nonexistent charities, identity thieves; every time he picked up the paper or talked to another cop there was something else. Sometimes, it seemed that the entire state was doomed to be remembered for a grand total of three things: hurricanes, orange juice, and people who tried to sell you swampland.

Tripp wasn't that crazy about orange juice, either.

So he took a special pride in taking down a con man, regarding it as not just in the public interest but good for Miami's public image, too. And Gordon Dettweiler—which was his actual name, strangely enough—had been taking advantage of just about everyone he met for a long, long time.

The On a Roll Bowl bowling alley seemed to be a genuine business, of which Dettweiler was the registered owner—but Tripp wasn't convinced. The tournament's cash prize smelled like bait to him, and he was sure there was a hook hidden inside the lure.

The first thing he checked out were the sponsors, the neighborhood businesses that were supposedly putting up the money. He tore a handbill advertising the tournament off a lamppost around the corner from the bowling alley; the sponsors were all listed at the bottom. Then he went door to door, asking each and every owner to verify that they were contributing and exactly how much.

He started to notice a trend almost immediately. He'd visit a small business—a dry cleaner or a corner store—and the owner would be reluctant to name an actual figure. When pressed, the dollar amount then named would seem much higher than the business could afford to donate.

Tripp took a break in a tiny restaurant, a hole in the wall selling Cuban sandwiches and slices of pizza. He studied the middle-aged Asian woman behind the lunch counter over his cup of coffee, and had an idea. The restaurant wasn't on Dettweiler's list of sponsors, but it was between two businesses that were.

"'Scuse me," said Tripp. He fished the handbill out of his pocket and unfolded it. "Was there a guy in here a while back, trying to get you to make a donation to this tournament's prize money?"

The woman glanced at the poster. "Yes, I remember him," she said. "Told him I wasn't interested."

"How much did he ask you for?"

She named a number a quarter of what the other businesses had quoted. "But he told me that because it was for charity, I could write it off on my income taxes—and he'd give me a receipt for four times as much as I paid. I told him to get lost."

"Good for you," said Tripp. "You did the right thing."

He tossed a twenty down on the counter, got up, and headed for the door.

"Don't you want your change?" she called after him.

"Keep it," Tripp said over his shoulder. "Honesty shouldn't always be its own reward."

When Adano Bermudez was arrested, his lawyer had ordered a medical evaluation as part of his defense. While Natalia couldn't get access to Bermudez's medical records, she could take a look at the evaluation.

What she found was that of the four most common symptoms of narcolepsy, Adano displayed only two. He didn't suffer hypnagogic hallucinations—nightmarish visions narcoleptics sometimes had when falling asleep or waking up—or automatic behavior, which was what most people called sleepwalking but which could in fact entail activities that ranged from eating to driving a car. What he did manifest was sleep paralysis and a condition called cataplexy. Sleep paralysis meant exactly that: When waking up, Adano would be unable to move or speak for several moments, even though fully conscious. Cataplexy was a condition that caused momentary muscle weakness, with a specific set of triggers for each individual. When tested, Adano had shown total muscle collapse when either anger or fear had been induced. Not only that, he'd reacted poorly to every kind of CNS stimulant or antidepressant tried, meaning that the normal chemical methods of controlling the disease weren't an option for him.

It wasn't the burst of laughter that made him fall asleep during the robbery, she thought. *It was fear. And according to this report, he reacts just as strongly to becoming angry—which means there's no way he could have killed Hiram Davey. That kind of violent outburst would have left him slumped on the floor, either asleep or paralyzed.*

She decided to pay a visit to Valera. "Hey, Maxine," she said, strolling into the DNA lab. "Got the bloodwork from the Davey case done yet?"

"Hours ago," Valera said, picking up a sheet of paper from beside the printer and handing it over. "I thought you'd have been by before now."

Natalia studied the sheet. "Haven't had a chance—been riding around with Frank, talking to suspects."

"Tripp? Lucky you." Valera sounded more envious than sarcastic.

"You're kidding. Frank?"

"I am most definitely not kidding. That build, that jaw, that gruff voice? He can be *my* daddy anytime."

"Okaaay . . . I see you isolated two different donors from the blood samples I sent you."

"Yeah. One matches the vic, the other's an unknown female."

"So the killer must have nicked herself—and that narrows my suspect list down to one. Thanks, Maxine."

"You're welcome. Now go back out into the big, sunny world and try not to forget us poor techs stuck in the lab while you get chauffeured around by a tall, rugged detective."

"I'll do my best," Natalia said with a grin.

"What?" said Tripp. "I got something stuck in my teeth?"

Natalia looked away and shook her head. "Never mind. Just thinking about something someone said . . ." She checked the Hummer's rearview mirror and changed lanes. She and Tripp were on their way back to Frog World to serve Sheila Smithwick with a warrant. "You uncover anything on Dettweiler yet?"

"Yeah. He's been taking in a lot less money from local merchants than he claimed, handing out inflated receipts they can use to get big deductions on their income tax returns. Almost impossible to prove, though."

"So if he isn't getting the money from donations, where's it coming from?"

Tripp scratched the side of his chin. "Well, the entry fee's pretty stiff, but there's no way to tell how many people have entered without getting a look at Dettweiler's books—and even then, I wouldn't trust what I read."

"You think he's planning on collecting the money and then disappearing?"

"Cut and run? No, I don't think so. He's the registered owner of the business, which gives him a lot less leeway to just pull up stakes and vanish. Something else is going on—I just haven't figured out what, yet."

"Well, unless he had a female accomplice, I don't think he was involved in Davey's murder. And Adano Bermudez and Joshua St. George are both excluded for medical reasons."

"We'll see," said Tripp.

This time, the front door was locked. Tripp pounded on it, to no effect. "Let's try around back," he said.

They found an emergency exit propped open with a two-by-four on the other side of the building. "Hello?" Natalia called out. "Ms. Smithwick? Are you here?"

They found her in the middle of the central pond. She was crouched naked on a lily pad–shaped island made of green concrete, and she had painted herself green. She had a large Tupperware container in one hand.

"Hi," she said cheerfully. "I heard you knocking, but I was in the middle of lunch." She dipped one hand into the container and came up with a handful of live crickets. She crammed them into her mouth and chewed, the occasional twitching leg sticking out between her lips.

"We . . . we have a warrant," said Natalia. "For a sample of your—blood?"

Smithwick finished her mouthful. "Did you know that when most frogs swallow, their *eyeballs* sink deeper into their *skulls*? It helps push the food down. Talk about having eyes bigger than your stomach, huh?" Her own eyes were wide and bright.

"Think she's faking?" Tripp whispered.

"If so, I admire her commitment," Natalia whispered back. "Ms. Smithwick? If you wouldn't mind coming over here—"

"Not just yet. After lunch, I always go swimming—I don't care *what* the doctors say." She dropped the container and launched herself into the shallow water. "Ribbet! Ribbet!" she cried. "I don't care what the doctors say! I don't! I don't!"

"You will," said Natalia with a sigh.

"You know we gotta catch her, right?" asked Tripp.

"You go left. I'll go right."

Wolfe stared at the big, dead fish in front of him. The lab didn't have the space to store it, so they'd put it in a refrigerated truck in the parking lot. Wolfe's breath puffed out in from of him, swirled around and up like lazy smoke. The truck was cold, but it was refreshing after the heat of the parking lot; Wolfe had broken into a sweat just walking from the building to the vehicle.

"What's your secret, Moby Dick?" he muttered to himself. *When I pushed Dragoslav, he hinted that there was something being smuggled, and we just weren't smart enough to find it. How did he put it?* "You can't see beyond your own prejudices." *Meaning it's our own thinking tripping us up, our own assumptions. So to solve the case, I have to think outside the box.*

Wolfe was an intelligent guy, but—like everyone—he had his blind spots. He also had OCD, obsessive-compulsive disorder, though it was firmly under control. When he'd first become a CSI, Horatio had told him that a touch of OCD made him a perfect candidate for the job; the intense focus and attention to detail the disorder sometimes induced were pluses in his line of work.

Most of the time, anyway. The downside was that sometimes Wolfe had a hard time seeing the bigger picture; he zeroed in on specifics but failed to notice the more unpredictable elements—like the eventual consequences of his actions. It had gotten him into trouble more than once.

And it was why he had a problem with gambling.

He knew he didn't seem like the type—all of his coworkers had been surprised when they'd found out. Gambling seemed like the kind of problem an on-the-edge rule breaker would have, not a clean-cut, button-down guy like Wolfe. But when you broke it down, it actually made a perverse kind of sense; crime scene science was all about trying to recognize patterns, to impose order on what seemed at first glance to be chaos. That was Wolfe's job, and when he did it well it rewarded him with a sense of satisfaction and accomplishment.

But gambling—gambling was like the dark mirror of science. You were still trying to impose order on chaos, still trying to see the pattern emerge from the random, but the tools you had to use weren't the same. Intellect was still involved, but so was intuition; control was important, but you had to take risks in order to win. It appealed to an aspect of Wolfe that didn't get much exercise, and once he'd started to experiment with it his obsessive-compulsive side took over. That was the trap he'd fallen into: His OCD insisted on total order, total control, and that was never possible with gambling. It had given him an itch that he could never fully scratch, and now he wished he'd never started in the first place. So far, he had it under control.

So far.

He stared down at the fish, trying to get that intuitive part of his mind working, the kind that sometimes spoke to him when he was playing, that told him to take another card or stand pat.

The fish stared back with one dead eye.

It wasn't talking.

15

HORATIO AND CALLEIGH studied the objects spread out over the surface of the light table, which included Timothy Breakwash's clothes and every item they had recovered from the balloon. The balloon itself was still in the possession of the FAA, but they had extensive photographs of it from every possible angle.

Horatio crossed his arms. "If Timothy Breakwash finally hit the jackpot, it's highly unlikely he'd take his own life. Therefore—impossible as it seems—he was murdered. The question is not only *how*, but *where* and *when*."

"Right," said Calleigh. "Because if he were killed earlier or later than we thought, the murder could have taken place on the ground."

"Let's start with later. The first person on the scene was Joel Greer, and witnesses say he was in an awful hurry to get there."

"He might just have been concerned for his boss."

"Yes—or he might have wanted to get there first so he could put a bullet in his head." Horatio stared down at the items on the table, his expression intent. "Let's say Breakwash is somehow incapacitated in midair. That would lead to a crash, giving Greer the opportunity to shoot an unconscious Breakwash at close range with a silenced weapon. If it was done quickly enough, no one would see or hear a thing."

"Two problems with that. First, it would have been far easier for Greer to shoot Breakwash at the beginnng of the flight instead of the end. Second, the tox screen for the vic came back negative for any kind of sedative or intoxicant."

"And if he'd been shot before the balloon launched, our witness with the telescope wouldn't have seen Breakwash moving around while the balloon was in flight."

"True," said Calleigh. "But the balloon was too far away for any real identification. Maybe the person he saw wasn't Breakwash at all."

"A second occupant? Now that's an interesting thought . . ."

"Let's say Breakwash was shot on the ground, in the basket. A second person flies the balloon and simulates a crash. Breakwash is out of sight on the bottom of the basket, and the pilot crouches down for the landing. Joel Greer is the first to arrive, and helps shield the pilot, who rolls out of the basket and then hides behind it—in all the confusion, he's mistaken for one of the people who rush over from their cars."

Horatio considered the theory. "It's possible," he conceded. "Witnesses, after all, are notoriously unreliable. But I know something that isn't."

Calleigh smiled. "Science?"

"Indeed. Let's give the FAA a call and see what they can tell us."

In the end, it took Tripp, Natalia, and two licensed mental health experts over an hour to corner and wrestle Sheila Smithwick into restraints. She was large, strong, and determined not to be caught—plus, whatever she'd coated her skin with was extremely slippery. While Natalia was taking the blood sample, the naked frog woman made croaking sounds that the CSI would have sworn a human throat was incapable of producing. Smithwick paused after one particularily loud burst and said, "Did you know that the larynx of the European tree frog takes up a fifth of its body?"

"No," Natalia said through gritted teeth. "I did not."

After she'd been taken away, Natalia and Tripp took a long look at each other. Both of them were soaking wet, their clothes smeared with mud and algae. Natalia burst out laughing, and Tripp started chuckling, too.

"You know," said Tripp, "I'm starting to think this whole case is one long practical joke orchestrated by Hiram Davey's ghost."

"Maybe so," said Natalia, "but we're going to have the last laugh."

Natalia ran the sample back to the lab, then headed home for a quick shower and a change of clothes. Sheila Smithwick hadn't been formally charged with anything—not yet—but she was being held for psychiatric evaluation. Natalia wondered what would become of Frog World; would it be just another abandoned roadside attraction, a half-built dream filled with empty terrariums and a dried-out pond? Maybe an ecological society would take it over, finish what Smithwick had started.

Natalia sighed. More likely, it would be torn down and replaced by condos or a hotel. This was Miami, after all.

Calleigh called the FAA investigator, William Pinlon. "Hi, Mister Pinlon? This is Calleigh Duquesne, from the Miami-Dade crime lab. I was hoping I could get some information from you regarding the balloon that came down on the highway the other day."

On the other end of the line, Pinlon sounded exactly as harried as he had at the crash site. "Right, right, the balloon. My people just finished up with that. I've got the report right here, just let me call it up . . . damn computer . . . okay, here it is. You want me to fax you a copy?"

"That would be lovely. Can I ask you a few quick questions first?"

"Uh . . . yeah, sure."

She only had a few. When he'd finished answering, she gave him the lab's fax number, thanked him, and hung up.

"Well?" asked Horatio.

"According to Mister Pinlon, all the data lined up. They looked at the altitude of the balloon, the distance it traveled, how much gas was consumed, and the prevailing winds for that morning. If there had been an extra person aboard, the additional weight would have forced the balloon to burn more fuel than it did."

"Which eliminates the second-passenger theory. I think we can safely say Breakwash was alone—which means he had to have been killed in midair."

"Maybe we're concentrating on the wrong details," said Calleigh thoughtfully. "Maybe he was shot from a distance, and the close-up GSR was faked?"

"He also had GSR on his hands. Maybe he was shooting back at the killer."

"But the FAA didn't find any bullet holes in the balloon—I checked. Which means our killer used a low-powered twenty-two rifle—as opposed to the higher caliber a professional shooter would choose—to make a near impossible shot at a moving target, and got it on the first try. And it *still* doesn't explain the GSR around the wound."

"So we're back where we started from," said Horatio.

Calleigh sighed. "Yeah, I guess so. What kind of approach do you want to take?"

Horatio looked at everything they'd gathered from the balloon. "We go over everything we have and see what we've missed," he said. "Whatever answers there are, they're right here. We just have to find them . . ."

Natalia stared at Valera in disbelief. "You're sure, Maxine?"

Valera gave her an apologetic smile. "Sorry, Natalia. The blood isn't a match."

"So Sheila Smithwick isn't our killer."

"No. Her blood also tested positive for traces of two antipsychotics, while the first sample was clean."

"Whatever she's taking, she isn't taking enough of it . . . thanks, Maxine."

She broke the bad news to Tripp in the hall. "So she may be crazy," finished Natalia, "but she's not a killer."

"Tell that to the crickets," said Tripp. "Now what? We've eliminated all our female suspects."

"Not quite. Marssai Guardon had no reason to kill Davey—but what about the *faux* Ms. Guardon?"

"The body double? She did say she'd be in a lot of trouble if her parents found out it was her in the porn video."

"And Marssai said Davey was going to spill the beans in his book. I think it's enough for a warrant."

Tripp nodded. "I'll give the judge a call."

"Thought I'd find you out here," Delko said. He stepped into the reefer truck and closed the door behind him. "I should have known better than to introduce an obsessive-compulsive to a really big fish. Are you going to start calling me Ishmael?"

Wolfe glanced over at his colleague. "You know, when this case started out, I was the one making the jokes."

"I know. Funny how things can turn around on you, huh?"

"At the moment, I'm not laughing."

"I know." Delko walked up to the large metal table the sunfish lay on and poked it with a finger. "If only we could drag it into the interview room and ask it a few questions, right? What's your name? What were you doing on that boat? What's your relationship with Jovan Dragoslav?"

Wolfe grinned despite himself. "At least we don't have to take its prints."

"There is that." Delko shook his head. "You know what this case reminds me of? There's this folk tale I read once, about a border guard. Every day, a local merchant carts a wheelbarrow full of sand up to the checkpoint. The border guard sifts through the sand carefully, searches the merchant, but he doesn't find anything. The next day the same thing happens, and the day after that. The guard is sure the merchant is smuggling contraband across the border, but he can't figure out how. Turns out the merchant is smuggling wheelbarrows."

"Great story—but that can't be the case here. This fish is basically worthless. It's common, not good eating, and riddled with parasites. Unless Dragoslav has tapped into a lucrative black market for shark tapeworms, I don't see what possible value this fish could have."

"You're right," Delko admitted. "It can't be the fish itself. And there's nothing hidden in it—we've even X-rayed the damn thing. So why was it on the ship? Is it just supposed to be distracting us from something else?"

"We've gone over the whole boat, too. I'm pretty sure that whatever the shipment was, it's on the bottom of the ocean now. Probably in several large, white plastic buckets that we have no hope of ever finding."

Delko shrugged. "I could suit up and look—but you're right. We don't know exactly where the boat was when it was hijacked, and we don't know if the buckets floated or sank. I guess we can console ourselves with the fact that whatever they held, Dragoslav can't get his hands on it, either."

"You know," said Wolfe, rubbing his hands together to warm them up, "that's just not much consolation at all."

*   *   *

"All right," said Horatio. "Let's go over every single item we recovered from the balloon. Flight manual."

Calleigh nodded. "Check."

"Water bottle."

"Right here, and containing approximately half a liter of water. Tested clean."

"One pair Nomex gloves."

"Got them. Epithelials inside match the vic."

"One Zippo lighter."

"Yes. Prints on it a match to the vic."

"Brunton wind speed and temperature meter."

"Got it."

"One length of nylon rope, approximately one hundred feet, with attached carabiners."

"Yep."

"One Suunto aluminum optical sighting compass."

"Uh-huh."

"One small instrument pouch with Velcro seal."

"Yes."

"And one suicide note, of dubious origin."

Calleigh nodded. "You know, balloonists are supposed to keep a flight log—but Breakwash's is missing."

Horatio examined the compass closely. "Yes, I noticed that. I assume that's because the actual location of Rodriguo's plane is in it—which means Breakwash would have kept it someplace safe. Someplace he didn't share with his partner . . . or his wife."

Calleigh picked up the photos of the basket she'd taken before the FAA hauled the balloon away. "I've been studying these pictures. Look at the spatter pattern on the edge of the basket and the frame of the gas burner."

Horatio took the pictures from her. "Consistent with Breakwash being shot in the head while in a standing position."

"I know—it's frustrating. I'm beginning to think we need to take a second look at the balloon itself."

"The FAA isn't ready to release it yet. But I still think there's something we're missing here . . ."

Horatio stopped, put the photos down. "Wait a minute. There *is* something missing here . . . something you'd expect to find in a hot-air balloon."

"What, H?"

Horatio smiled. "The murder weapon. Only that's not what it would have looked like to Timothy Breakwash . . . what's one of the main reasons people go up in balloons?"

"The view," said Calleigh. She saw Horatio's point an instant later, and a smile blossomed on her face as understanding did the same behind it. "A view that extends a long way in every direction. You'd want something to bring parts of it into better focus."

"So you carry binoculars," said Horatio.

The simulation wasn't hard to rig. Calleigh set up her own basket in the ballistics lab, with a dummy

standing in it. The other part took her a little
longer, but not nearly as long as Horatio would
have guessed.

"Okay," said Calleigh. "Timothy Breakwash
would have been standing. He spots something on
the ground far enough away that he wants a better
look." She pulled up a microphone stand on wheels
with a pair of binoculars clamped to the top, making sure the eyepieces lined up with the dummy's
head. "He looks through them, but something's
wrong. One of the lenses seems to be blocked.
Without even thinking about it, he does the first
thing anyone does; he fiddles with the focus knob
in the middle."

Calleigh stood to one side and put on a pair of
protective headphones, while Horatio did the same.
Then she picked up a six-foot-long stick with some
cloth wrapped around the end and used the padded
surface to carefully nudge the focus knob a few de-
grees to the left.

Blam!

The ballistic dummy jerked backward and fell
over, coming to rest with its back leaning against
the far edge of the basket. The binoculars shot
backward on their wheeled stand, spinning at the
same time.

Horatio took off his ear protectors. "And that's
how you fake a suicide in midair. You plant the
note beforehand, then get the victim to shoot himself in the head."

"It wasn't hard to build, either." Calleigh walked over to the mounted binoculars and undid the clamp holding them in place. "I hollowed out one side and mounted a spring-loaded striker with a single twenty-two cartridge in a short length of pipe—basically a zip gun. A little bit of fishing line wrapped around the focus knob tied to a stick holding the spring in place, and that's it. One shot straight through the eye."

"And the recoil sends the murder weapon into the swamp below." Horatio nodded. "Okay. Now we know how it was done. But we still don't know who did it."

"Or why. Presumably it has something to do with Rodriguo's treasure, which makes our two prime suspects the two people who knew Timothy had found it."

"But we also know that neither Randilyn or Fredo knows the location of the treasure—Fredo wouldn't have tortured Randilyn if he knew, and she would have given him the information if she had it."

Calleigh paced around the basket, her brow furrowed in thought. "So either Randilyn is a lot tougher than we thought—or she knows the location, told Fredo, and lied about it afterward."

"I don't think so," Horatio said quietly. "The torture went on for a long time, which means either she didn't talk or she couldn't—which means neither of them know where the treasure is."

"And therefore neither of them would kill the only person who did. There's only one possibility I'm seeing, Horatio."

He nodded. "There must be another partner. That person must know where the treasure is, and eliminated Breakwash to keep it to themselves."

"Which brings us back to Joel Greer, Lee Kwok, or Sylvester Perrone."

"Yes. I think maybe we need to take a closer look at all three—specifically in the areas of treasure hunting and gunsmithing. See if any of them has any diving experience, or has rented any heavy equipment recently—winches, flotation tanks, anything to do with salvage."

"I'm on it."

"Mister Perrone," said Horatio. "I was wondering if I could have a word."

Sylvester Perrone looked up from his clipboard. He stood beside a rectangular concrete tank, the lip around two feet off the ground, one of dozens arranged in a grid. Each was about twice the size of a child's wading pool, and Horatio could see the silver flicker of fish beneath the surface.

"Lieutenant Caine," Perrone said, his voice friendly. "Is the word one I'll like hearing?"

"That depends. How do you feel about murder?"

Perrone's sunny smile faded away. "What? You don't think I had anything to do with what happened to Tim, do you?"

"What I know, Mister Perrone, is that the first time I talked to you you tried to mislead me. I would advise against doing it now."

"Look, I told you—I was just trying to keep a lid on any rumors that would hurt my business. I was up-front about everything else, including what I told you about Tim."

Horatio put his hands on his hips. "What you didn't mention was how badly Sweetbright Aquaculture is doing financially. You're about to go under, Mister Perrone—unless you get a sudden and extremely large influx of cash."

Perrone's eyes hardened. "That's not going to happen, Lieutenant. I built Sweetbright myself, from the ground up, and I'm not giving up without a fight."

"No matter who gets in your way?"

"The only people getting in my way are my creditors, and I don't think killing them off would do me any good. Neither, for that matter, would killing Tim."

"Not because of *Pfiesteria* infection, no. All of Tim's data indicated he hadn't found any signs of contamination, and I don't think he was planning on blackmailing you—Timothy had his own plans for getting rich."

Perrone snorted. "Tim didn't have plans—he had dreams. Wild, unrealistic dreams about striking it rich overnight with some grandiose scheme. He was a nice guy, but I can't say I had a lot of respect for him. You know what his biggest problem was? He refused to consider the possibility of failure. I don't just mean he was optimistic, I mean he had this kind of mental block—like if he admitted that something could go wrong, then it would. He was so afraid of the downside of any project he'd just pretend it didn't exist. You can't run a business like that."

"You sound somewhat bitter, Mister Perrone."

"Do I?" Perrone shook his head. "Just frustrated, I guess. It takes a lot of hard work to succeed, and I've put in my years. I didn't just quit the first time something went wrong, and I've always tried to stay aware of any potential problems before they happened. In the end, it looks like my way of doing things might not be any more successful than Tim's."

"I can see how that would be infuriating, Mister Perrone. Especially if Timothy's methods proved, in the end, to bear fruit."

Perrone looked confused. "What's that supposed to mean?"

"It means, Mister Perrone, that Timothy Breakwash discovered something. Something important."

"What, you mean one of his crazy ideas finally paid off?"

"It did—and it's why he was killed. But the discovery I was referring to wasn't what Timothy found, it's what he learned." Horatio took out his sunglasses, unfolded the arms slowly. "That if you chase a dream long enough, sometimes you can catch it. Unfortunately, somebody else wanted that dream badly enough to commit murder. Someone who needed money. Someone with a grudge."

"Meaning me? That's insane."

"Is it? I understand you recently purchased some salvage equipment, specifically a barge with a heavy-duty winch. An odd—and expensive— choice for a businessman facing bankruptcy."

Perrone shook his head in annoyance and glanced down at his clipboard. "That's what I am, Lieutenant, a businessman. And that's what that purchase was—a business expense. I got it for a song from an associate, and in my line of work I can write off a boat at tax time. I plan on selling it for a profit after that, and I've already got someone lined up. There's nothing illegal about any of that."

"Illegal, no." Horatio slipped on his sunglasses. "Suspicious, yes. I'll be in touch, Mister Perrone."

Calleigh stood three paces behind the man with the gun. She was sure he hadn't heard her approach.

He spun around quickly when she touched his shoulder, but didn't point his weapon at her. She smiled and showed him her ID, then waited for him to remove the bright orange ear protectors he wore. "Mister Kwok? I'm CSI Calleigh Duquesne. I believe you talked with my boss earlier?"

Lee Kwok glanced around the shooting range as if he expected to see Horatio lurking somewhere in the background, then said, "Uh, yes, I did. What can I do for you?"

"Why don't we go somewhere we can talk? A gun range isn't really the best place for a conversation."

"Sure. They've got a lounge, we can talk there."

The lounge was called the Shootin' Gallery, and had the brightly lit, oak-and-brick look of an English pub that had wandered into the wrong country. Calleigh pulled up a wooden chair at a small, round table and motioned for Kwok to join her. He was dressed in jeans and a T-shirt with the name of some research conference on it, and looked distinctly uncomfortable.

"I—uh, I'm not sure what this is about," he said as he sat down. "I thought I already cleared everything up with Lieutenant Caine."

"This is just a follow-up visit," Calleigh said cheerfully. "You know, like going to the doctor. Just making sure we didn't miss anything the first time."

"Oh. I see."

Calleigh pulled out a notebook and consulted it. "So, Mister Kwok. You and Timothy Breakwash went to school together?"

"Yes. I'm still working on my Ph.D."

"Okay. I understand that when Timothy needed access to some equipment, you helped him out?"

"I didn't think I was doing anything wrong."

"No, of course not. Just a favor for a friend—we all do it. Even police officers." She smiled at him, and he smiled back tentatively.

"Beyond that, you saw him socially, too, right? You two hung around together occasionally?"

"Not very often. I had a beer with him now and then."

"Did you ever shoot together? Here, maybe?"

"No. I don't think Tim was much for guns. He owned one—a twenty-two, I think—but I doubt he ever even fired it."

The waiter showed up and took their orders. Kwok had an imported beer, Calleigh a club soda. She took a sip and then asked, "Mister Kwok, I understand your own experience with firearms is a little more extensive."

Kwok shrugged. "It's my hobby. I own quite a few."

"Is that so?" Calleigh let her smile get a little warmer. "I have quite an extensive collection myself. You ever hit any of the gun shows?"

"Oh, sure. I always hit the Southern Classic at the Dade County Fairgrounds. Picked up some nice pieces there."

"I like the Suncoast shows, myself. They've got some good older stuff."

They talked guns for a while, until Calleigh could see she'd gained Kwok's respect. Then she casually asked, "You know one of the things I find really interesting? Homemade firearms. You know, the ones that show real ingenuity."

"Oh, you mean guns built into canes, that kind of thing?"

"All sorts of objects. I've even seen guns built into remote controls—you know, the kind on a key chain you use to set your car alarm?"

"Wow, that's pretty small." Kwok grinned. "Of course, the scientific principle behind a gun is pretty basic. All you really need is a bullet, a barrel, a propellant, and something to set it off."

"Ever made anything yourself?"

"Me? When I was younger, sure. Cobbled together a zip gun out of an old piece of lead pipe, a shotgun shell, and some surgical tubing—the elastic kind they use for slingshots. Almost blew my own hand off."

"Well, I hope you're more careful these days."

"Don't worry, I am."

"I'm not the worrying type, Mister Kwok," said Calleigh. "I've found that sooner or later, things have a tendency to work themselves out."

"You believe in karma?"

Calleigh finished her drink and got to her feet. The smile she gave Kwok was just a touch cooler than before. "No. Justice."

16

"WE NEED TO FIND those binoculars," said Calleigh. She spread out a gridded map on the light table of the Everglades area she'd already searched.

Horatio bent over it, touched one point with a finger. "This is where you encountered Fredo Bolivar?"

"Yes. You think he was there to recover the murder weapon?"

"No, I think he was there looking for the treasure. He might have been tracking the balloon from the ground and trying to figure out what his partner knew but hadn't told him."

"Not a bad plan—unless Breakwash knew he was being tracked and was trying to throw him off the trail."

Horatio straightened up. "We don't have the balloon's flight plan, but there must be a more accurate way to track the path it followed."

"If Breakwash had used a cell phone instead of a radio, we might have been able to use GPS—actually, many balloonists now carry a GPS transponder. But FAA regs don't insist on it, and apparently neither did Tim Breakwash."

"Maybe, maybe not," said Horatio thoughtfully. "If you were searching for a site on the ground you wanted to be able to find later, you'd need accurate coordinates. Maybe the binoculars aren't the only thing missing from the balloon."

"In that case, the transponder should have been in the basket when the balloon crashed."

"Unless it was removed," said Horatio. "And there's only one person who could have done that . . ."

Horatio was waiting outside the hospital room when an upset-looking Joel Greer came out—so upset, in fact, that he walked right past Horatio without seeing him.

"Joel," said Horatio.

The young man stopped and looked back. "Lieutenant Caine," he said. He tried to smile. "I didn't notice you there."

"But I noticed you. Here to see Mrs. Breakwash?"

"Yeah. She—she needs her friends right now. After everything she's gone through."

"That's true. But you and Randilyn are more than just friends—aren't you, Joel?"

"What?"

Horatio took a step forward. "I took a look at your phone records, Joel. You and Randilyn spend a lot of time talking to each other."

"Well, of course we do. I worked for the Break-washes. If I couldn't reach Tim I'd phone his wife's cell."

"At three A.M.? I don't think so, Joel. You don't have a forty-five-minute conversation with the boss's wife in the middle of the night unless you're talking about a lot more than work."

Fear flashed across Joel's face and was replaced by defiance. "Yeah. Yeah, okay, I admit it. Me and Randy are in love. She'd had enough of Tim's get-rich-quick ideas—she wanted someone she could count on."

"Count on to do *what*, Joel?"

"To be there for her. Tim took her for granted—he didn't understand how hard it was for her. He was always wrapped up in his own little world, off in the clouds."

"And you," said Horatio, "were down on the ground with his wife."

"She deserved better, Lieutenant."

"Most of us do, Joel. The question is, how far are we willing to go to get it?"

"I didn't kill Tim."

"Maybe not. But you did steal the GPS transponder from the balloon after it crashed."

"Why would I do that?"

"Good question. Maybe because you knew about the treasure, and thought the transponder would tell you where it was. Maybe because you knew the transponder could lead us to the weapon that killed your boss. Or maybe just because someone told you to . . . but that doesn't really matter right now. What matters now is that I know you have it—and I want it."

"I don't—"

Horatio reached into his breast pocket and pulled out a folded piece of paper. "This is a warrant to search your vehicle and residence, Joel. I'm betting I find what I'm looking for."

Defeat registered in Joel's eyes. "And if—if you do?"

"Then our next conversation," said Horatio, "won't be quite as pleasant."

They found the GPS transponder in a desk drawer in Joel Greer's small apartment, and took Greer into custody. Horatio sent the transponder to the AV lab; Cooper was able to pull coordinates for Timothy Breakwash's last journey off it, finally giving them a definite flight path to follow. The murder weapon was still missing, but now they had a much better idea of where it might be. Horatio made some calls and prepared to return to the swamp.

A few hours later at the edge of the Everglades, Horatio surveyed his troops. They consisted of twenty police academy cadets, plus Calleigh, Wolfe, and Delko. "Okay. I know some of you have been out here before, without any success. We're going to try again, and this time we know exactly what we're looking for: a pair of binoculars. Our previous calculations of the search area were off by nearly twenty percent, which means most of the ground you'll be covering will be new. Stay alert, keep an eye out for snakes and gators, and be aware that there may be others searching for the same thing we are. Eric, you'll be coordinating any water searches that have to be made; Mister Wolfe, you're with me. Calleigh's the primary—anything you find, report to her."

Wolfe walked over as the searchers dispersed. "What do you need, H?"

"Thank you for lending a hand, Mister Wolfe. I'll let you get back to your own investigation shortly."

Wolfe shrugged. "Glad to help. Delko and I are kind of stuck at the moment, anyway—maybe this'll shake something loose."

"You never can tell, Mister Wolfe, you never can tell . . . Calleigh and Eric can handle the swamp search. I need you to check on something else for me."

"Okay—but why me?"

Horatio smiled. "Because it's a job that requires obsessive attention to detail. While Calleigh could certainly handle it, I need her in the field—and sometimes, you have to play to your team's strengths."

"I'm flattered—I think. What's the job?"

"I need you to go through every website Timothy Breakwash had bookmarked and look through all his paperwork and reference material. If he could find Rodriguo's treasure, then so can we."

Wolfe nodded. "Re-create his research, and hopefully come to the same conclusion. Like staging a re-enactment of a crime scene."

"Exactly, Mister Wolfe. Because whoever killed Timothy Breakwash is going to be headed for the site he discovered . . . and I intend to be there to greet them."

"So Wolfe gets to do research," Delko grumbled, "while we have to search a swamp. Figures."

"Oh, come on, Eric," said Calleigh. She was a few steps behind him, applying some extra mosquito repellent as she walked. "It's not so bad. You've got me for company, right?"

Delko smiled ruefully. "Yeah, I guess. At least I don't have to lug all my equipment by myself."

"Eric Delko. I am *not* a pack horse."

"No, that's the cadet's responsibility—yours is to keep them in line."

"So I'm a cowgirl?"

"I'll get you a hat and some boots."

"Just make sure they match. I hate leading a roundup in the wrong accessories."

He laughed. "All right, I'll quit complaining."

She grinned and rubbed some bug repellent on

her throat. "At least you get to spend some time in the water, away from Florida's national bird."

"You think the mosquitoes are bad? Try leeches. Not to mention water moccasins, snapping turtles, and the occasional alligator."

"I thought you said you weren't going to complain anymore."

"That wasn't a complaint. That was my job description."

The heat was brutal. Swarms of gnats hovered around their heads like a haze of smoke, and the air seemed thick and heavy. The humid, rotting smell of vegetation was so strong Delko thought he could taste it as well as smell it. Even the sounds of the Everglades seemed slow and hypnotic, a buzzing, sloshing melody only occasionally punctuated by the shrill cry of a bird or animal.

It wasn't long before they came to the first deep pool and Eric had to suit up. He knew visibility would be poor, but he'd be relying more on his waterproofed metal detector than his eyes.

"Keep an eye out for gators," he told Calleigh as he slipped on his mask.

"Got you covered," she answered, patting her sidearm. Normally Delko would have preferred his spotter to carry a rifle—but if Calleigh thought she was carrying enough stopping power for a large, hungry lizard, Delko knew better than to argue.

He bit down on his mouthpiece and waded in.

*   *   *

Horatio had his own task to accomplish.

He hadn't confronted Randilyn at the hospital when he'd spoken to Joel Greer, because according to the nurse on duty she was heavily sedated and only semiconscious. But that's where he was headed now, because Randilyn Breakwash was the one piece of the puzzle he couldn't quite figure out.

He mulled it over as he drove. She clearly had a great deal of resentment toward her deceased husband, but that didn't mean she'd killed him; Horatio would have been more suspicious if she'd appeared overcome with remorse. Instead, she seemed angry that Timothy had died, a much more honest response that Horatio had seen many times before. Survivors were often angry; angry at the victim for leaving them, angry at themselves for all the things they never said or did. Angry they couldn't save the one they loved, or even angry they didn't get to end the life of someone they hated.

A lot of that anger was frequently misplaced guilt, and Randilyn certainly had reason to feel that. *The question is,* Horatio thought, *what is it she's guilty of? An affair with another man, or the death of her husband?*

He kept coming back to the torture. It seemed to him that it proved conclusively that neither Randilyn nor Fredo could be the killer. Such an extreme act wouldn't be undertaken unless absolutely necessary; the fact that Fredo had gone to such lengths meant he didn't know where the treasure was, and Randilyn's injuries were horrifying enough to convince Horatio she would have talked if she could have.

Maybe one of them killed Timothy because they thought they knew *the location of the treasure, but were then proven wrong?* Horatio considered the idea— then rejected it. While Tim might have been smart enough to set up a decoy, the killer was too careful to fall for such a trap; the elaborate method of the murder proved that. Whoever had killed Timothy Breakwash was a thorough planner.

That left Joel Greer, Lee Kwok, and Sylvester Perrone. The first was sleeping with the victim's wife, the second had experience with firearms and science, the third needed the money and had access to salvage equipment. *Which one is the third partner?*

He didn't know. He suspected that neither Fredo Bolivar nor Randilyn Breakwash knew either, but it was possible Randilyn had information she didn't know was valuable. Horatio intended to confront her about her affair with Joel Greer and see if he could learn anything new.

He thought about all the suffering Fredo Bolivar had put Randilyn through, trying to get her to give information she didn't have. Bolivar hadn't realized one of the truths Horatio lived with every day: Getting the answers you needed wasn't so much a matter of how you asked, but of choosing the right questions in the first place.

"Questions, questions, questions," Wolfe muttered to himself. "Too many questions . . ."

He was at a workstation in the layout room. The light table behind him was piled high with books, stacks of file folders and magazines, all of it from Timothy Breakwash's study. Wolfe had spent the first hour just dividing it into different categories, and now he was doing the same for the computer files.

He was looking through Breakwash's emails at the moment. The man seemed to have corresponded with hundreds of people on all sorts of topics, but Wolfe was concentrating on the last six months and anything that might be connected to Rodriguo's treasure: missing Cuban art, smuggling stories, information on plane crashes in Florida. There was a ton of material to go through, but he finally hit gold when he noticed a bunch of emails from one particular edress, swamphunter@floridacrimehistory.com. They'd carried on a lengthy correspondence concerning Rodriguo, a subject swamphunter seemed to know a lot about:

> Rodriguo was the last and best of the so-called "cocaine cowboys." He was innovative, fearless, and smart. Law enforcement was never able to even get a picture of him, let alone catch him.

Estimates of his net worth at the time he disappeared run as high as five hundred million dollars—amazing for someone who was really no more than an ambitious smuggler. The money is no doubt long gone, but I'm convinced at least a quarter of his fortune was spent on art—Rodriguo's Legacy, as it's sometimes called. It was intended to buy his way into Castro's inner circle, where he could retire without fear of reprisal from the U.S. Some people ask why he would choose to retire in a communist country where luxuries are controlled, when he could live like a king somewhere else. I believe the answer is simple: Cuba was Rodriguo's home. It's where he came from and where he wanted to return to. I think he was tired of the high life, tired of the danger and pressure of who he'd become—and going back to his homeland with a few hundred million in his pocket would give him all the security he'd ever need.

"Sounds like a fan," Wolfe murmured. "Or maybe somebody a little closer . . ."

Calleigh was the one who found it.

It was in one of the areas they hadn't searched the first two times, half buried in a patch of mud. Calleigh called out for everyone to stop, knelt, and carefully pulled it out of the muck.

The binoculars were pretty much exactly as

she'd predicted: shattered glass in one eyepiece and what looked like the end of a metal pipe in the interior. There was a piece of fishing line wound around the focus knob, leading to a tiny hole drilled in the doctored side.

"You called it," said Delko. He was dressed in his wetsuit, flippers slung over his back; he'd had to dive so often he'd given up changing between times, just had one of the cadets haul his tanks between pools. "Just like what you came up with in the lab."

Calleigh slipped the muddy binoculars into an evidence pouch. "With one major difference—this pair killed a man."

"Think we can pull anything useful off it?"

"Won't know until I get it back to the lab."

"The sooner, the better," Delko said with a grin.

Calleigh called Horatio on her way back to her Hummer. "Horatio? We've got it. We were right."

"Good work. I'm at the hospital."

"You speak with Randilyn Breakwash?"

"That was my intention . . . but she's no longer here. It seems that she checked herself out, against the advice of her doctors. Joel Greer must have spoken to her."

"You think she's running?"

"I don't know. I'm on my way to her residence—if she's not there, we have to assume she's in the wind. Get those binoculars into the lab and make them talk."

"I'm on my way."

*   *   *

"Cooper, you got a minute?" asked Wolfe from the doorway.

Cooper didn't answer, studying the screen in front of him intently. Wolfe walked into the AV lab, noticed the earplugs in the tech's ears, and tugged on one, pulling it free and spilling tinny music into the air. Cooper looked up, startled, and swiveled in his chair. "Oh, hey, Wolfe. What's up?"

"I hate to take you away from—is that Beyoncé?"

Cooper tapped a key and the image vanished, replaced by a graph. "Music video. Helps me relax between projects."

Wolfe folded his arms. "Relax? Or goof off?"

"You say tomato, I say potato. Or rutabaga, or some other appropriate vegetable. I never really got the hang of that saying."

"I need to know who Timothy Breakwash was corresponding with on the Internet before he was killed." He gave Cooper the information he had on swamphunter. "Think you can track it down?"

"You're in luck. The IP address is local—which makes sense for something named floridacrimehistory.com—so it's not like I'm trying to trace a website out of the Netherlands." Cooper tapped away at his keyboard. "Okay, here's the address of the company that owns the domain name. Ask them nice and maybe they'll cough up swamphunter's info— if not, you'll have to get a warrant."

"I'll try the polite way, first. Considering the topic of the website, they might be friendly to law enforcement."

"Or lawbreakers." Cooper shrugged. "Apples and oranges. Or maybe pomegranates and pineapples."

Wolfe shook his head. "Do me a favor—stay away from the produce section, okay?"

Wolfe's instincts proved correct. The owner of the website—a portly, ginger-haired man wearing an NYPD T-shirt and baseball cap—was more than happy to help, giving Wolfe swamphunter's real name, address, and phone number.

It wasn't who Wolfe expected.

Horatio pulled his Hummer into the Breakwash driveway. The garage door was wide open, revealing not only Timothy Breakwash's home lab, but another kind of vehicle entirely: the balloon that had carried its owner's body back to Earth.

"Hello? Mrs. Breakwash?" Horatio approached the garage cautiously, but there didn't seem to be anyone around. He stood at the threshold for a moment, hands on hips, then moved to the front door and knocked. No answer.

He returned to the garage and walked inside. The balloon had apparently arrived as a neatly wrapped bundle of fabric, but it had been pulled apart since then. Folds of brightly colored polyester spilled across the floor and draped over the basket.

Horatio pulled out his cell phone and punched in

a number. "Yes, Mister Pinlon, please . . . hello, this is Lieutenant Horatio Caine. I have a question about the balloon investigation you're conducting. It's my understanding you were to turn the balloon itself over to the Miami-Dade crime lab once you were finished with it. Uh-huh. Well, I'm looking at it right now, and it's not in my lab. It's been returned to the next of kin of its former owner . . . yes, I understand that's the normal protocol, but not when a crime has been committed." Horatio listened, then sighed. "Yes, of course. Bureaucratic oversight. Unfortunately, your mistake may have just cost me my prime suspect."

Horatio disconnected, then took a closer look at the balloon. A ragged chunk of the envelope was missing, apparently cut out. *Of course. He concealed the coordinates of the downed plane in the balloon, probably written on the nylon itself. Whoever cut this scrap out is no doubt headed there right now.*

They had the murder weapon; the killer had the location of the treasure. But there was still one piece missing—Timothy Breakwash's flight log. Joel Greer didn't have it, and it hadn't been found at the scene or in the balloon. Where would Breakwash have hidden it?

There was only one place Horatio could think of: at the site of the treasure itself. After all, Breakwash wouldn't need the coordinates—those were with the balloon. But the flight log would still be valuable to him, too valuable to destroy; it was, after all, a chronicle of his success after years of failure. It was the document he could hold up later and say, *This is how it happened. This is where I was and what I was doing when all my dreams came true.*

Horatio eyed the cut fabric draped over the edge of the basket. "That was the high point of your life, wasn't it?" he said softly. "But what goes up . . . must come down."

Wolfe had been sure swamphunter would turn out to be Fredo Bolivar, but he'd been wrong. Swamphunter was a retired DEA agent named Garrett Mc-Culver—the same one Horatio had gone to as a source.

It made sense, Wolfe had to admit. These days, everyone turned to the Internet for research, and it was only natural that two people obsessed with the same subject would meet online. Neither one would know anything about the other; an ex-cop and an ex-con could become friends without ever meeting face-to-face or even knowing the other's real name. But . . .

But the online name McCulver had chosen both-ered Wolfe.

He thought about it as he drove out to McCul-ver's place. Swamphunter. Maybe McCulver liked to shoot ducks in the 'Glades, or even bag himself some venison every season.

Or maybe he was more interested in hunting something else.

McCulver had quit the DEA out of disgust with how they operated, or so Wolfe had heard; Calleigh had mentioned some of the details of the case in the break room. Wolfe had no love for drugs—being an obsessive-compulsive gave his brain enough problems, thank you—but he had to admit he had his own reservations about the drug war and how it was being conducted. Confiscating a dealer's expensive toys made sense on the surface, but combining that with a zero-tolerance policy meant someone could lose his house or business if so much as a single joint were found, and Wolfe had seen exactly that happen. But the thing that bothered Wolfe the most was what happened to all the houses and cars and boats confiscated by the DEA: They were sold at auction . . . and the profits went directly into the DEA's budget. It was a self-reinforcing system that had reminded Wolfe of the case he and Delko were working.

"Of course it does," Calleigh had said. "You guys are dealing with pirates, and the DEA are privateers: pirates with a government license to operate. Countries used to provide what was known as a letter of marque to pirates, who were then authorized to plunder ships from other countries—or at least those nations they weren't on friendly terms with. The privateers kept the proceeds, just like the DEA does today—but instead of being at war with Spain or France, we've declared hostilities against the drug cartels."

"Or anyone with a package of rolling papers," Wolfe had pointed out.

"Well, that's the problem with employing pirates—sorry, privateers. Once you give them the authority and incentive to take what they want, it's kind of hard to rein them in. A lot of privateers acted exactly the same as pirates, attacking any ship that came along. Eventually it was agreed to be a bad idea all around and countries stopped employing them."

McCulver had seen that process firsthand, and according to Calleigh it hadn't sat well with him. Wolfe had read all the emails swamphunter and Breakwash had exchanged, and it was obvious the ex-cop had a great deal of respect for the smuggler he had pursued but never caught. It was as if, over the years, McCulver had gradually lost faith in those he worked with, and come to admire the criminal he was supposed to bring down.

Wolfe shook his head. If the DEA were pirates, what did that make Rodriguo in McCulver's eyes? A victim? Or an antihero trading drug profits for art, risking everything for a chance at a new life in his homeland?

Wolfe didn't know. He also didn't know exactly how deeply McCulver was involved—there were gaps in the emails that suggested some of them had been deleted, though that was just guesswork. What he did know was that McCulver wasn't answering his phone, so he was going out to see him in person.

He parked the Hummer in front of McCulver's small place and got out. A beat-up Jeep was pulled into the driveway, but Wolfe didn't know if it was McCulver's or not.

He knocked on the front door and waited. No answer. Wolfe listened intently, trying to judge if there was nobody at home or if McCulver was just avoiding company. He thought he heard music, but it was so faint it might have been coming from somewhere else—McCulver's place was right on the shore, and sound sometimes carried in funny ways over the water.

He tried the door. Locked.

The windows on the front of the house were blocked with blinds. Wolfe made his way around the side of the house and was rewarded with a window looking into an empty bathroom. He kept moving, reached the corner, and took a cautious look around it. There was a small deck looking out on the shore, with a gull perched on a Styrofoam cooler. It noticed him and cocked its head in an inquisitive way, as if it had more of a right to be there than he did. Two empty lawn chairs were the only other thing on the deck, but the patio door was ajar.

Wolfe stepped onto the deck, prompting the gull to take wing with a loud, piercing cry. "Hello?" Wolfe called out. "Mister McCulver? Anyone home?"

Still no answer, but now he could tell the music

was definitely coming from inside. The Rolling
Stones' "Satisfaction," sounding like it was being
funneled through a very small speaker.

Wolfe glanced around, trying to decide what to
do. He had a bad feeling about the situation—
somehow, he didn't think an ex-cop like McCulver
would leave his house open like this. He took a
deep breath, drew his gun, and stepped inside.

The living room wasn't large, nor was it tidy.
Newspapers were stacked on the couch, the coffee
table was crowded with empty beer cans and a
stack of pizza cartons, the rug looked like it hadn't
been vacuumed in months. The bright, flickering
hues of a computer screen in the corner caught his
attention; online advertising cycling around the pe-
riphery of a webpage. He walked over for a closer
look and saw the source of the music: a pair of
headphones plugged into the computer.

"Hold it right there," a voice said to his left.

Wolfe turned his head slightly. Garrett McCulver
stood in the hall, a .45 automatic in his hand.

It was aimed at Wolfe's heart.

17

CHERISE DAMEO looked so nervous sitting in the interview room that Natalia almost felt sorry for her. Tripp, on the other hand, was looking at her like she was a red piñata and he was a bull with a baseball bat.

"So, Cherise," said Natalia. "We got the results back from the blood sample we took."

Cherise tried to smile. "So, how long do I have to live, Doc?"

Natalia didn't smile back. "That depends on the appeals process, I guess. And whether you get the death penalty."

"Wh-what?"

"Your blood was a match to blood found at the crime scene of Hiram Davey's murder. His book was going to reveal you were the body double in Marssai Guardon's X-rated video, and that would have gotten you in deep trouble with your folks—deeper than you could handle. So you killed him, and stole his laptop."

"No! That's—that's not what happened at all!"

Tripp leaned forward. "No? You had a lot to lose, Cherise. Miami's a real playground, as long as you have money—but once the 'rents cut off your allowance, you're not allowed in the sandbox anymore. No more parties, no more clubbing, no more drinking Cristal with celebrities by poolside. You couldn't handle saying good-bye to all that, so you said it to Hi Davey instead."

"You've got it all *wrong*. I didn't kill *anyone*." She started to cry.

"Your blood says otherwise," said Natalia.

"My blood? I can explain that."

"Go ahead," Tripp growled.

"Okay, I was at Davey's place. And I *did* go there because I was afraid he was going to tell people about me in his book. Marssai thought the whole thing was just a big joke, but I'm not like her—she's got all these plans to make money, but I don't. I couldn't stand being broke, I just couldn't."

"So far, you're not helping your case much," said Tripp.

"Okay, okay. It's just—this is *embarrassing*, all right? I convinced Davey to change his mind."

Natalia raised an eyebrow.

"Yes, I *slept* with him, okay? I figured if I was nice to him, he'd be nice back. I mean, it wasn't like he was covering up some big crime, right? All he had to do was not use my real name."

"And the blood?" asked Natalia.

"I was nervous. We were cutting up some limes to do tequila shots and I cut myself. You know how you can do that sometimes, and if the knife is sharp enough you don't even notice right away? Look." She held up her hand—the index finger had a Band-Aid wrapped around it. "Can't you do some kind of CSI test thingy to prove I'm telling the truth?"

"Let me take a look at that," said Natalia. Cherise held out her hand and Natalia carefully peeled the Band-Aid back. The skin beneath was white and wrinkled, with jagged edges around the wound itself. "Cherise, what kind of knife were you cutting the limes with?"

"A steak knife. You know, one of those ones with the ripply blades, like a saw or something."

Natalia sighed. "Well, this cut is consistent with one made by a serrated knife—and Davey's wounds were made by a straight-edged blade. I guess you're telling the truth."

"Oh, thank you. Thank you," said Cherise. She took a long, shaky breath. "I was so afraid."

"It's all right," said Tripp. His own face had softened. "Maybe you should rethink some of the people you hang around with, though. Keep running with that crowd, and sooner or later you won't be so lucky."

"I will. I will, I promise."

"So what time did you leave Davey's place?" asked Natalia.

"I didn't stay for long afterward—I told him I had a party I had to go to. It was around eleven, I think. I was a little worried he might want to come with me, but he didn't even ask. He just looked kind of sad when he said goodnight."

"Well," said Tripp, "Davey might have been a goofball, but he wasn't stupid. I think he knew the score."

"He didn't *have* to sleep with me," said Cherise, a hint of defensiveness in her voice.

"No, he didn't," said Tripp. "But sometimes, being used is better than being alone."

Despite the heat, despite having to dive in murky pools that might hold any number of hostile or poisonous animals, Delko was almost sorry when Calleigh found the binoculars. Diving always helped center him, cleared away any mental cobwebs. When he was underwater, it was like some part of him woke up, a part that had been patiently waiting for him to return to the sea—or it might be just the focus that came with knowing he was in a dangerous environment, where inattention to any detail might kill him.

Maybe it was that focus that finally gave him the clue to solving the Dragoslav case, or maybe it was just dumb luck that he noticed something in the water with him. He paid no attention to it at the time, but the image of it kept coming back to his mind's eye, even after he'd left the 'Glades and returned to the lab. He thought it was just simple natural beauty at first, the way it had diffused the sunlight shining through it from above, but the image was accompanied by a nagging feeling of something left undone, something important he'd forgotten. Even more frustrating, for some reason he associated the image with—of all things—wheelbarrows.

And then he remembered the story he'd told Wolfe, and everything clicked into place.

He actually laughed out loud, causing the only other person in the lab—Natalia—to look up from her notes. "I miss something?" she asked, smiling.

"No, *I* did. Something obvious. Something right in front of my face the whole time."

"If it was a snake, it would have bit you?"

"Not a snake," said Delko. "A fish."

Natalia nodded. "Ah, the infamous fish I've been hearing about. Sounds like a case my vic would have loved."

"Hiram Davey, right? How's that going?"

Natalia sighed. "Coming along. We've narrowed the suspects down to a crazy woman obsessed with frogs or a career con man. I'll let you know."

"Frogs, huh? So I guess you're looking for who croaked him."

Natalia gave him a look.

Delko grinned. "Hey, I've been getting hit with fish jokes for the last two days."

"So you take it out on me?"

"Sorry. Didn't think you were so sensitive."

She frowned. "I'm not. I mean, I can take a joke as well as—"

"'Cause you seem a little . . . jumpy. Or would that be hoppy?"

Her look turned into a glare. "Oh, very clever. Fish boy."

"Frog princess."

"*Sushi* scientist!"

Frank Tripp walked through the door. "Get a room," he said. "One with a waterbed, from the sounds of things . . . Natalia, the warrant's ready. I'm just heading over to the bowling alley."

"I'll come with you. Later, Aquaman."

"I'll pass along your regards to any tadpoles I run into," he called after her.

Natalia was doing her own version of fishing—which had less to do with a hook and a line than throwing a stick of dynamite into the water and seeing what floated to the surface. She already knew about Gordon Dettweiler's previous arrests; now she was going to use that knowledge to apply some pressure. Based on Dettweiler's prison record and his possible involvement in a homicide, she'd obtained a warrant to search his home, his vehicles, and his place of business, looking for either the knife used to murder

Hiram Davey or the laptop that had been stolen from Davey's home. She didn't think she'd find either, but it would let her shut down the alley for the day while it was searched; that wouldn't look good to all the community businesses contributing to the bowling tournament. Maybe if she pushed him hard enough, she could get him to make a mistake.

Natalia handed the warrant to Dettweiler at On a Roll Bowl personally. He read it with a growing look of dismay on his face, which gave Natalia a great deal more satisfaction than she'd expected.

"This is—this is harassment," said Dettweiler. "You want to search my home, my car, and my boat? Fine. But at least let me keep the alley open."

Frank Tripp, standing behind Natalia, shook his head. "'Fraid not. This place is closed, as of now."

"For how long?"

"Until we're done," said Natalia sweetly. "We'll let you know."

"This ain't over," Dettweiler growled. He stuffed the warrant in the back pocket of his jeans and stalked off.

"You play hardball," Tripp said, watching Dettweiler leave. "I think you just stomped all the good out of that good ol' boy."

"I may have a manicure," said Natalia, "but I can still throw a punch."

Natalia honestly didn't expect to find anything in Gordon Dettweiler's house, vehicles, or business; if he'd killed Hiram Davey, he was too smart to make a mistake like keeping the murder weapon or the laptop around. But even smart killers slipped up, and it was her job to spot those slips.

She searched the house first. It was nothing re-markable, a two-bedroom bungalow on the out-skirts of Homestead, but it was well-defended; Dettweiler had installed bars on all the windows, steel-cored doors at the front and back with heavy-duty locks, and a top-of-the-line security system. "What are you protecting?" she murmured to her-self as she stepped through the front door and dis-abled the alarm system with the code she'd been given.

Whatever it was, she didn't find it. She confis-cated all the knives in the kitchen, but didn't find anything like a laptop. It was hard to believe the house belonged to someone with Dettweiler's folksy personality; the resident seemed to favor ex-pensive wines, Danish Modern furniture, and French cuisine. If it weren't for other indicators—a photo of him with a woman, his name on discarded junk mail, and the label of a prescription cream in the bathroom—Natalia wouldn't have believed he actually lived there. Gordon Dettweiler was clearly a very different person in private than in public—as no doubt previous victims of his scams had already found out.

The boat and four-by-four he drove were more in keeping with his down-home persona, sporting a gun rack and winch on the SUV and plenty of bass-fishing equipment on the boat. That made sense; they were places he interacted with the world, places where his carefully designed façade was on full view. Natalia began to understand why the house had been so heavily fortified—it was where he kept the real Gordon Dettweiler, the one who read the *Wall Street Journal* and listened to classical music. The boat looked like he lived aboard it at least part of the time, and she was willing to bet none of his "friends" had ever set foot in Dettweiler's house—if they even knew he had one.

She took some filleting knives from the boat, then moved on to the bowling alley. It had a lunch counter, and she confiscated everything with an edge she could find. Tripp walked through the front door just as she was bagging the last blade.

"Any luck?" he asked.

"Won't know for sure until I process everything at the lab. But so far, it doesn't look good."

Tripp glanced over at the empty lanes. "You know, I've been giving this a lot of thought. The only way I can figure out for Dettweiler to make a profit out of this tournament is if he controls who wins."

Natalia walked out from behind the lunch counter. "What, you mean, like paying someone to throw a game?"

"Nah, that wouldn't work in a tournament. You'd have to give someone an unbeatable edge, then bet heavily on them. If they were in on it, you wouldn't have to worry about the prize money either—just divide up the entry fees and whatever sponsor money you'd managed to generate. The gambling profits would be the big payout."

Natalia frowned. "How, Frank? I mean, it's a pretty simple game—what do you do, glue the other guys' pins to the floor?"

"I don't know. But this might be our chance to find out."

"What do you have in mind?"

"The warrant specifies that we're looking for a laptop or a knife, right? Well, there's all kinds of maintenance spaces behind and beneath these alleys—perfect hiding place for a murder weapon or a missing piece of hardware."

"You sound like you have something in mind, Frank."

Tripp scratched his chin. "Noticed something when we served the warrant—Dettweiler's pal Leroy was rolling a few, at the same lane he was the first time we showed up. Threw a strike, then sat down like it tuckered him right out."

"I don't follow."

"Let's just say I'd like to take a closer look at the lane. Indulge me, okay?"

"Sure, Frank. Let's check it out."

Access to the space behind the pins was through a door between two of the lanes. The room was narrow, dirty, and crowded with machinery, illuminated by a bare bulb in a wire cage.

"This is it right here," said Tripp. "Lane twelve."

Natalia pulled out a flashlight and shone it on the pin machinery. "I don't really know what I'm looking at here, Frank."

"I do," he said. "My cousin owned a bowling alley in El Paso. Worked there summers when I was a kid." He knelt down and said, "Let me have that flashlight for a second, will you?"

She handed it over, and he shone it at the lip of polished wood where the lane itself ended. "Uh-huh," he said. "You see that?"

Natalia leaned over and took a closer look. "Is that what I think it is?"

"If you think it's the reason Hi Davey was killed," said Tripp, "it most definitely is."

18

DELKO FOUND JOVAN Dragoslav at a restaurant—not surprisingly, one of the most expensive and exclusive dining establishments in Miami. When the maître d' asked him if he had a reservation, Delko showed him his badge. The man glanced at the two uniformed officers behind him and said, "Table for three?"

"We won't be staying," said Delko. "As a matter of fact, you'll have a table opening up in just a minute."

Delko made his way through a maze of white-clothed tables, most of them empty—it was too early for the dinner rush and too late for the lunch crowd. Dragoslav was sitting at a table next to the window, looking out over the ocean; the restaurant was on the twentieth floor of a skyscraper, with an impressive seaside view. His companion was blonde, beautiful, young enough to be his daughter but apparently old enough to drink champagne. Delko thought she looked familiar, but that happened a lot in Miami; you saw a stunningly attractive woman who reminded you of someone, and then realized you were thinking of an actress or a singer or a model—not even someone famous, necessarily, just someone you'd seen in a toothpaste ad or a music video. You weren't so much recognizing them as identifying which tribe they belonged to.

"Mister Dragoslav," said Delko. "Enjoying the cuisine?"

Dragoslav regarded him coldly. "I was, until now. I warned your partner that I would pursue charges against him if he continued to harass me, and that applies to you as well."

"Oh, this isn't harassment. This is an arrest. Mind if I sit down?" He pulled out a chair and sat in it without waiting for permission.

"Go ahead, do your best to humiliate me," said Dragoslav. "The greater the spectacle, the more ammunition I have. I look forward to asking for your badge as a souvenir."

"I wouldn't go reserving a spot in your trophy case just yet. In fact, you'd be better served by enjoying what's left of your meal while I talk. It might be the last good one you're going to have for a while."

"Truly? That seems unlikely."

"Yeah, well, this whole case has been unlikely. I have to admit, trying to figure out just what it was you were smuggling drove me about half crazy. I knew it had something to do with that moonfish— or sunfish, or even toppled-car fish—you had in that concealed freezer, but I just couldn't figure out what. And then it hit me—wheelbarrows."

"I beg your pardon?"

"You know the story about the guy smuggling wheelbarrows? Border guard so focused on the content of the wheelbarrow he overlooked the thing itself? That's kind of what you were doing, except I didn't look quite hard enough. You weren't smuggling wheelbarrows, you were smuggling wheelbarrow *wheels*."

"You are not making any sense."

Delko reached over and plucked a peeled shrimp from Dragoslav's plate. He popped it into his mouth and chewed. "That's really good," he said approvingly. "You always demand the best, right? I saw the buffet you had laid out on the boat—impressive. But then, you were about to sign a deal with a guy who thought of himself as a gourmet, so you had to step up. Brought in all kinds of goodies: expensive cheeses, foie gras, truffles . . . and seafood."

"There is nothing illegal about any of that." Dragoslav was good; his face gave nothing away.

"You know what I said about wheelbarrow wheels? I'm going to stretch the metaphor just a little bit more and change it to wheelbarrow bearings. You know, the little round things inside the wheel itself?" Delko smiled—a wide, expectant smile.

Dragoslav refused to play. "If you have an accusation to make, Officer, then do so. This is beginning to bore me."

"Have it your way." Delko leaned back in his chair. "I knew the fish was important, but I didn't know why. It's an unusual creature, and for a while that threw me—I wasn't sure which odd feature made you choose it. Was it the number of parasites it hosts? The fact that its flesh can produce tetrodotoxin poisoning? Or was it maybe something as simple as its sheer size?"

Delko shook his head. "No. It was because the ocean sunfish is the most fecund animal on the planet, capable of producing more than three hundred million eggs at a time. Eggs that you scooped out and replaced . . . with more fish eggs."

Dragoslav finally returned Delko's smile. It was the look of a man who has just been beaten at chess but still considers himself the superior player.

"Beluga caviar," said Delko. "The sturgeon that produces it has become so rare that in 2006 its eggs actually became an illegal substance in the U.S. The ban was lifted the next year, but even then only a very small amount was allowed to be imported into the country. That was good news to black marketeers; the legal caviar trade generates around a hundred million dollars annually, but the illegal version makes five times that. At a street value of over seven thousand dollars a kilo, I figure the shipment you brought in was probably worth around one point two million. And once you had your distribution network in place—the Luccinis' trucks and Wolchkowski's supermarkets—you could count on a nice, steady stream of income."

"And how do you propose to prove this? Considering that no such caviar was found on my ship."

"Because you dumped it overboard when the shooting started? Sorry, Jovan. There were more than enough eggs left on the inside of the sunfish's ovary for me to collect a sample, and DNA testing established exactly which species they came from. You're under arrest for the illegal importation of a restricted substance."

"For which I will receive a fine, no doubt," said Dragoslav. He yawned theatrically.

"Oh, it's not the fine you'll care about. It's the fact that now that I've figured your method out, you can't use it anymore. That's going to cost you a lot of money. Not to mention losing face with the Luccinis—they don't like dealing with failures. So all in all, I figure I just gave your organization a big, nasty black eye."

Delko motioned to the officers waiting behind him. "Hook him up."

After Dragoslav had been handcuffed and taken away, his dining companion—who had watched the entire conversation with wide, disbelieving eyes—waved at Delko as he was about to leave. "Excuse me," she said. "Umm—who's going to pay for this?" She indicated the half-eaten meal on the table in front of her.

Delko shrugged. "I guess he will," he said. "One way or another."

"Does this mean I finally get my bowling alley back?" Gordon Dettweiler asked. He smiled genially, as if the Miami-Dade Police Department were doing him a favor he greatly appreciated.

"Not just yet," said Natalia. She motioned Dettweiler inside the On a Roll Bowl, then closed and locked the door behind him. "We've got a little experiment we'd like you to see."

Frank Tripp was waiting in the booth in front of lane eleven. "Hey there, Gord. Glad you could make it."

"I hope you folks are about done," said Dettweiler. "I'd like to get back to business—lot of people need to get their practice in before the tournament, you know."

"Is that so?" said Natalia. "Well, bowling was never my game. How about you, Frank?"

"Never had much interest, myself," said Tripp.

Dettweiler chuckled. "Well, I suppose it's not everyone's slice of pie—"

"Know what I always liked?" asked Natalia. "Marbles."

"Sure," said Frank. "Played it all the time as a kid. Best in my neighborhood."

"Oh, I think I could have taken you."

"Doubt it."

"Matter of fact, I could *still* take you."

"Think so, huh? Care to make a little wager on it?"

"Absolutely." Natalia turned to Dettweiler, whose friendly smile was starting to look a little confused. "You a gambling man, Gord?"

"I don't really see what this has to do—"

"Tell you what, Frank," said Natalia. She walked up to the edge of lane eleven and pulled a short cardboard tube from her purse—the core of a roll of toilet paper. "I'll bet you a steak dinner I can put a marble through this roll from the length of an alley away. One shot. What do you say?"

"You're on."

Natalia walked the length of the alley and placed the tube where the headpin usually was, then walked back. "Lucky for us, I even have a marble with me." She produced a cat's-eye from her pocket and held it up. "See?"

The look on Dettweiler's face was now a carefully composed smile.

Natalia knelt and placed the marble carefully at the toe line. She lined up her shot, then flicked the marble with her forefinger. It made it about three-quarters of the way down the lane before rolling into the gutter.

"Tough luck," said Tripp. "I prefer a nice sirloin. Medium rare."

"Oh, come on, Frank." Natalia got to her feet. "I

was just getting warmed up. How about giving me another chance?"

"I'll take a second steak dinner if you want to risk it."

"I was thinking of more interesting terms this time. Say, for instance—Mister Dettweiler's freedom?"

"Now hold on a sec—" Dettweiler began.

"Fine with me," Tripp interrupted. "Same conditions?"

"No, I think this time we'll change things around a bit. First, let's use a different location." She walked back toward the pins, picked up the tube, and moved it over to lane twelve before returning to where Tripp and Dettweiler waited.

"Don't see as how that should make a difference," said Tripp.

"Now, I'm afraid that was my last marble—and I don't think the ball return is going to cough it up. But I've got something just as good." She pulled a small plastic baggie full of ball bearings out of her purse. "That okay with you, Frank?"

"I don't know, Natalia. Doesn't seem quite right to me."

"Oh? Tell you what, Frank—how about if I put *ten* of these through that tube? That satisfy you?"

"Yeah, that seems fair. What do you think, Gord?"

Dettweiler didn't answer. He looked like a cruise ship novice who'd spent all his time at the buffet just before the sea turned rough.

Natalia grabbed a handful of ball bearings. She rolled one after another in quick succession down the lane, not even pausing to aim. Every single one shot straight down the center and through the tube at the end.

"Well," said Tripp. He turned his head and stared at Dettweiler. "How about that. You're one hell of a marble player, Natalia."

"Well, it helps when there's an electromagnetic strip right down the center of the alley," said Natalia. She smiled at Dettweiler like a cat considering an extremely plump mouse. "And if you were the one who assigns lanes during a tournament, you could even make sure that your buddy with the custom-made ball—a ball with a layer of iron close to the surface—always got that particular lane when it mattered the most."

Dettweiler's grin had returned, though it didn't look nearly as confident as it had before. "Oh, this is all just a misunderstanding. That's not an electromagnetic strip, it's a *static* electric strip; all alleys have 'em; it's to prevent dust buildup on the lanes." Shaking his head, he walked behind the lunch counter and reached for a drawer. "This'll explain everything—"

"If you're looking for the gun," said Tripp, "It's not there anymore. Though I was tempted to have Natalia leave it where it was; I'd love an excuse to put a few holes in you."

"Static electric strip?" said Natalia. "Please.

You're talking to a scientist, not one of your marks."

Dettweiler sighed. "Look, that's a very fancy theory and all, but I don't *have* a custom-made ball full of iron—"

"No," said Natalia, "but your friend Leroy does. I know, because that ball is sitting in my lab right now, right beside an X-ray machine that told me exactly what was inside. Frank got suspicious when he noticed Leroy resting between turns—but he wasn't resting. He was just waiting for his ball to come back, because it's the only one he practices with."

Dettweiler nodded. "Leroy. Of course. You know, I never did trust him—"

Tripp cut him off. "You can save the finger-pointing for the trial. And I'm not talking about intent to defraud, either; you're going down for the murder of Hiram Davey."

"Murder? How the hell do you get murder from a trick bowling ball?"

"You didn't murder Davey with a bowling ball," said Natalia. "You used a knife. You were careful about getting rid of the murder weapon and Davey's laptop, but you didn't eliminate the one witness to the crime—because you needed him to win the tournament."

Natalia crossed her arms. "Leroy's in custody right now. He's already given us a statement describing how you killed Davey because you were worried his book would reveal your scam."

Dettweiler snorted. "Is that all? Sounds like it's my word against his. I'll take my chances in front of a jury—I have a way with people, you know? Leroy, on the other hand, is both dumb and ugly."

Natalia nodded. "You're right, Gord. Leroy isn't that bright, or that tough. We brought him in for questioning and told him we knew all about the tournament con, and he cracked like an egg. I guess that's what you get for picking a sidekick you can push around, huh? Turns out it's just as easy for them to be pushed around by someone else. You, on the other hand, are a master manipulator—as proven by your two prior convictions. Which one of you do you think the jury is going to believe planned an elaborate scam like this?"

Dettweiler's smile only got wider. "I guess we'll see."

"Yes, we will," said Tripp. He pulled out his handcuffs and advanced. "And Natalia and I will be sitting in the front row when it happens. This'll be your third strike, Dettweiler—but now, it's a whole different ball game."

"I've got a print," said Calleigh. She looked up from pieces of the binoculars she'd meticulously disassembled. "On the inside of the lens, on the doctored side."

Horatio nodded. "Which means it must belong to our killer. Do we have a match?"

"Running it through AFIS now."

The system found a match quickly. Horatio studied the screen with narrowed eyes. "Randilyn Breakwash. Well, now we know . . ."

"But that doesn't make sense," said Calleigh.

"Sometimes *people* don't make sense," said Horatio. "But the evidence always does. We just have to look at it in the right way."

"Maybe Randilyn can shed some light on the subject."

"I'm sure she can—but first we have to find her. She apparently found the coordinates to the treasure hidden in the balloon and is no doubt on her way there now. We're going to have difficulty intercepting her . . . unless Mister Wolfe was able to complete his assignment."

"Who the hell are you?" Garrett McCulver snapped.

"I'm CSI Ryan Wolfe," Wolfe said. "Can I show you my badge?"

"Take it out slowly."

Wolfe did so, then handed it over. McCulver glanced at it, then lowered his gun. "You work with Caine, right?"

"Yeah. He's got me following up some leads. One of them led here."

McCulver motioned to the sofa. "Have a seat." He sank into a lounger himself, and put the gun down on a table beside it—still within easy reach, Wolfe noted. "This about Rodriguo again?"

"That's right. You post on floridacrimehistory.com as swamphunter, right?"

"You're pretty sharp. Yeah, that's me—why?"

"Because our vic in the case was someone you knew as skyhigh88."

McCulver looked intrigued. "Really? I should have guessed—he was the only one in the forums more interested in Rodriguo than me. And he hasn't posted anything in the last few days."

"That's because someone shot him in the eye with a pair of rigged binoculars. We think the same person is headed for the site of Rodriguo's treasure right now—but we don't know where that is."

"That's why you're here, huh?" McCulver shook his head. "I've been looking for Rodriguo's stash for over twenty years. You think I can just pull it out of thin air now?"

"Not thin air. Research. I've gone through all Breakwash's notes. If you and I put our heads together, maybe we can arrive at the same conclusions he did."

McCulver considered it for all of two seconds, then grinned. "Hell, yes."

"Great. Uh, you wouldn't mind putting the gun away now, would you?"

Wolfe took McCulver and all his material to the lab; Horatio met them at the door. "Good to see you again, Mister McCulver."

"You too, Horatio. Or should I call you H?"

Horatio smiled. "If you're on my team, H is fine."

They spread everything they had on the layout table: maps, books, old newspaper clippings, and magazine articles. Wolfe sifted through data at a workstation at one end, while McCulver tapped away at a laptop at the other. Calleigh and Horatio went through the paperwork, looking for the clue that had led Timothy Breakwash to his break-through—and ultimately, his death. Delko, his own case wrapped up, pitched in as well.

"All right," said McCulver. "Before we dive into this, there's a little something I'd like to read out loud. Skyhigh88—that is, Timothy Breakwash—sent it to me shortly after we started corresponding. Horatio and Wolfe have already read it, but you two haven't." He indicated Calleigh and Delko with a nod. "Listen up. A lot of this is speculation, but it's based on the best facts anyone's been able to un-earth, and it's the closest thing to a re-creation we're going to get concerning Rodriguo and what happened to him and his treasure."

McCulver cleared his throat, then began.

"November 23, 1988. Midnight. The hurricane season in Florida officially ended over three weeks ago, but a tropical wave in the Caribbean has just generated the eleventh storm of the year, a cyclone named Keith. Keith is an anomaly; the last time a tropical storm made landfall in the continental U.S. this late in the season was in 1925. On a small private landing strip near Pahokee, a plane is being loaded with a very special cargo.

"The plane is almost certainly a Cessna Skyhawk 172, one of the most popular light aircraft ever produced. With over forty thousand of them being made since 1956, the disappearance of a single plane during an unregistered flight is easy to cover up. The year before, a student named Mathias Rust flew one into Soviet airspace, landing near Red Square without being intercepted by the Russian military; the pilot of this Cessna hopes to do the same thing in Cuba, though he's more concerned about Coast Guard planes than Soviet Migs. His name—the only name known by his friends, his lovers, his business associates—is Rodriguo.

"By the few descriptions that exist, he is a handsome man. Tall, well-built, clean-shaven. More importantly, he is a dangerous man in a dangerous business, and his risks have paid off; he is worth somewhere in the neighborhood of half a billion dollars. Approximately one-fifth of that wealth is now aboard the plane he is about to fly to his new home, in the form of paintings and pearls that once belonged to Spanish royalty. He is the only one at the airstrip—he will enter this new life alone.

"Rodriguo is a brave man, but he is not foolhardy. He is a careful planner and has been preparing for this voyage for the past several years. No one but several high-level officials in the Cuban government and Castro himself knows he is coming; none of his closest associates even know he's been investing heavily in art. Tonight, Rodriguo dies—and is reborn as someone else.

"But Fate has its own designs for Rodriguo's last flight.

"Tropical storm Keith makes landfall near Sarasota, on the east coast of Florida. It crosses the center of the state, producing winds up to seventy miles an hour—not hurricane force, but more than enough to cause a small aircraft problems. Rodriguo must have known about the storm as it developed, but decided to fly anyway. He's planned for too long, and one last risk is hardly enough to stop him.

"No flight plan was filed. No crash was recorded. Officially, tropical storm Keith was responsible for no deaths. But for one man in a small aircraft, flying low over the Everglades to evade radar, it was more than deadly enough.

"Cyclones can produce many kinds of weather: thunderstorms, hail, vertical wind shear. Which factor knocked Rodriguo out of the sky is unknown, but he almost certainly went down in the Everglades or the Atlantic. I believe his final resting place is the 'Glades, if for no other reason than no aircraft wreckage washed up on Florida's shores in the next few weeks. That, and the fact that if he'd managed to reach the ocean, Rodriguo would have been past the worst of the storm.

"What were his final moments like? Did he laugh, acknowledging that he'd met the one opponent he couldn't beat, Mother Nature herself? Or did he curse, fighting the controls and his own destiny as the plane hurtled toward the swamp?

"Those details can never be known. What can be known is where that plane went down—and what it carried. Somewhere in the shadowy depths of the Everglades lies the remains of a Cessna and her pilot, their corpses standing guard over one of the greatest undiscovered treasures in the Sunshine State. Waiting for someone to figure out their secret . . . waiting for someone to finally write an ending to the saga of Rodriguo."

McCulver finished and looked up. There was silence for a moment, and then Horatio said, "Those words were written by a man with a dream—a dream he was killed for. Let's get to work."

Wolfe compared emails from Breakwash's files and McCulver's records. Sure enough, a number of exchanges had been deleted from the balloonist's email but not from the ex-cop's.

"He must have been trying to get rid of anything that might give the location away," said Wolfe.

Horatio studied the screen over Wolfe's shoulder. "Which means that at this point he must have already found the plane."

McCulver stood on Wolfe's other side, a Styrofoam cup of coffee in his hand. "Not much in the message as far as clues go. He just wonders if Rodriguo had a lucky number."

"That's not all, though," Calleigh pointed out. McCulver stepped aside to give her a better view of the monitor. "He also wonders about Rodriguo's sense of irony."

Delko was at the light table with a large, detailed map of the Everglades. "Too bad the FAA doesn't require a flight plan with every balloon launch," he said. "We could track his movements a lot more closely."

Calleigh nodded. "Maybe we can, anyway." She took out her cell phone.

"Who are you calling?" asked Delko.

"Someone I know in Customs. I think what we need is a helping hand from Fat Albert—hello?"

"Fat Albert?" said Wolfe. "We're asking a cartoon for assistance?"

Delko grinned. "Fat Albert is the nickname given the aerostat that broadcasts Radio Marti into Cuba. The Cuban government jams the transmissions, but that hasn't stopped the U.S. from trying; they broadcast a television signal, too. The blimp they use is twice the size of Goodyear's and on the end of a fifteen-thousand-foot cable tethered at Cudjoe Key."

"Yes," said Horatio. "But more importantly, it's also a radar platform specifically tasked with detecting low-altitude, slow-moving aircraft. It's meant to observe potential drug smugglers, but it should work just as well for us."

McCulver chuckled. "Use a balloon to track a balloon. Perfect."

Calleigh hung up. "They're sending the data to our server. If we're right about the date Breakwash found the plane, it has to be somewhere on his flight path."

"I've got it," said Wolfe. He put the data up on the monitor.

"There," said Horatio, tapping the monitor. "Breakwash mentioned a lucky number and irony. Meaning Rodriguo had the bad luck to crash somewhere near Seven Palm Lake."

"You really think that's it?" asked McCulver.

"I do," said Horatio, already heading for the door. "Eric, bring your gear. Mister Wolfe, get us a chopper. Calleigh, I need you to follow up in the lab."

"On what?"

"Randilyn Breakwash," said Horatio. "She's our prime suspect for her husband's murder, but the evidence contradicts that. We've overlooked something—find out what."

"I'm on it," she said.

Wolfe contacted the special patrol bureau and got them on one of MDPD's Bell 206 L-4 helicopters. Even though McCulver was now a civilian, Horatio invited him along—he couldn't deny the man the chance to finally lay Rodriguo's ghost to rest.

Seven Palm Lake was an area filled with mangroves, islands of vegetation separated by intricate channels of water. The closest town was Flamingo, a tiny settlement that had once boasted a marina, lodge, campground, and housing for park rangers—until Hurricane Wilma had passed through and knocked most of the buildings flat. Only the marina and a small store were in operation now, and Horatio had the helicopter land on the only road into town. Flamingo was its southernmost tip, with Florida City at the other end of its thirty-eight-mile length.

There were several vehicles parked beside the small marina, and one at the store. Horatio noted that one of them—a large truck with rental plates—had an empty boat trailer hitched to it. "Mister Wolfe," Horatio said as they got out of the chopper, "talk to the store's proprietor and ask if anyone of Randilyn's description has been through here. Eric, see what you can do about renting that airboat at the marina; we don't have time to get one through official channels."

"Can I help?" McCulver asked.

"Can you drive an airboat?"

McCulver grinned. "Practically grew up on one."

"Go with Eric."

Horatio pulled out his phone as he walked up to the rental truck. "Calleigh? I need you to run a plate for me."

As he'd expected, Calleigh told him the truck had been rented to Randilyn Breakwash. "Got something else for you, too, H. Think I've figured out who the third partner has to be . . ."

Horatio listened. "Yes, that makes sense. Good

work. I'll let you know how things go at this end."
He snapped his phone shut just as Wolfe and Eric
returned.

"A woman fitting Randilyn's description came
through here a few hours ago, towing a boat on a
trailer," said Wolfe. "A tugboat. She offloaded it and
headed east."

Horatio nodded. "Of course. Shallow draft,
strong motor. Eric?"

"The airboat's ours. McCulver's firing it up right
now."

"Good. Eric, put your diving gear aboard; you
and I are going with McCulver. Mister Wolfe,
you're our eyes in the air. Go."

Wolfe spotted the tugboat in a fairly wide channel
amid the mangroves. He grabbed the heavy-duty
walkie-talkie and told Horatio, talking loudly to be
heard above the rotors. Horatio acknowledged and
directed McCulver which direction to head in, then
told Wolfe to head back to Flamingo; there wasn't
much he could do to help now. There was also little
point in stealth—both the airboat and chopper
could be heard coming from miles away.

Randilyn Breakwash, dressed in a wetsuit, came
out of the wheelhouse as they approached. The
sleeves of the suit were cut off, exposing her burn-
spotted arms, and she held one cupped hand palm
up in front of her. She didn't look surprised, just
defeated.

"Randilyn," said Horatio as McCulver cut the motor and the airboat drifted up to bump against the tug. "I'm afraid your treasure hunt is over."

She looked at him with dull eyes. "It's gone."

Behind the tug, the tip of one white wing projected a few feet above the water. Horatio could see how easily it could be missed, or mistaken for something else from a distance.

Randilyn held out her cupped hand. "This is what I found. It was in a small leather pouch around the pilot's neck."

Horatio stepped aboard and took her hand gently. Cradled in it were a bunch of white shards, gleaming iridescently in the sun.

"The crash must have crushed them between his breastbone and the throttle," she said. *"La Pellegrina. La Huerfana.* Both of them, destroyed."

"And the paintings?" asked Horatio.

"Underwater for two decades. Ruined." The look on her face was twisting from shock to anger. "He knew. He *knew*! He knew there was nothing left, knew it had all been a waste of time—"

"Yes," said Horatio. "But he didn't know you were planning on killing him, did he?"

"You don't understand. I stood by him for so many years. All those crazy ideas, all those plans . . . I really believed in him, you know? At first. But somehow, my whole life slipped away waiting for Tim to strike it rich, for one of his ideas to pay off. I just couldn't do it anymore. I stopped thinking about Tim's treasure hunting as any kind of possibility and started looking at it as a vice, like gambling. And if he deserved his vice, I deserved one of my own."

"Is that when you started up with Joel Greer?"

She looked away. "Yes. I was never serious about Joel. I just wanted something . . . something of my own. My own secret treasure."

"But then your husband found the real thing. And you were the first one he confided in."

"Not the first." Randilyn shook her head. "He had a partner. He wouldn't tell me who, just said he'd never have found the plane without him. Said he had inside information no one else did."

Horatio nodded. "Fredo Bolivar, the man who tortured you. But you couldn't tell him what you didn't know, could you?"

McCulver jumped aboard the tug. "Hold on, Horatio. I know I'm coming late to this game, but I'm getting confused. Did she know where the treasure was or not?"

"She knew the coordinates, yes. A simple series of numbers, longitude and latitude. Probably the most important numbers she ever had to memorize, and just to be safe she and her husband wrote them down inside a venting flap in the balloon. But then an unexpected factor was introduced; another partner. More accurately, a silent partner."

"Who?" asked McCulver.

"Pfiesteria piscicida," said Horatio. "The cell from

hell. Timothy Breakwash had samples of it in his lab. They were simply for comparison, but all the biohazard labels made you suspicious, didn't it, Randilyn? You thought Tim was holding something back. You did a little surreptitious investigating— and exposed yourself to the organism."

"I didn't think it was dangerous," she said. "The way Tim talked about it, it mainly affected fish."

"Mainly, yes. But *Pfiesteria* has also been known to cause neurological symptoms in people. One of those symptoms is headaches. And another," said Horatio, "is temporary amnesia."

Delko had joined them aboard the boat. "She forgot the coordinates?"

"That's right. And by the time she realized it, it was too late; Timothy had already triggered her trap. Don't bother denying it, Randilyn—we found the doctored binoculars, and we have your prints on the mechanism."

Delko had an evidence envelope ready; he took Randilyn's hand and dumped what she held into it. Then he pulled out a set of handcuffs. "You're under arrest," he told her.

"So this is it," said McCulver. He stared at the wingtip as if he couldn't believe it was real. "Rodriguo's really down there."

"The one that got away," said Horatio. "Seems he didn't get quite as far as he'd planned."

McCulver nodded. "Never thought I'd see the day. Guess I have you to thank, Horatio."

"We couldn't have done it without your help."

"What happens now?"

"Well, I have to escort Mrs. Breakwash back to Miami. Eric will stay behind to start processing the site; I'd appreciate it if you could be his spotter while he's in the water."

"Wouldn't miss it for the world. But I thought you needed me to pilot the airboat?"

Horatio smiled. "You're mistaken, Mister McCulver." He stepped back into the airboat, and took out his sunglasses. "Enjoy your big fish." He put them on, then helped Randilyn into the boat.

He radioed ahead while Delko offloaded his diving gear, made sure Wolfe would be waiting with the chopper in Flamingo. Randilyn Breakwash, her hands cuffed in front of her, sat in the prow and stared silently ahead. Horatio started up the engine.

The airboat made too much of a racket to talk, but Horatio didn't know what he'd ask her, anyway. *Was it worth it? How did it feel, to betray the one you loved for so long, only to have your own mind betray you?*

He found himself thinking about memory, about how it was a map of the past that led to places both valued and treacherous. It seemed to him that painful memories remained the sharpest, while the good ones, the ones you most wanted to remember, faded faster than the rest. He could still remember the exact sound his dog had made as his father kicked it . . . but the other day, no matter how hard he tried, he couldn't remember the color of the dress Marisol had worn on their first date. It was a small detail, an unimportant bit of trivia, but it bothered him deeply. It was an erosion of something good and fine in his life, an erosion that would continue year after year until even her face would be hazy.

It was simple biology, he knew. An organism that remembers what causes it pain is an organism that survives. It was science, not philosophy.

He took a deep breath of the rich Everglades air, and tried to remember Marisol's perfume. *There. Lilac, with a touch of vanilla. Not gone yet . . .*

Not yet.